MY UNDEAD HEART

ELDERGROM

BOOK 1

ISBN 978-1-66782-141-2
eBook 978-1-66782-142-9

These three volumes are derived from notes and recordings and interviews made with the main participants, as patiently archived, consolidated, and organized by Mary Ellen Maven, Chief Archivist, Continental Grid LLC., Westborough, Massachusetts.

CHAPTER 1
KELLY

Monday Night

I woke up in my hospital bed with the feeling there was someone else in the room with me. It was the second night after my heart transplant. It wasn't just that someone else was there with me. I didn't know who he could be—but I felt like I should.

The two previous days were lost to me. The day of my surgery and the next spent in recovery, I was at a low ebb. I was groggy and in discomfort. My ribcage felt abused. Pain medications had me knocked out most of the time.

It was that next night, when I was slightly more alert and comfortable, that I realized I had a visitor. The heart rate monitor next to me showed my pulse rising. I had that rush of rhythm you get when you realize you're getting the birthday present you'd hoped for, or that you're holding the cards that will win the poker pot. Something was coming.

Nurse Masako came to my doorway.

"Kelly, are you feeling okay? Your pulse is up." Her presence made an enormous difference. I was reassured by being cared for by another woman in her late twenties.

That had been the third time I'd woken up that night, but it was the first time I remembered dreaming. Someone had just walked over my grave. No, it wasn't just someone—it was he. Whoever he was, he was near. My heart knew him. It knew he was close.

But that must have been a dream because there was no one else there. I told Masako I was okay. She inspected my vital signs and double-checked the monitoring connections, commenting as she worked.

"This connection looks good. That lead pad is reconnected. Your vitals look great!" She left me feeling reassured.

It was nearly three in the morning. The room lights were dimmed, but it wasn't so dark that I'd miss someone in the shadows. My new heart began beating just a little faster again. He was coming.

No, he must be here.

I didn't see him right away. My eyes weren't being called to where he was standing. I was certain he was there, but it wasn't until I paid attention to my racing heart that I was able to see him.

His long pale face was taut with surprise. He stood just left of the foot of my bed, maybe eight feet away. We were looking at each other eye to eye. This seemed to startle him, like I was winking at him through a two-way mirror. A warm smile took shape on his face. In fact, he looked amused.

"You're not Wendy," he said. He kept looking at me. He tilted his head one way or another, as if the correct angle might reveal something hidden about me.

"I'm Kelly," I said. He needed to know that. I was in no hurry to see him leave, though, as he was the first non-medical person I'd seen in a month.

"Kelly." He said it as if he were savoring the sound of it. "Forgive me, Kelly. I thought someone else was here. Apparently, I got—bad information."

"That's okay," I said. "I hope she's okay."

"Who? Oh, Wendy."

"She's here in the hospital?"

"I didn't think so. I guess intuition drew me here somehow. I wasn't expecting to hear from her until this time tomorrow. Odd. Somehow, I thought she was here, even though that wasn't the plan." He paused and thought. "She'll be okay, I'm sure."

I saw him more clearly. His features were precise and balanced, like he was best of breed. His dark hair was long, framing the light brown skin of his face in chestnut brown. He was both lean and powerful, like an oarsman or a fencer. He'd closed his eyes briefly.

"You are?" I asked after an awkward moment.

"Yes, you can still see me," he said, still looking at me like there was someone hiding behind me. Then he focused on me. "Happy to meet you." He bowed just so slightly and said, "Roberto."

The door opened and Nurse Masako came to my side looking concerned.

"Kelly? How are you feeling?"

I told her I was okay, and she went ahead with her usual check of my IV line, electrodes, and sensors. The overhead lights buzzed as the room grew brighter. I didn't see Roberto.

"Masako, the man who was just standing here?" I asked. "Where did he go?"

She looked surprised. "Sorry, Hon, I didn't see anyone. Your vitals were elevated again, so I thought I'd check in. Who was he?"

I said I didn't know. I told her what I'd seen, and that made her unhappy. She promised she'd call Security.

3

"First let me get your temperature," she said, passing the device's wand across my forehead. She approved of the result. "Are you thirsty?"

I was thirsty all the time, but I didn't tolerate a lot of water. I agreed to a juice box with a sippy straw. She was back with it in a moment. It tasted like the bug juice from middle-school summer camp, a happy time, when I was still healthy. My heart monitor showed I was calming down. Then I recalled Roberto's face. The monitoring equipment confirmed what I felt. My heart sped up when I thought of him.

Masako returned with two Security staffers about fifteen minutes later. A young man and a young woman, both in guard uniforms, made a quick scan of the area and started in on me with a list of questions. Masako, my impatient defender, kept their intrusion brief. We sent them away with "pale skin, long brown hair", and "male, well-spoken." I didn't volunteer that he'd given me his name. I did say that I didn't know him and didn't recognize him. I left out that I was happy to meet him. Also, I didn't mention that hard-to-see-at-first business. I was overdue for sleep. I drifted off as soon as Masako left me.

KELLY
Tuesday Sunset

My new heart stopped beating at sunset on the third day after my transplant surgery.

The previous two days I'd felt exhausted, beaten, nearly empty. True, the new heart was beating on its own. But who knew for how long? Hadn't it just come from a dead person? In my depleted condition, that was as clearly as I was seeing matters.

My father looked much less stressed. I started thinking I might really be okay, though, when Daddy came in to visit looking relaxed. At his afternoon visit, he came in with a couple of new car magazines, likely bought at the hospital gift shop. He was taking a few moments to contemplate the latest 550-horsepower gas-guzzler. He regularly drove a sensible six-cylinder car, but he was expert on tuning high-performance vehicles. As a hobby, he built up his sixties station wagon into a drag strip car. He joked that seismographs spiked when it backfired.

I was happy he'd stopped worrying about me for a few minutes. He'd rarely leave time for his own life. He'd raised me, putting his life second after Mom died from cancer. I was just old enough to start causing trouble—but I never did after that. I love him so much. Daddy did everything for me that Mom had asked of him, and more. I vowed to stay alive to keep him from another big hurt.

Late in the afternoon, Daddy left me to have dinner in the hospital cafeteria.

That's when the weird thing happened. The sun set a few minutes after he left.

My heart quit. The cardiac monitor alarm sounded after a few seconds. I heard voices on the hospital PA system and saw a red light flashing in the hallway. A man's voice on the intercom by my head said, "Hold on, we're coming."

This next part is so fascinating and strange. My heart wasn't beating, but I was feeling great despite the continued stillness in my chest. It was as if all the clouds had just vanished from the sky. I didn't hurt.

Then something moved in my chest, though, and that alarmed me. The heart shifted this way and that, like it was testing its connection to the veins and arteries that anchored it. It wasn't painful, but I was distressed by the bizarre sensation.

Soon I was panting. I wanted air, but I knew I needed something even more than that. The heart had to do something different. I was afraid I would die around it.

What it did next felt like it was inhaling. It then anchored itself in its new home. It laid its claws or teeth or little hooks or whatever into the tissue and bone surrounding it. It pulled everything in tight around itself. It felt like my chest had sunk. A stinging sensation began shooting back and forth in my surgical incision. My new heart had taken custody of my chest.

It knotted up, slurped, and spit out its first swallow of blood. I was panting. My arms and legs and neck swelled. The heart clenched over and over again, stumbling through a series of unorganized random beats. It felt like hours went by while the possessed heart finally settled for a steady rhythm. Once it got going, it sped up like someone twisted the throttle on a motorcycle. My face flushed and my kidneys ached. I needed to pee.

A man in a surgical mask pushing a crash cart stormed into my room. Masako and another nurse I'd seen before rushed to my bed, Masako looking right at me, while the other nurse reviewed my tubes and wires.

Masako said, "Kelly, are you with us? Say yes if you understand me."
A normal-feeling pulse began just then. The heart slowed, each beat feeling
a little less aggressive than the one before.

I felt good.

"Yes," I answered. No problem.

"I think it's a monitor malfunction," the second nurse said. She was
matter of fact. "I mean, have you ever seen this before? BP of one-ninety-five
over sixty-three. It's like she's relaxed but pushing an automobile." That was
about right.

"Pulse one-eighty," Masako said. "No—wait. It's down to one-forty
plus. Still dropping. Yes, it's got to be a malfunction."

"Get her carotid pulse, then cuff her other arm," the masked man said.
He had to be a doctor. "Let's verify."

It all checked out. Their manual instruments had confirmed what the
monitors were reporting. They printed out the graph of my event, muttered
and speculated, and agreed they'd need to study it more. They brought in
another monitoring system as a precaution, and the readings appeared
equally reasonable. They left me attached to the new one and rolled the
suspect one away. I think they were amazed more by the graph than by how
well I said I felt. Masako came in about half an hour later to see how I was.
"I'm actually pretty good." In fact, I felt ready to leave the hospital. It was the
best I'd felt in years. It's just that it was a few weeks earlier than predicted.

Still, my heart beat hard and sometimes fast all night long. The heart
that was dying in my chest had never beaten with the determination of this
one. The nurses kept me laying there all night, feeling like I was running a
marathon even though I wasn't moving. Doctors came by once an hour. I was
becoming dehydrated and sweated up the bed. An internist ordered more
fluids pumped into me.

It would have solved it all if they'd just let me get up, chug a sports drink, and then jog a few miles. It caused them deep concern and confusion when I proposed it. My father had always said I was quite willful. It took all the focus I could muster, though, to stay in that bed until sunrise.

DWIGHT
Also on Tuesday Evening

"Hello, Dwight? Are you there?"

I was surprised to hear Wendy's voice on my phone. First of all, the caller ID said it was Modern Memorials calling and I'd never heard of them. I screen business phone calls with my landline's answering machine since I don't often answer. At the time I was busy feeding my fish. My aquatic family fills twenty-four tanks, and they need regularly scheduled attention. Aquarium care was my profession at that time.

Also, Wendy was dead, or so I'd heard. This was another reason I was surprised to hear from her. I'd gotten the news the day before. Still, hearing her voice saying my name decided it. I picked up.

"Wendy Allard?" I asked.

"Wow. Hey, Dwight. What's happening? Listen, Dwight, I know I might not be your favorite person anymore, but I really need your help. Can you come across town and pick me up? I need a ride—like right now?"

Not my favorite person? Only at those times when I wasn't thinking about her—and that was rare. That status of favorite was hers automatically. After getting the news she'd died, I'd spent Monday night going through my photo collection. I had hundreds of pictures of her, thanks to the righteous reach of my telephoto lens.

I suppose you could say I'd been stalking her, but that never seemed to come up as an issue. We'd both been students at Springfield State. She'd started two years later than I had. It had been three years since I'd first caught sight of her.

She arrived on campus in the fall in full gothic splendor. I made photographic record of it. Jet black hair, a tiny black dress over tight black jeans, silvery gray lipstick and maroon smoke eye shadow all harmonized perfectly

9

in this lady of darkness. I had Kinko's print that picture poster-sized, which I set up as the centerpiece of my shrine to her in the basement of my town-house, just to the side of the stairs. When I'd heard she'd died, I went down there to contemplate my loss. I almost cried.

It was easy getting a crush on her in the first place. Wendy was the counter-culture queen of Springfield State. When most girls were getting training bras, she was probably getting her first tattoo. She had half a dozen piercings visible by the time she was a senior in high school. When Springfield High School got a metal detector, she became the argument against one, because it would trigger every time, causing delays. It was unthinkable to have to search her every day to make sure none of the other ones she had hidden turned into handguns or machetes.

I thought she didn't like me. I'd figured that out a couple of years ago. I'd been publicly humiliated. She left me sitting for over two hours at Rocket Burger waiting for her, but she never showed up. It was her friends that set me up—she claimed she knew nothing about it—but that seemed unlikely because the rest of the students clearly did.

"Pick you up?" I asked. I was worried I was being set up again. "Now? Uh… look. I have a question. I'd heard you died."

"Let's talk about that later, okay? So, will you come? Please?"

"Where are you?" I asked. Her directions weren't useful, but she was totally certain of the address. Modern Memorials was in a building complex in North Springfield Technical Park. She said to hurry, and to bring towels and blankets because she was really wet. I loaded up and drove.

I was suspicious of course, but the call did come from a business phone. She'd called from where I was driving to. My caller ID was the proof. Wendy had to have been there.

Thick gray smoke was leaking from under the edges of the roof of Modern Memorials as I was arriving. There were two loading dock bays on the front of the building. One was at the right height for box trucks. The other one was set lower, probably so a hearse could back up to it.

That lower door was open. As I pulled up, my headlights lit the inside of the space. I saw someone coming toward me, bent at the waist, hands clutching chest and stomach. It wasn't clear right away that it was Wendy. I got out of my car to help whoever it was. Blood soaked the front of her clothing, and she was blackened with soot and charring. Some of her long hair had burned away from the top of her head.

"Dwight," she said. "You came." Then I knew it really was Wendy. It was her voice. She was hurt bad and needed help. I thought to have her lie down right there, but the billows of smoke told me it was time to get out. I took her by the arm and steered her out. The loading bay had several dozen coffins stacked up. Near the stack of coffins, there was a man lying there dressed only in his undershirt, boxers, and socks. He wasn't moving. On the back wall, flames were shooting out of what looked like a furnace or oven. The wall above it was solid flame reaching all the way up to the ceiling.

"What about him?" I had to shout to be heard over the crackling of the flames. She shook her head to say it was hopeless. I helped her out of the building, supporting her by the shoulders. She was having trouble standing upright. She held my left arm so tight I thought the bones might break.

I got her to my car. Smoke swirled up from her head and neck. I pressed a towel against the smoldering spots. She hissed with discomfort. I spread the spare blankets I'd brought along over the back seat and had her lie down. "I'll call 9-1-1," I said, "but I'll pull back away from this first. What happened?"

"No. No 9-1-1. What day is it?"

"It's Tuesday. Tuesday night."

"The third night," she said. Her voice was soft. Then, sounding very urgent, she said, "There was some big screw up, I guess. I think I may be in trouble. Please—help me, Dwight. Get me away from here."

Even when she was cold and condescending toward me, she would be hard to deny. But now she sounded so frightened and desperate, I did as she asked and drove us away.

Her stink was making me nauseous. You know that metallic odor of clotting blood? And she smelled of scorched hair and charred meat and smoldering plastic. There was this rancid smell too, like the grease disposal behind a highway diner. I rolled down my window.

I drove us out of the industrial park and headed toward Central Hospital. I told Wendy I was taking her there.

"Oh please, no. Please don't do that! Can you just take me to your place? Let me lie down for a while. Things aren't what they look like."

"What do you think they look like?" I asked. "You're joking, right? 'Cause from here, it looks like you've been assaulted, stabbed, and set fire to."

"How much did you see back there?" Wendy asked.

"I saw a building with smoke coming out, a loading dock with a stack of coffins, and there you were, walking out all blackened and bloody. I think that's a really good reason to go to the hospital."

"A hospital doesn't help people like me, Dwight. I'm already dead."

I helped Wendy lie down on the kitchen floor. My townhouse has a ground floor entrance from the car port that opens into the kitchen, so I was able to walk her in. Blood sloshed out of her stomach wound. Keeping her flat reduced the spilling. I turned on the exhaust fan over my stove to reduce the stink.

Wendy wasn't as disoriented as I'd have expected from someone risen from the dead. I had questions, but my priority was the same as hers: to see how badly she was hurt.

I almost didn't recognize her. A lot of her hair was fried away. Both of her cheeks were blackened, and one had a thin crack. Her lips were charred. There was blood on her teeth. Bloodshot brown eyes looked at me through singed eyelids. For a moment, I thought I saw two extra teeth behind her front teeth, but I wasn't sure. I looked a second time but didn't see them.

She had on a once-white lab coat, stained with dried blood and fresh. The trousers she had on looked like they were borrowed from a construction worker. Her hands were black and brown, from soot and scabs. The fingertips of her left hand were burned down to boney points.

She had oversized men's work shoes on. I slipped them off her. The tops of her feet were bare, but there was bubbled-up black membrane wrapping around the sides and bottom of each foot. Her shoes must have melted onto her feet.

"How bad is it, Dwight?" I was going to have to look at her chest.

"Let go of the coat. I need to see." She took her hands away, leaving it to me to open the coat.

I was kneeling on the floor next to her. I opened the right flap of the stained lab coat toward me, and then the left flap away from me, revealing the remains of a black lace blouse. I was careful not to reveal the parts I used to dream of seeing.

Through the lace, I saw she'd been cut open from collarbone to navel. On the TV crime investigation shows they show corpses all neatly sewn up after an autopsy, but Wendy's chest was left hanging open.

"There's stuff missing, isn't there?" she asked. Her diaphragm muscle squeezed up toward her ribs as she spoke. I couldn't see much else.

"You've got lungs, anyway." I didn't really know what I should be looking for. "Look, I've got an anatomy book. I'll get that, and scissors. And a flashlight—so I can see what the story is." I was back in under a minute.

I laid the book open to the thorax diagram for guidance and began cutting through the charred black lace with the scissors. I beamed the flashlight into her wound, but the details I needed were obscured.

"Uh, Wendy? So I can see what's going on, I need a better look. We need to prop you open."

She reached for her chest with both hands, stuck her fingers into the gap, and pulled her rib cage further open. Something snapped. It sounded like a kernel of corn popping.

"Does that help?" she asked.

It didn't help. I'd fainted.

I don't think I was out that long. My brain must have overloaded. She was propped up on her elbows, talking to me.

"Dwight! Dwight, please. Don't fall apart on me now. I need you." Blood frothed from the gap in her belly.

"Okay, yes. I'm okay," I said, though I was far from it. "I—I'll start at the top. Go a little more slowly this time."

"Like this?" She pulled her ribcage open again. I pretended I didn't hear the grinding sound. Using the flashlight and my anatomy book, I started my inventory. I used a pencil to make notes in the book about what was present and what was missing. However, I tossed the pencil after I used it to push her intestines aside to search for her pancreas. I didn't find it, but I kept looking for all the standard parts.

I sat back when I was done. I was feeling better, despite the horrific task I'd just completed. I guess I get a lift out of learning something new.

Since I'm something of a science geek, I can tell you that the brain has an area for rational processing and an area for emotional processing. The words I'd heard made sense to the rational part, except for the dead-but-still-speaking business. My emotional part was really agitated.

"So—it's bad, isn't it?" She asked.

"Well, the good news is you're still conscious and able to speak. And you've still got lungs and a stomach. On the downside, most of the other parts are gone."

"Damn. What's gone?"

I didn't want to say it.

"Your heart is missing. So's your liver, your pancreas, and your kidneys. Seems that's all transplantable stuff. I'm surprised they didn't take your corneas and your thigh bones."

"Oh crap," Wendy said. "I'm still going to die, aren't I?"

I thought about that. What had already happened was impossible. Going by the surgical cut down her middle, qualified authorities had already declared her dead. Her prize organs had been harvested, and she'd been shipped to a crematorium. Still, she was able to call me and ask for a ride.

"Wendy how did this start?"

"You mean what happened tonight?" I nodded yes.

"I woke up all on fire. I was in this wooden box, and it was falling apart onto me. Coals were falling on me. My feet were burning. My hands were cooked into claws—like this." She held up her hands. I saw bare bone on some of the fingertips of her left hand.

"My hair was burning, and my blouse was smoking." She looked down at her chest. "It was such beautiful lace. Vintage Victorian. Really rare. I freaked out, you know? I just went wild, breaking up the box, knocking everything away. I tried to sit up and banged my head on a metal ceiling. I was lying on metal rollers. All around pipes were shooting flames right at me. I was in this huge oven.

"I saw a door by my feet. I scrambled along on the rollers and kicked at the door. It took so long to open. My feet hurt bad because my shoes were on fire. I kept kicking anyway and the door finally popped open. When I got out, I couldn't stand up straight. Bent over felt better, but then I saw I was sliced open. If I tried to straighten up, I'd lurch backward. Plus. my feet and clothing were still on fire.

"Then this cold white cloud hit me. It felt so good. The flames went out."

"Someone was there with a fire extinguisher?"

"Yeah, the guy who was cooking me. He said, 'Oh my Guh…Guh… I'm sorry, I'm sorry!'" I think she was trying to say God. "Was that him on the floor?" I asked.

"This is his coat," she said pointing to the blood-splattered lab coat. "These are his pants." She pulled her belly open with one hand and dipped the index finger of her other into the puddle in her belly.

"This is his blood…" I saw amazement on her face. She was starting to understand what she'd done.

"I had to feed," Wendy said. Her voice was really loud. "I was just doing it. I grabbed him and pulled him down on the floor. I have these fangs that flip out from inside my mouth. I grabbed him while he was still putting out the flames on me and bit him on the neck."

"Did that help?" I wanted her answer to be no.

"I think so. I was so desperate—I couldn't help it. Nothing could have stopped me. I drank and drank until the blood leaked out." She pointed to the slit in her chest. "He went limp. It was disgusting. I just tossed him away when he went dry. For a few seconds, I felt calm. Then I noticed the fire was spreading. I knew I needed to call someone for help."

"How are you feeling now?" What I was actually thinking was, "how long until you kill me?"

"G... G...." She looked puzzled, confused why the word would make her choke. She couldn't say God. She looked up at me.

"Damn it, Dwight, have you been listening at all?" Her face froze for a second after she said it. "G...I need to be put back together. I'm going to need more blood. And I've got to find Roberto. He was supposed to meet me when I woke up."

I was not going to be sick. I promised myself I'd hang on. "Okay, listen. You've heard the list of what's missing. On the plus side, your stomach is still connected to your esophagus and your intestines. Also, your lungs are both there and working—otherwise, you wouldn't be talking. Do you have any idea where the missing parts might be?"

"No."

"Where did you last see them?" My mother's favorite question.

"Asshole. I died and someone steals my organs. I wake up in a burning wood box, sliced open like a fish, and you're wisecracking. You are this far from becoming my next meal."

Bad news. I didn't see the gap between her fingertips. Worse news was she'd just confirmed that I might have a place in her food chain. I instantly missed the comforting, though misplaced, illusion of friendship.

"Wendy, I need to understand. You knew you were going to die?"

"Well, yeah. Roberto is so exciting. He's so sexy, and he loves me. We're going to be a couple for all of eternity. Death will never part us. It brings us together. We decided to do it last Thursday. He drained me some each night. He said he'd be at my coffin at sunset after my third day dead, and I'd wake up to see him smiling down at me."

"You can close up, Wendy. I've got the list." She worked her two halves back together, depositing more red-brown fingerprints on her faded skin.

"Wendy, are you… were you an organ donor? Was that on your driver's license?"

"No! I'd never let myself be cut up and passed around. Ick."

"Your parents might have released you for donation."

"Not likely. They're traveling. They took a cruise to Antarctica, of all places. I waited to do this when they had no way to interfere."

Who else would have the right to let her be harvested, I wondered?

"Wendy, did you give someone else power-of-attorney while they were away?"

A light went on behind her eyes. "Well, yes. My sister Tisha—older stepsister Tisha. Bitch-burn-in-hell Tisha. We set up to make medical decisions for each other while Dad and New Wife are away. If one of us had an accident."

"Could she have decided to offer you up as an organ donor and then be cremated?"

Wendy's eyes glazed over. She lay back inside the levy of blood-soaked blankets and towels, staring off into space. Her breathing grew stronger and stronger.

"Of course," she said at last. "Bitch sister has ignored everything I've ever said. I left a note saying no organ donation. And of course, no cremation. And I ordered up a big honking party at Morty Coil's along with the funeral service. I should have woken up there with Roberto next to my coffin."

"Don't know if one is planned, but I wasn't invited," I said.

"I should have put you on the list. You're not so bad. Sorry."

"Thanks," I said. I hope my smile looked gracious, not forced.

"So, Dwight, what's your plan? How are you going to get my organs back?"

I'd figured out this much: the goth queen of Springfield County College had died, gotten her organs harvested, and, while being cremated, was resurrected as a vampire. Then she sucks a crematorium worker dry and comes to my apartment, splashing his blood on me and on my life, expecting my help. She could have killed me—and she hadn't said she wouldn't. I didn't understand how or why she was alive.

I quickly understood I was her nearest food source. I have always wanted to avoid conflicts of interest where it's my life that's at stake. I thought it would be a fine time to leave. I considered telling her, "I'd be delighted to get out and look for those organs, Miss Allard. How about I get back to you in a few days? I'll text when I've got something. They're bound to turn up."

Instead, I said, "So, I'll be going out to track those organs down. I just need to feed my fish and then I'll be on my way. It's just a minute. Then I'll be doing everything I can to restore you. It's awful this happened. Really unfair."

"You can feed your fish," she said. She appeared to be tightening up. I sensed my death coming in a point-blank blast. "But you're not going anywhere near them till those organs are back in. Your brain can work fine from here. Get someone to help you. You have friends, right? Here, give me your phone." She held out her hand for it. I surrendered it.

She explored it for a few seconds and then made a call. I strained to hear the voice that answered.

"Hi!" she said. "I'm Wendy Allard. You're Tanner, right? Have we met?"

"Um… I heard you were dead," I heard Tanner say. "What are you doing with Dwight's cell?"

"I'm badly injured and Dwight is helping me out. He could really use your help. Can you please come right away? Please hurry. Yes, to Dwight's place, okay? Great."

Ten minutes later, she had me unlock the kitchen door, leaving it slightly open. I should have run then, but Tanner might've been walking into certain death. I wouldn't trade his life for mine.

"Dwight! Hey man!" That was Tanner at the door. In a flash, her iron grip was on my arm, holding me in place.

"Tell him to lock the door behind him and come in here," Wendy hissed.

"Lock the door behind you." I called out. "Then get in here." Already I was seeing I'd probably made a mistake.

Then Tanner was looking over my shoulder. I was kneeling over Wendy. The levy of towels and napkins around her was clot brown. The slit in her chest bubbled and hissed with her breathing. Sooty gray and black skin contrasted with the bright red flecks of blood spraying out of her chest.

"Tanner, I think you remember Wendy. Wendy, meet Tanner. You see, I got word she died, but then a while ago, she calls up and asks to come over. She's got a problem."

I saw I'd gotten a little bit ahead of Tanner.

"There're some parts missing, aren't there?" he said.

"He's a quick study," Wendy said, laying her hands over the gap in her belly.

"Yes," I said. "The most popular transplant organs are no longer on board. Heart, liver, kidneys, pancreas… they're all missing."

"Lungs. They left the…" she said.

"True," I said. The situation really needed a positive spin. "The lungs are pumping, and her digestive tract is almost intact."

"And she's still alive. You know, Dwight, this is a really bad situation, and I really truly wish I wasn't here right now. I'm just…"

A flapping sound made me think a giant bird had flown into me, because now I was lying on my back with Tanner under me. Wendy had her vise grip on his ankle. She had reached between my knees and grabbed him, knocking us both over.

"Oh no, no, no, Tanner," she said. "You're staying with me—just in case Dwight gets distracted and doesn't come back quick with my organs. I might get thirsty." She said it like she'd just remembered she was out of bottled water.

"Sure thing, then. I'll just feed my fish and then go out and find your heart and stuff. It'll just take…"

"Screw the fish, Dwight," Tanner said. His voice was edged with fright. "I'll feed them. Dwight, go wherever you have to go now. Please. Go. And Wendy! You don't need to hold my ankle so hard. I think you might break it."

CHAPTER 2
ROBERTO

Also On Tuesday Evening

13 Rue Morgue. Morty Coil's doors opened at 6:30 p.m., and I entered an hour later, shadowing a group of people. No reason for anyone to look at nobody-here-right-now. On the far side of the group of mourners, I read the video displays for each of three funeral suites. Two appeared to be in use. I checked the vacant one as well, but the names on the video displays all were missing Wendy's name or the family name Allard. Two of the rooms I checked had coffins, both lit by an overhead bank of colored spotlights.

The room on my right was backlit in orange, with purple at the corners. People wearing bright orange football jerseys were entering. The coffin was closed. The display on the wall outside was showing a video of a young man running the length of a football field, just beating the defenders to the end zone. The clip ended and the name Siggy Andersen filled the screen in white letters on black. The football video restarted.

The room ahead of me, according to the video display on the wall, was the next-to-final resting place for Amanda Bergen—unless she was Wendy. The open casket was lit in rose and peach, blending into the white floor-to-ceiling curtains behind it.

People were seated, looking reflective. In their grief, no one noticed as I went straight to the open casket and used the kneeler. If those people were Wendy's mourners, I didn't recognize them. I believed I'd met most of her friends. Something was very wrong. There were no goths or nerds in the room. Mostly, they were thirty-something professional types.

A glance into the coffin showed me it wasn't Wendy.

I stood again as quickly as I'd knelt, repelled by the essence of the prayers for the dead that had soaked into the padded velvet rail. It was reflex, not plan, that got me off the kneeler. In times of stress—before I was transitioned—I took comfort in praying at my church. Kneeling was how I focused best, but this kneeler drove me away.

Suddenly everyone seemed to be looking at me.

There's a peculiar invisibility I can have when my mental focus is just right. I call it "nobody-here-right-now." It's a calm mental state, where I'm following my intention but I'm not preoccupied with purpose—just completing my itinerary. I flow through crowds of people unnoticed. When that frame of mind dissolves, though, it can be like a spotlight shining on me. That spotlight had just come on. Dozens of eyes were on me so I hurried out of the room.

Back in the entry, the doors to the third room, on the left, were closed. That room's video display was dark. I tried the door. It was unlocked. The room was laid out like the other two I'd seen. Guessing there had to be more than one door in each room, I separated the curtains behind the empty coffin stand and found both an elevator and a door to a stairwell. I prefer stairs. Elevators advertise to the entire building that someone is in motion.

I descended to the next level down. A corridor took me to a pair of glass doors that were probably right under the front entrance of the building. Opening them and stepping in, on my left I saw two staff members at the far end of a long clinical-looking room. It was a bright area, appointed with brushed stainless fixtures and white-enameled walls. Many displays and banks of status lights and readouts gave the appearance of a state-of-the-art facility, the likely envy of the morgue staff of any local hospital.

A young man and a young woman, both wearing white lab coats, were standing at their computer workstations, facing each other. They were surrounded by three walls of brushed-steel lockers. Doors on the two back corners of the room probably allowed gurneys or coffins to be rolled in and out.

Just above each locker was a display showing the name of its occupant, arrival date, and a number code. Each door had a credit card–sized slot leaking red laser light. I read every display in a matter of seconds. No Wendy Allard. There were two occupied lockers that had no names.

I approached the two workers, coming up behind the man. The woman spotted me over his shoulder. Her nametag said Annie.

"Father in heaven! Basil—behind you!" Annie yelled. She grabbed at a tubular container on her desk and held out a wooden cross the size of a rolled-up newspaper. The cross lit up. Its near-black-hole awfulness scorched me like a flamethrower. The cross was glowing with a kind of light that casts no shadows. The radiance formed a ball of light around her, reaching nearly halfway to me.

I stumbled back toward the glass doors, putting three more yards between the cross and me. I wanted to retreat from the undiluted grace it radiated, channeled from a divine realm I'll never see. It felt like the glow it gave off would pull me apart cell by cell.

No doubting Thomasina, I saw Annie's face change. Belief was transforming into certainty. All was justified and proven—the divine repels the undead. The power and brilliance of her cross strengthened, pressing me back even harder.

Basil turned and faced me. "Oh God. Annie, is that a…"

He remembered something, and a second later, another cross was being offered for my contemplation. I felt the weight of a second one pressing on me. I wanted to leave, but I did have a reason for coming that far. At least I would be out the door before they could touch me.

"Hi. Sorry to spook you folks," I said. I remember sounding somewhat hoarse. "Forgive me for arriving unannounced. Look—I'm not going to hurt you or try to convert you or anything like that. I just need to find the remains of my friend. Could you just open up those lockers for a moment? Just need to see…"

"What do we do, Annie?" Basil asked. "The hygiene manual doesn't cover this."

"You agree on what we're seeing here? He's classic OTG, Basil."

"Oh hell, you're right," he said. The light around his cross brightened, expanding a few feet outward. "You're always right. I don't suppose we'll be processing this one."

"Well, you two have raised all kinds of questions for me," I said. "What do you mean by OTG?" Was this the same thing my maker Jack had told me about?

"Off The Grid," Basil said. "You're not being tracked or monitored. Right?"

"That's how I like it. So, how about opening the lockers? Really, I won't be a problem."

"Not unless you're on the Access List of a registered client," Annie said. "Basil, keep your cross between us and him." She propped up her cross next to her keyboard. "Who are you looking for?" I wondered if she was faking curiosity while trying to figure out what to do about me.

"Wendy Allard," I said.

Annie stopped typing. Her display filled with text. "I should have guessed this would be it. Ms. Allard came in profiling as a potential revenant. We did the field exam, got the next of kin's verbal okay, and had the infected material processed."

"What are you talking about? Field exam? What do you mean by processed? Do you kids play doctor with the dead bodies?"

"I resent that," Basil's cross shook as he spoke to me. "And I noticed you didn't ask what revenant means. Annie and I represent the central part of the state to the Continental Grid Hygiene Outreach Committee. It's an important service of our parent company, CG. I think it doesn't get enough publicity, really."

Annie took over. "Since you are OTG, maybe you don't know about Continental Grid." She thought for a moment. "Knowing about them wouldn't help you much, I guess. Here's the thing. Revenant management is something they do really well."

Jack Murphy had explained to me—while he wasn't killing me—that Continental Grid—CG, he called it—was hunting him down. Somehow, they must have been able to find him without using his sire to sniff him out. Or maybe Murphy was somehow destroyed.

"The young woman you're looking for?" Annie said. "She came in harvested. The hospital didn't close her up—I guess they thought that might save us time with the embalming, but very unprofessional. We had no processing decision at that time. They sent along the clothes she died in. Odd thing was, we already had an order on file from the client asking for no embalming. That didn't add up if she was an organ donor, so that was a red flag.

"The main sign was the bite marks on her arms and inner thighs." Annie was looking at her computer display again. "Basil called Ms. Allard's executrix—a stepsister, as I recall—and faxed us a release, so we forwarded her for processing." She picked up her cross again and turned toward me. Hers was much brighter than Basil's, but they were both painful.

I asked, "Are you going to tell me what that means?"

"We had her remains cremated."

"When?" I asked.

"Her remains were sent out by the afternoon shift."

"Where?"

"Modern Memorials, North Springfield Technical Park. If you hurry, you might see them boxing up her ashes. It's on the other side of the city. Sorry for your loss. God rest her soul—and yours. Now please go away."

Those words made me flinch for a moment. It was the first time since I'd died that someone had spoken about my soul. It hurt. Thinking about it filled my head with noise.

What kind of monsters were these people? They spent their nights examining corpses for bite marks or interesting tattoos and destroying those who might become vampires. I thought they might be thieves also. They'd cancelled Wendy's grand funeral and wedding service. They'd taken frightening and presumptive actions. They owed her greater respect. They also owed her a refund.

Basil looked at Annie. "What can we do about him?"

"About whom?" she replied. That was the last thing I heard as the glass doors swung shut behind me.

I needed a car. It was too far to run without my speed drawing attention, and as far as I knew then, I wasn't able to fly. I was exhausted from the pressure of Annie and Basil's crosses. The more they talked, the more they believed, and the more painful the pressure got to be.

On the street nearby, I found a whale of a car—a 90's Ford Crown Victoria—with the keys still in the ignition. It started flawlessly, and I was enjoying warm air from the dashboard. I knew the industrial park containing Modern Memorials quite well. It was where I'd worked with Jack Murphy— my vampire "sire." We'd both been doing roadwork on the night shift there. More about that another time.

I tore across town, fearing I'd be late. Wendy should have reanimated several hours earlier. Waking up anyplace other than Morty Coil's™ would be a deep shock to her.

Flashing lights, police vehicles with loudspeakers, and fire trucks filled the parking lot at Modern Memorials. There were nearly a dozen first responders. I thought I'd come to the wrong place, but then I was able to see the sign. I pulled into a parking slot in front of a nearby insurance agency, got out, and walked. As I got closer, I saw steam and grayish smoke rising from the building's charred façade and roof. I went into the nobody-here-right-now frame of mind and entered the building. I meandered to the building's main door looking at no one in particular. The focused state of the firefighters and cops made it easy to move about inside.

In the loading dock area, I saw EMTs, three cops, and two firefighters standing around the prone body of a man. He was face down on the concrete, wearing only boxer shorts and a white tee shirt, maybe four yards from the ruptured door to a furnace. The door looked like it had been smashed repeatedly with a sledgehammer.

A fair-skinned man lay in a puddle of blood. There were scorch marks on his clothing and flesh. However, though severely injured, he was still alive.

The living might not have noticed it, but living prey is of critical importance to me. They'd all assumed the man was dead. As nobody-here-right-now, I eased my way past the cluster of emergency professionals.

I looked inside the furnace. The layout suggested that coffins—probably wooden—were rolled into the furnace where an array of gas burners jetted flames inward from the three sides and down from above. The charred corners and intact bottom of the box indicated the process had been interrupted. The pipes feeding the burners were bent and mangled. The oven door, hanging by just one hinge, had been beaten open. Someone pounded it out from the inside. I tested the metal of the door and found it sturdy. Someone as strong as me had been inside the oven and fought her way out. Wendy had reanimated inside this oven. I tried to imagine how bad that would feel.

"Hey buddy, step back from that," an authoritative voice said. "What's your business?" Standing over the underwear man was a police officer. He was looking right at me. I'd forgotten myself. I'd felt empathy and that let me become noticeable.

"That guy on the ground is still alive. You need to get him help now," I said. As they looked back at the victim, I dashed out of the building, returned to my borrowed Crown Victoria, and drove off. I was grateful that my speed overcame their reaction time.

The scene I'd just left told me that Wendy had reanimated and was out there somewhere, disoriented and drunk from the blood of the man on the floor. I felt badly: I'd wanted to do much better for her. Things of that sort had gone awry for me since I died.

I drove to Wendy's home, where she'd lived in the basement level. That was so she'd have her own private entrance. She could've had a room in the main part of the Clark household, but that would have increased contact with her stepsister and stepfather.

No one was home. Wendy's mother and stepfather were away, and wicked stepsister rarely missed an evening out. She did a lot of networking.

I spent a few of the early morning hours driving by Wendy's favorite clubs and the homes of those few friends of hers that I'd met, but I never felt a connection. Soon, Springfield started turning out its lights. The Ford ran low on gas. I was forced to abandon it. Again, I was nearly broke, and I didn't dare leave a stolen car near where I'd be hiding. I'd travel the last few miles to a hiding place on foot. Searching for Wendy would have to wait until the next sunset.

DWIGHT
Also Later Tuesday Night

I'd heard of Morty Coil's™ before. I'd never had any interest in going there, but I would have if Wendy had put me on the invite list. Instead, she'd sent me there to ask about what went wrong. I'll bet this was their first consumer complaint from beyond the grave. I might have gone there anyway, but she gave me no choice—Tanner was her hostage.

I found Annie and Basil down in the lower level in the meat locker area. Annie was on the phone, and Basil was focused on typing at his keyboard. As I came through the glass doors, Basil noticed me.

"Wow! Dwight Witken?" he said. "How've you been? Sorry, didn't see you coming. We're on something urgent. What brings you here?"

I knew Annie and Basil from Springfield County College. I was going to have to be nice to them. They both were a year behind me, and they were decisive in choosing the mortuary science program. I was fairly sure they were just friends and not a couple.

We didn't have the geek bond going, so the friendliness I heard in his greeting surprised me. More than warm, though, he sounded stressed.

"I was hoping to find out about Wendy Allard's funeral," I said. "I thought it was supposed to have been tonight." They both stopped what they were doing to look at me. Annie said a few quick words to the phone and set it down.

"Unfortunate, that," Annie said. "Can you hold on a minute, Dwight?" She ended the call and turned her attention back to me. "You may not know that part of what we do deals with public health issues." Annie had often been preachy. "We hold back the decay and corruption that eventually overtakes us all." It sounded like she was reciting a lesson. "Sometimes, remains are more dangerously corrupted, and Wendy Allard was one of those cases. We made

32

the assessment and reviewed it with her next of kin. She took our advice and let us send Miss Allard out for processing. The funeral has been cancelled. She said a memorial service will be announced when their parents return from an overseas vacation."

That sounded strange. I began feeling irritated at her being preachy with me. I realized I was seeing too much of a world I didn't want to believe existed. It was exciting and terrifying. The deal-with-the-devil part of the bargain, though, was that I had the girl of my dreams—admittedly, lying there eviscerated on my kitchen floor and holding my best friend by the throat. So, I refocused on my objective: getting Wendy's organs back before she gives in and drinks Tanner's blood. Also, I thought it'd be great to help her out.

"So, cremation solves health problems? So that I don't have to guess and show my ignorance, what is the contagion you're fighting?"

Basil looked like he really needed to confide in someone. "Extra-biological revivification," he said. "When we were new at this, we took our volunteer work seriously, but honestly, it felt like planning for space aliens: it may never happen, and it won't be on any schedule you can control. Then yesterday morning we received remains with all the warning signs—and a complication."

"You're still talking about Wendy, aren't you" I asked.

Annie and Basil were instantly concerned. They both whipped out white crosses and held them out toward me.

"Was she your girlfriend?" Basil asked.

"Just gathering some facts for a friend of the family. You think she was going to come back from being dead? Chillax, will you? Hey, are those things loaded?" I asked, trying to lighten his mood. Basil was frozen in place. Fear was all over him.

Annie spoke. "We're not expert yet. We heard it's a good career move to volunteer in the industry, you know, to get known. So, we both signed up for the H O C. Bill, the owner of this Morty's franchise? He's supportive. We took CG's basic safety course, but yesterday was the first time our training found something. It looked like we had a potential revenant in one of our lockers. We're still coming to terms with it." Basil was trembling, but Annie looked rock steady.

"So, her funeral was cancelled, right? Whose idea was that?" I asked.

"Has to be next of kin or an executor," Annie answered. "Gotta check." She started typing at her computer but stopped. A memory had kicked in. "Leticia Clark," she said. "That's the name. We double-checked because the family names didn't match. Miss Allard was survived by a stepsister who had proof she was the executrix. The remains arrived here Monday, and we checked her out that night. We got the stepsister on the phone the next day, and it took her half the day to get us proof of her status. Kind of nerve wracking, you know, worrying that the remains are going to reanimate and fight their way out of the locker. At least, the death certificate was accurate. Only one night had gone by when she arrived." Basil relaxed a little, losing some of the slouch he'd held himself in.

"It all went kind of weird," Basil said. "When her remains arrived, we did the inspection, agreed there was a risk, and placed the call to Ms. Clark. She wasn't interested in going forward with the funeral, especially with our recommendation. Surprisingly, she really focused on the refund when she found out the funeral was pre-paid."

"Pretty damn strange," I said.

"Basil," Annie said. "It wouldn't have made much sense to continue with the original plan. With the remains harvested like that, we'd have to do a lot of restoration before presenting her. Just as well it was cancelled if she wasn't planning to embalm. The main point was she would become a revenant

34

and would use Morty Coil's for her coming out party. That is not happening while we're on the H.O.C."

"H.O.C? What was that again?" I asked.

"Hygiene Outreach Committee, sponsored by Continental Grid," she said. "They've trained us to keep our eyes open for these situations."

"I'm surprised you're not more surprised, Dwight," Basil said. "You're handling this news well for a man of science."

"Science is a method," I said, offering a memory from a two-credit seminar on the scientific method. "It's an approach for developing knowledge, not a blockchain of guarantees. Look, guys, we were in some of the same classes. You're both bright enough and your hands went up as fast as mine. You know we just don't know everything yet. Yeah, I'm kind of amazed, though." Basil stood a bit taller, reassured by what I'd just said. Reality had just gone all pear-shaped on him.

"Yeah, that's good," Basil said. "I'm kind of freaked out by all this. Miss Allard's remains came in Monday, and we sent her out for processing Tuesday afternoon. Then, maybe two hours ago," Basil looked to Annie who confirmed with a nod, "a genuine OTG revenant just walks in through that door looking for her too..." Basil looked at me like he'd just seen me clearly for the first time. "Now you're here on the same subject." He held out the cross and took a timid step toward me.

"It's all good, Basil," I said. "Wow, dude. All right. Bring it." I held out my hand, showing I was willing to touch the cross. I figured I was safe because I hadn't been bitten yet.

Basil's confidence improved. He approached me. I held out my hand, reaching for the cross. He laid it across my open palm.

"Pffth!" Tiny coils of smoke squirted out between my fingers when I closed my hand around it. It felt way hot, so I moved it to my other hand. I heard "Pffth!" again. Another wisp of smoke accompanied the sound—the cross was burning traces of Wendy's dried blood on my insufficiently spotless hands. Nothing happened to me. I didn't burn.

I offered the cross back to Basil. He looked concerned. I guess he hadn't heard about smoke. Neither had I.

"No big thing," I said. "I had some kosher franks for dinner. So, wow, yeah. You had a real vampire come here earlier, right? O T B you said?"

"No," Basil said, "O T G. Means 'Off The Grid.' That's a revenant that has never been captured or is not supervised in any way. We were taught we might see a potential revenant once or twice in our lifetimes, but that we'd probably never see an animated one. So that was wrong. We know he's out there."

Basil explained the visit and how they'd driven an undead creature off with their crosses. If that was Roberto, Wendy's maker, they'd sent him off on a wild goose chase. He'd find nothing at Modern Memorials except firemen.

"So, it sounds like a lot went wrong for Wendy," I said.

"Sure did," Annie said. "She got harvested, despite the request on file here. She came in with marks showing she was probably contagious. Her stepsister—we applaud her for doing the right thing—agreed we should process immediately. And she said 'Cancel the funeral, including the catering. I don't know her friends.' She got worked up when we told her 15 percent of the deposit was non-refundable. She agreed, though, when we said we would send a check right away. No love there. So, everything got cancelled."

"Where'd her organs go?" I asked.

"I couldn't tell you where they ended up," she said, "but she was harvested at Central County General. I hope they did some good. The lives they save may offset a life gone to waste."

"What's your interest in this, Dwight?" Basil asked. "I didn't know she was in your circle."

"Like I said, I'm looking into it for a friend. I thought Wendy was an okay person, despite some issues we had," I said. "No, we were never involved, but I guess she respected my intelligence." Knowing that didn't do me much good. She expected me to find her scattered organs and reassemble her. She had Tanner for leverage.

Time to get on with it. Morning was a handful of hours away and I had no idea how long she'd survive with those organs missing.

"I guess I'm just closing a chapter of my life," I said to Basil. "I always had hope..." It hadn't been a reasonable hope. Annie and Basil just looked at me. Way too emo.

"Well, gotta be going," I said. "Have a better one." I congratulated them on their bravery, said goodbye and hustled over to the hospital.

DWIGHT
Wednesday, Just Before Dawn

The only two ways into the hospital at that hour of the morning was the main entrance or the emergency room. Both brightly lit entrances were on neighboring drive-throughs. I found space in the parking lot. I left my car farther away, as the surveillance recordings might not be low resolution. When a group of three people arrived at the main entrance, I tailgated them into the lobby.

Getting the organs seemed much harder than simply walking in. I couldn't just tap on the front door and say I was there to pick up an organ. Then I realized, yes, maybe I could.

After reading the lobby directory, I decided that the thoracic surgery unit appeared to be my most logical destination. I went to the front desk and announced to the woman on duty that I was there to courier a transplant to Veterans Hospital in the next town over.

"Third Parker, Suite 360a, Dr. DeSaul," she said.

"Where do I sign in?"

"You do the paperwork up there. Elevators three and four are on."

I was definitely nervous. I'd have been more comfortable being arrested at that point, but my audacity was succeeding. I could snoop around the hospital for recently collected organs—if they were still here.

I admit I was a bit stupefied by that time. My background in science led me to believe something like vampires shouldn't exist. But then I'd looked into the chest cavity of a woman who should have been dead, yet she was able to talk to me, manipulate me, and even intimidate me, all while still missing five critical organs. I'd just lied my way into a hospital, about to commit a…I didn't know. I'd always wanted a relationship with Wendy, but it didn't need to be so creepy.

The elevator opened on the third floor and suite 360a was a few steps down the hall. The open door showed a waiting area with a glassed-in reception area at the far end. Nobody was at the desk, but there was a doorbell mounted on the glass with a label reading "Attendant." I wanted to turn around and walk away, but I didn't have the nerve to go home empty-handed. I felt safer staying there a few more minutes. After changing my mind a number of times evenly divisible by two, I pressed the button. I heard a man's voice call back in response to the ring.

"Be there in a moment." A frail guy my age came up behind the glass a few seconds later. "Picking up?" he asked. The nametag on his clean white lab coat read, "Devin."

"Yes," I said. "Thanks for being ready."

"No problem. It's always 'beat the clock' when it comes to transplants. Which service sent you?"

"Uh, ummm…Damn," I said, "Sorry, it's slipped my mind, I freelance for so many. It went in one ear, out the other."

"Would it be Action Medical Transfer? I remember they called in for the liver we just harvested."

"Action," I confirmed. "That's them. You said harvested today?"

"Right, from a fifty-two-year-old heart disease case."

"Hmm," I said, "Doesn't sound right. Can I come back there and take a look around?"

Frail Guy looked very offended.

"Just joking! Wow, Devin, you've been here a few too many long nights."

"Oh, okay. Sure." He didn't look at all agreeable.

"Look, I may have crossed up my orders. I'll go back to my car and check my paperwork. Be back in a few."

Once I was back in my vintage LeMans, I drove out onto the central artery, a four-lane road with a jersey barrier down the center, broken up by traffic lights every five blocks or so. I didn't have enough knowledge of the hospital's systems to make the needed connection. Force was out of the question if I was going to find any other parts.

This left me without custody of any of the five internal organs important to the creature that might kill my best friend if she was unhappy or got the munchies.

I excel at solving problems if they're interesting—and this was interesting—but this one was way too complex for me to get my usual "Eureka!" Maybe the police could sort it out. I needed to save Tanner. I also still wanted Wendy—or thought I did. Besides her dying and reanimating nothing much had changed about my feelings for her. But if the police saved Tanner and controlled Wendy until they got her to the hospital, maybe she would be reunited with her organs. Of course, at that point I'd no longer be her savior: I'd be the guy who ratted her out to the police, got her jailed for kidnapping Tanner and for murdering some poor crematorium worker, and for conspiring to falsify public records—specifically, her death certificate.

"But this'll be good for you, Wendy," I'd have to say. "You need to take responsibility for your actions just the same as if you were still alive." Maybe she'd appreciate my maturity and insight.

I was still driving and thinking. What would happen if I did the right thing and called the police? I guessed it might go something like this:

> Police dispatcher: "Springfield Police. This call is being recorded. What's your situation?"
>
> Dwight (that's me): "There's a woman in my townhouse who's badly injured. She's missing some important internal organs which are probably still at

Central Hospital. We need to get them re-installed before dawn. Oh, and don't scare her or she'll kill my friend Tanner."

That approach quickly discouraged me, though I could manage to avoid saying the word vampire. If I faced the inevitable—that Wendy is out my league and would never be mine—I had to do right by Tanner. That call might've gone like this:

Police dispatcher: "Springfield Police. This call is being recorded. What's your situation?

Dwight (me again): "My friend is in danger. He's being held hostage by a dangerous woman who might kill him soon."

Police dispatcher: "What is your name? Where are you?

Dwight: "I'm Dwight Witken. I'm on Route 4a bypass, heading toward Hibbard Plaza."

Police dispatcher: "Where is your friend? Has anyone been hurt?"

Dwight: "He's at my house. The woman has a major wound in the abdomen."

Police dispatcher: "She's the hostage?"

Dwight: "No she's holding my friend Tanner hostage. You've got to hurry. She's getting desperate, and she could kill him."

Police dispatcher: "Where are they?"

Dwight: "They're at 92 Urbandale Road, unit 17-1."

Police dispatcher: "What are their names?"

Dwight: "Lehane Tanner. Wendy Allard."

Police dispatcher: "Is anyone armed? Are there weapons? How would she carry out her threat?"

Dwight: "There are some kitchen knives, but I doubt she'll let him get them. She is unarmed."

Police dispatcher: "How would she make good on her threat to kill him?"

Up until that last point, it was going fairly well. I was sure I could count on the police to do what they do best, which in this case would have been to get everyone—me included—under control and then sort it out as time allowed. Control the situation, segregate the interested parties, get their stories separately, and then try to reconcile them. In two hours, it would be sunrise, and Tanner might be dead before the cops ever set foot inside. Wendy believed she would go up in smoke if exposed to sunlight. Calling the police might be the right thing to do, but I'd probably be dooming one, if not both, of them. I turned around and drove for home. I'd have to improvise.

CHAPTER 3
DWIGHT

Wednesday, early morning

"You haven't got them!" Wendy was still alert. Upset too. "Oh fuck. I am so screwed. I feel so sluggish. Let me drink from Tanner or I'm going to be entirely out of it." She was flat on the floor where I'd last seen her. Tanner was sitting on the floor next to her, his back against a kitchen cabinet, his belt noosed around his neck. Wendy started pulling him toward her. Tanner braced with his arms, but her strength and the noose forced him closer. She dropped her jaw open wide. Two fangs flipped down inside her mouth, reaching past her upper lip.

I thrilled at her lethal beauty, still visible somehow through the soot and charring, but the trance broke as I saw Tanner's peril.

"Not so fast!" I shouted. She paused. "Let me ask you. How much worse off are you than when I picked you up? Give him some slack while we talk about this." She gave his leash some slack.

"Oh, thank God," Tanner said. Wendy squinted back at me.

"My legs are getting numb. I'm feeling weaker. I'm thirsty—I need to do some more sucking."

43

"But you're still alive, right?" I said, "or reanimated, or whatever it is that makes you go, right? You've got five major organs missing, but you're still able to talk with me and even reason with me. That's a huge advantage compared to being dead." I decided not to force a smile with my punch line. The emotional look on her face told me I did right.

"Think about how I see it, Dwight. I'm scared. I just finished dying what seems like what—maybe ten hours ago? That's what if feels like to me. I'm cut up, emptied out and hungry for blood, and I don't know where Roberto is. I need my organs and I need Roberto. I need blood." She started reeling Tanner in.

"Stop that, damn it!" Once again, she stopped. "Listen to me. Tanner, you too—let's think this through." I'd never seen Tanner look scared before. "Wendy, this vampire Roberto—he bit you early Sunday night, right? Now it's early Wednesday, and the story is you were dead until ten hours ago. Right so far?"

"Sure, I guess," she said.

"That's how I got it," Tanner said. He was very attentive.

"Would you agree this is not something biological? It is something supernatural, whatever that means? You might have been in a coma or in some hypnotic state, but with your heart, liver, kidneys, and pancreas gone, you should have been—and stayed—stone cold dead. But you're not. So, you are able to operate outside the rules of biology and physics that apply to Tanner and me. I'm not happy about this, but seeing is believing, I guess."

"What's your point?" Her voice was heated.

"My point is that maybe I can help you feel better now, and keep you going while I figure out how to get your organs back. I can try to get the information about where they went." I didn't want to tell her they all might have been transplanted.

"Look, since you've been getting along this well without five organs, restoring the function of even one organ should be a noticeable improvement. Do you understand what I'm saying?"

"I think so…"

"Do you really think you'll die—or whatever it is that happens—if you don't bite Tanner? Do you know it for a fact?"

"Well, no, but considering how this has been going…"

"So just stay calm. I've got a few ideas." Actually, I had no ideas. "I just need to snoop around in my workshop for a few things. Don't bite Tanner, okay?"

"I won't—not right now."

"Thanks again," Tanner said. His eyes told me he knew this was a temporary reprieve.

I hurried to my study, and immediately remembered the incomplete job I'd done feeding my fish. I hadn't gotten to the saltwater tanks yet. The food was next to a tank I was prepping for another saltwater habitat. I had several spools of surgical hosing for custom fitting a new high-performance circulation pump on the table, and some sheets of mylar mirror backing for the tank.

I'd left the new pump sitting out next to its shipping box. I'd been admiring its sleek egg-shaped layout and excellent workmanship. It was quiet ("Magnetically Driven!" it said on the box), high capacity, and transfers liquid at up to a hundred gallons per hour.

A quick online check revealed a human heart moves about seventy gallons an hour, so—within limits. Rummaging through my toolbox, I came up with a bundle of nylon cable ties. I returned to the kitchen.

"I have here what you might call a jury-rigged heart. Tanner, I'm going to need your help."

"You're kidding me," Wendy said. "What the hell is that?"

"It's a magnetic drive aquarium pump, salt water resistant, and designed for three years of uninterrupted operation. It's yours now—or I can see if we can find you a used beef heart in the supermarket tomorrow morning."

"Where is Roberto? I have no idea what to do." She was looking panicked again. The slack had gone out of the belt connecting her to Tanner.

"Wendy. Listen. Roberto or no, it's your decision and you need to decide now. Let Tanner help me help you. I'm pulling for you."

"You are? After what's happened between us?" Did she mean standing me up?

"You're still a human being," I said.

"I don't think so."

"I still care." It was true, though it was embarrassing to say.

"I needed a geek to get me through this," she said. "I chose the best one I knew. I hoped you were the right one. Okay. Do it."

"Let Tanner go, please," I said. She dropped the belt. Tanner moved to hands and knees, removed the belt, and eased himself into standing position. He looked stiff.

"You okay, Tanner?" I asked.

"I'm the most normal person in the room, aren't I? Gotta pee."

He scrambled out to the bathroom.

By the time he returned, I had collected my toolbox and brought it into the kitchen where I attached a clip-on light to the nearest cabinet door. Following my instructions, Wendy placed her fingers into her wound and spread her chest cavity open. I tried to not think about the grating sound.

We wedged a couple of shot glasses between her ribs to hold her open, letting her release her grip. I rolled her onto her right side to drain the pooled blood away from the cavity left by her missing heart. I looped a cable tie around the cutoff end of the right coronary artery, pushed the intake end of the pump into the tube, and pulled the cable tie tight around the intake flange. Once I located the pulmonary artery, I did the same with the pump's output. After double-checking all the clamps, I plugged her into the wall outlet.

Wendy's eyes went wide. A deep hum resounded from her chest. Her skin turned whiter. She grabbed my arm.

Her withered black fingers were irresistible, digging deep into my wrist. My hand turned red. She dragged me toward her, with no more effort than it would take to remove a tissue from its box. Her eyes glistening, she dropped her jaw open. She curled back her upper lip, and her fangs pivoted down behind her human teeth. She pulled me down toward her.

The bass note burbling in her chest stopped. Her eyes dulled and her grip weakened. I pulled away. Air whistled out of her as she collapsed back onto the floor.

"No, no. Not nice to try to bite Dwight," Tanner said, wagging the end of the power cord that had been driving her blood pump. "That looked like it felt better maybe?" he asked.

"Yes. Yes, it did. It was wonderful," Wendy answered. "You could turn it back on. Maybe turn down the speed. I promise I won't bite. I'm sorry. It's just reflex, I guess anyway. Like after I came out of that oven. I couldn't help that."

"What do you think, Dwight?" Tanner asked. "I can't give you a whole lot of perspective on this. She seems repentant."

"Plug her in," I said. Tanner restored power.

"Unplug me!" she shouted. She was reaching for me but dropped back when Tanner unplugged her again.

"What?" I asked.

"As soon as you turn it on, my thirst skyrockets. It takes over and it's all I want. I feel incredible with it on—really good—and I must drink."

"You're thirsty now?" I asked.

"Always, but I have some control this way. I feel weaker than when I woke up—like I'll run down and stop. I so need to see Roberto."

"Do you think you can keep from killing me if I give you my arm to drink from?"

"You'd let me? Oh Dwight. No. Not with the pump on. But I think I can control it this way. It's what I'm craving."

I said, "I guess that's what you signed up for, isn't it? You gave up life for nights on the run, frantic for blood. I don't get it."

Her widened eyes showed me the painful revelation, or at least that's how I read it. What had she gained by giving up life? She looked lost.

"Sure, Wendy. I'll do it for you. Try to think this way, okay? Say to yourself, 'I'm accepting a pint of blood from him.' Don't make it about taking it, okay? Imagine being grateful for each swallow." I got that tactic from a TV shrink's show about food addictions. His fat cat demeanor made me think he needed to follow the same advice.

I unbuttoned my cuff, rolled up my right sleeve, and lay down next to her on the floor, angling myself against her. I held my naked arm before her face.

"Tanner. If she goes more than thirty swallows, pull me away from her, okay?"

"I'll keep count," he said with little enthusiasm. He must have been remembering her strength.

"Thanks, Dwight." She pulled my arm to her mouth, her fangs unerringly lancing the big vein at my elbow. I jumped at the initial twinge, but quickly relaxed as she sucked and swallowed. Tanner's count went to twenty. She was going fast.

"Wendy! Stop!" I said. "You've gotta stop now." I was becoming scared.

She swallowed twice more. Then she stopped and released my arm.

"You said thirty, Dwight," she said. "That was twenty-two."

"If you couldn't stop at twenty, you might not stop at thirty either. Better to check before I got too weak. How do you feel?"

"Better."

KELLY
Wednesday Sunrise

The heart had been erratic all night, but its strangest behavior came near dawn. There was a sudden change where it felt like I was on a treadmill going seventy miles per hour. Everything felt consistent and steady. Ten seconds later it stopped. I felt it again a minute later, but only for a few seconds. A few minutes later, I was soaring. I was comfortable and powerful and surfing on the shimmer of the northern lights. I was irresistible and unstoppable.

The sensation lasted about a minute. Was that someone else having sex, I wondered? Do vampires do that?

I felt good. I'd felt energized before, but now I was feeling nourished, less anxious. The hospital still had me on a liquid diet. Dad had fed me milk soup at dinnertime. I was still hungry for something real—like a rare steak maybe—but the urgency had gone away.

Then for about half an hour I was back on the treadmill. Once again, the rolling rhythm had me desperate to get up and walk. Running would have been even better.

The sensation stopped just as suddenly as it began. Once again it came on, and stopped right away. That happened two more times.

DWIGHT

Day 4: Wednesday Near Dawn

"I'll find you something to wear," I said.

"Size six. An eight's okay if it's on the discount racks. Black, long sleeves, mid-calf to above knee. Not too high on the waist, okay? My boobs don't need any more emphasis. And maybe something with a lace or mesh panel to cover the split here," she said, indicating the surgical incision in her chest. The silver duct tape closing it didn't look that good.

"I mean something, I've got here," I said, numbed by the awkwardness of it all. I craved the approval of the most dangerous human-shaped creature I've ever seen. The hardest part to ignore was that Wendy, the princess of darkness I'd admired for so long, was gutted and charred. Not so pretty at that moment, but still Wendy.

My athletic gear had little to offer. My retired ultimate Frisbee gear gave minimal coverage. Thinking that way reminded me of my best black ensemble. I fetched a suitcase from the attic storage and fished out my karate uniform. Heavy black top, gusseted drawstring pants, and black belt was what I wore in one of my father's favorite photos of me. Two years of regular attendance and I was awarded my black belt right on schedule. One month later, a punk who knew Thai boxing beat the snot out of me at the campus beer cellar. I never told Dad and I never again volunteered to fight.

I pulled out a black zippered fleece I wore on winter days, a pair of my black socks, and a pair of black Chucks. When I returned to the kitchen with my fashion triumph, Wendy was talking to her friend Rose on my cell.

Wendy was saying, "No, he finished me off just before dawn. It took him three nights to drink me—yeah, I cheated by drinking some water. It slowed things down. Wow he got weird. What? Yes. It did hurt at first."

She saw the clothing I was carrying. "What the hell is that?" She said to me. "Rose—I gotta call you back." She put my phone down. "You can't be serious."

"Look Wendy. It's only fifteen or twenty minutes till sunrise. We need to get you settled and away from any possible sunlight or reflections. That's the way this works right? Sleep by day, sunlight fatal or very painful, something like that?"

"Yes. We are creatures of the night," she said, a lilt creeping into her delivery, that certain *je-ne-sais-noir* tone of hers that turned my head the moment its sound kissed my ears.

"Sorry, it's what I've got that's black. It's okay if they get, um, soiled. We need to get you changed and downstairs where you'll be safe. We'll need to help you down."

"Oh. Wow. Damn it all, I would not want to be caught dead dressed like that. But some of this stuff is burned onto me."

Tanner and I set to work on her lab coat and trousers with scissors, hoping to not jostle her too much. A few times I caused her pain when I cut too close to the cloth sticking to her arms. Even when we hurt her, though, she didn't get upset. She seemed almost curious about pain, like the quality of it had changed somehow.

We soon had her uncovered. At the completion of this phase there was an awkward pause.

"Nice," said Tanner.

"I never dreamed..." I began.

"Oh, come on, Dwight," she said. "You've never undressed me in your mind? I always thought you were the geek with testosterone. I guess from where your eyes are and from Tanner's heavy breathing that my boobs are still okay. I guess that's something. Hey, do you have a mirror?"

I almost said yes, thinking about the reflective backing for my new tank. She nearly charmed me, but she didn't need to see the charring and blisters on her cheeks.

"There's a mirror in the bathroom, but right now, you've got a problem with standing up. They messed up your abdominal support when they cleaned you out. Okay? So, let's slip you into something more comfortable.

We couldn't get her into the karate pants and fleece without disturbing some of her injuries. She reacted several times but let go of it quickly. The fleece was easier to put on than the pants, as the skin of her upper body had taken less damage from the oven. I tied the karate belt around her midsection, making an extra loop to use up its length. Wendy's midsection compressed as I knotted the belt. Her empty gut and split stomach muscles made her waist hourglass narrow. If she noticed, she said nothing.

What she did notice was the duct tape. "It makes my skin look yellowish," she said. "And it keeps coming unstuck. The edges are curling up." I made a mental note to do something about that, but we had more immediate problems to address first, like keeping her safe during the day.

We connected her to an extension cord we ran up from the basement. With me lifting her around her shoulders and Tanner taking her legs, we carried her down the stairs without dropping her or tangling the electrical cord around our legs. We laid her on my old sleeping bag, which Tanner spread out over the top of my washer and dryer. I hoped she wouldn't leak too much blood on it. There was still laundry in there.

She asked for my cell to make a call to Rose. Tanner stayed with her while I went up to the kitchen to get it. Sunlight had just hit my living room window.

"Hey, Dwight," Tanner said, "She conked out. Her pump's still running, but she just quit." She was flat on her back, her blackened hands curled near her chin. I tugged on a wrist. It felt rubbery. I shook her by the shoulders a few times. It was like shaking a sandbag.

"Wendy?" No response. I shook her harder. Tanner put his hand on my shoulder. He looked serious.

"Dude, maybe we should set fire to this place and leave," he said. "This was an incredibly scary night, and even unplugged she's dangerous. Your clothes dryer uses gas, right?"

"Hey, no talking like that, especially where she could hear us," I said. "Who knows how something incredible like her works? This shouldn't be, but still, here we are, playing dress the dolly with a damaged vampire."

"I need sleep," Tanner said. His eyes were glazing over. "Clean clothes. A spotless mind wipe. Maybe some oatmeal with raisins and almond butter. Check in with you later." He started up the stairs.

"Hey, Tanner? Sorry I got you into this." He stopped on the stairs and looked back at me. "I mean, she snared my cell phone and guessed she'd have a good shot at getting whoever was first on favorites."

"She's brilliant, man," Tanner said. "Got to admit. She said she was at your place, and could I please oh please come over. My bad for taking the bait. You know, at first, I kind of wondered if you'd kidnapped her." He shook his head. "Got that way wrong, didn't I? Sorry. Well, so long as we can unplug her and stay out of her reach, we have some degree of control. I'm hanging with you for now. I get your bed, though. Dude, you owe me that. Anyway, what's next?"

"With Wendy? Get her organs back into her for sure. I don't know how ready the hospital is going to be for reinstalling organs into someone they decided was dead. There might be some inconvenient pauses while they review policy and go fishing for an insurance approval."

Tanner smiled back at me. I did not expect that. Not at such a weird time. He amazed me. Despite the scare she gave him, he was resilient enough to further assist me in the noble cause. He helped me measure and trim the plastic hoses and caps we used to reclose or lock off connections to her missing organs. First, we clamped off all the leaks in her circulatory system. Next. we did her digestive tract and then duct-taped her abdomen closed.

We switched her pump off. Tanner flicked the switch on and off and then handed it to me. I tried the same thing two more times. No difference. She was out. Off. We left her powered down for the day.

She was rigid. We moved her arms or turned her head with great effort, but a minute later, she'd return to her original posture. Her mouth was parted enough to allow a glimpse at her fangs, tucked away against the roof of her mouth, no longer poking into her luscious lower lip.

I contemplated her restoration while Tanner went upstairs to sleep on my bed. I imagined I would win Wendy over if I just could figure out how to put her back together before that Roberto guy finally showed up.

KELLY
Wednesday Morning

The day shift nurses came by first thing in the morning, intent on changing my dressing and inspecting the wound's drainage. There was immediate consternation when they lifted the old bandages away from my ribcage. "Betsy, are you seeing this?" One nurse asked.

"How can that be?" Betsy said.

I was unable to see. They were standing over me, their hands over my chest, and I couldn't make out what had caught her attention. The first nurse, Amanda, was daubing the wound with a cold foaming antiseptic.

"What is it?" I asked.

Betsy looked away, avoiding me and the other nurse. She hesitated.

"The—uh—appearance of your wound is…atypical."

Bleeding? Infection? Gangrene? My stomach knotted up. "What…?"

More hesitation. "Amanda?" nurse Betsy asked.

"Yes. Well. It looks like you've healed up—almost completely. It's just… It's unusual."

I saw a pink line about the width of a pencil mark running from between my collarbones down to the top of my belly. Off both side of the line was a fringe of thin white fibers, each nearly as long as an eyelash. It was not obvious that my ribcage had been cracked open. In fact, my chest felt strong. This was not what the surgeon said it would look like. The drain tube was just lying there, next to the end of the pink line of scar, its bulbed end visible. It had been ejected.

Medical people must have this quiet horror-proof bunker state into which they enter, embargoing worries and fears and the impact of the unthinkably awful things they are obligated to tell patients and family. When they're in that zone, patients can tell. I knew I could. I wasn't even a little uncertain. The faint seam running down the center of my ribcage was more disturbing than any horror movie I'd seen. However, the medical people had the numbers taking their side: "temperature normal, BP normal, oxygenation at ninety-seven percent, pulse under seventy, blood chemistry normal. White cell count is normal. Your red cell count is down a bit—transfusion probably lagging your needs by a unit." They'd say this in a hopeful way, believing that a positive spin would help make it all good. I wondered if that meant they'd give me more blood.

I had to ask, "What happened that made it close up like that? I was told it'd be weeks—it looks like it healed up a year ago."

Amanda and Betsy had busied themselves with keyboard entry and monitor checks. They exchanged a glance between them at my question, but no one volunteered an answer.

As they left, they promised that my surgeon would give me more detail when he came by on his rounds. I hoped Masako would be on duty again that night. She would be straight with me.

Dr. Sanders, my heart surgeon, showed up very quickly. The anesthesiologist and the assisting surgeons joined him. Together, they looked at my chest. Then each took a turn examining and thumping it and listening to it with a stethoscope. Nobody was saying anything. Dr. Sanders left, and the head of nursing came in. Next, the hospital's ombudsman dropped in as the assisting surgeon left. People tagged in throughout the day, but I learned nothing more.

The hospital's legal team must have done a fine job preparing them for my questions. What a relief it was when Daddy inserted himself in the room after having restrained himself most of the day. Once he's determined to do something, he'll make it happen, and he decided he was going to see me. Instantly, I was calmer, and when I asked the staff for time alone with him, they were happy to comply.

"Daddy," I said once we were alone, "I'm feeling amazingly well. Miraculously well, and the staff here can't figure it out. To a person they've been saying things like this:

> 'Each individual demonstrates his or her own unique response to every known procedure. We're pleased to note that you're doing very well, and are getting all the benefits expected from the transplant. You received your signed copy of the surgical waiver, right? Ah yes, here's a copy. We regret we cannot make predictability the primary success criteria for transplant proce-dures. You'll be fine.'"

You may know I once was a reporter, but I also had opportunity to editorialize, and I did so for Daddy. He rewarded me with his proud smile.

"Coming from their leather chairs in legal or administration to my bedside, each one gave me the party line. No one has been able to say why I've healed so fast. What they say essentially is, 'whatever's happened—even if you decide it's bad, it's not going to be something that's our fault.'"

I explained, but Daddy hadn't yet seen the scar. He'd spent enough time in the waiting room to know the staff was not telling him everything, but once he was with me, he declined my offer to look. No self-respecting man of his generation would consider looking on his daughter's nakedness, or even an uncovered strip of skin that acknowledged her sensual identity.

After filling him in as best I could, he decided to go look for Dr. Sanders. Daddy wanted to get his own read on what was going on. The nursing staff managed to placate him while indicating some tests were still being arranged for me. A male orderly wheeled me away before Daddy got back.

I asked the orderly where we were going. A nurse would usually drop by to let me know of some upcoming test or medication, but this time I was whisked away without preamble.

"Just a routine test. Nothing to worry about." He was looking at me like I had a spitting cobra hiding under my johnnie.

My dad had taught me how to translate such talk. I imagined the orderly's real words: "Well, no, they don't know what's going on. If it were you, I'd worry. Hell, it's not me and I'm worried."

First, there were some X-rays, after which they injected me with something the color of grout. "Bullets? Shrapnel? BBs? Any metal plates, pins?" the technician asked. Then she started checking me all over for earrings and piercings, asking again if I had any metal fragments in my body. I answered no again and was then treated to fifty minutes of an MRI machine banging away. At each stop, I'd ask the technician what they'd found. "The radiologist hasn't seen it yet," she'd tell me. "We'll get you back to your room once he's verified the images."

KELLY
Wednesday Twilight

I waited for over an hour for the return trip to my room. Finally, the overdue orderly arrived to roll me back to my room. I'd have preferred to jog there, but that was "against regs." I'd have preferred to put him on the gurney and do the pushing, but even I knew that was out of character for me. As a healthy teen, I don't recall being all that engaged with physical activity. I was once fit enough to run cross-country, but I never was an all-round athlete.

On the way out of the radiology area, I asked the technician, "What did they find?"

"They haven't done the report yet," she said. Her eyes were on her clipboard. I think it was my report she was studying.

"You said that they'd send me back once they looked, and now you're sending me back. That means they looked, right?" She glanced back at me for a second. She returned her eyes to her clipboard, but seemed more engaged in deciding something than understanding the data.

"Your doctor will be giving you the results," the tech said, in her filtered-for-bad-news voice. She surrendered me to the male orderly and didn't look at me again until I was nearly out of the room.

On the return trip to my room, I got wheeled through the rehab area on the same level. The space was open to the west and well lit, with frequent skylights and a solarium area with comfy-looking chairs. The space was illuminated in the reddish orange of the late afternoon sun. I thought a lot of healing had occurred in that space. It felt more like a spa than a hospital. I wanted to stop there. I got the orderly to pause for a moment.

The sun was setting, dropping behind a ridge of distant hills. A riot of colors played on the horizon. Blue melted into a bright flash of green, which an instant later became yellow. Then I saw orange and finally a deep red lighting the underside of the few clouds on the horizon. The last rays of sunlight were playing in the area when the orderly insisted we get on back to my room.

As he rolled me back into the corridor, purple crept into the mix. My heart stopped paying attention to me. I heard the change in the audio beep of my heart monitor. The orderly's eyes went wide. He'd heard it too. It was beating at half speed, and with a degree of authority that felt like a drop forge pounding out steel parts.

"You're going to be okay, miss," he said as he hustled the gurney back to my room. "Code yellow!" he called out as he passed the nursing station. "Code yellow Austin 503."

Aside from feeling strange about how my heartbeat was ignoring me, I started feeling quite well. Powerful. I wanted to get up and jog a few miles to loosen up.

He got me back into the room. I wanted to get off the gurney, stand up, and maybe stretch a little bit. They wouldn't let me get up. I had to lie in place while a parade of experts came by. One after another became hushed and quiet as they examined me. They hung up films from X-rays and the recent MRI, and a few fluoroscopes on backlit panels on either side of my bed. There was a lot of murmuring and mumbling, and many incomplete questions or unfinished statements. Dr. Sanders made an appearance. He looked a bit lost. Keeping his voice low, I still heard him saying, "we'll have to wait and see," to everyone who queried him.

There was a lot of discussion, but none of it was including me.

"What is going on?" I asked, directing it no one in particular. I got no response, but everyone stopped speaking.

"What the hell is going on?" I screamed. Everyone froze in place. I was impressed at how loud I was. So were the people around me. Eyes were wide. I had their attention.

The physicians traded a series of glances, but Dr. Sanders got the short straw.

"There is some concern about these repeated—arrhythmias, let's call them. I think we may have to do a small exploratory procedure…see if there's a nerve pinch or blood vessel that is blocked or bleeding out. We'd like to do it tonight, if you're feeling up to it."

"You want to re-open my chest?" My voice cracked as I said it. Pressure started building in my ribcage.

"Yes…" he said.

Imagine the worst pain you ever felt. Did it come as a surprise? The worst ones do that, and I was feeling my worst pain ever. Before his "yes" completed…

I felt twisted up inside, like I was vomiting, except in was all inside my ribcage. It was the most painful cramp ever, and it wouldn't hold still.

Grunch. Grunch. The bones in my chest ground together, trying to pull further back from the surface. But then some twisted and pivoted outward. My bones were breaking. Skin lifted and split. Blood seeped out and around the protruding shards of bone touching air for the first time. A nurse stepped in to untie my johnnie and roll the front down. Seeing the slow-motion horror moving on my chest, she stepped back from my bedside.

It felt like someone was trying to open my ribcage from the inside with a crowbar and pliers. It was simply the worst hurt of all time. I couldn't speak, think, or breathe. I must have moaned. The pain was too big to be in any one place. Pain was everywhere.

The splintered bones tore twisted and pivoted, like they were threatening a potential intruder. Everyone in the room stood back. I heard a sigh and a thump. Someone fainted and had hit the floor.

I heard murmurs of fright from one of the nurses. No one was moving.

Then the bloody white slinters submerged, sliding back through the wounds they'd created, flesh closing behind them. I felt something still moving inside me, but it hurt less and less. I still saw movement below my skin as if wee snakes were moving beneath it. The stinging on my chest faded, replaced by a welcome numbness.

After most everyone was still standing back. The nurse on my left was nearest. Her eyes were wide. Her jaw hung slack. "What is doing that? How can it move like that?" she said, looking at Dr. Sanders. "Oh please, God, this can't be happening."

"Code! Code…something!" another nurse shouted.

What had happened on my chest was obscene. No one should be looking at my nakedness and the writhing of my wound. I pulled my johnnie back up over my chest and held it closed. Sweat blossomed from my scalp, and I fought to hold still. The movement had slowed even more, then stopped. What had been agony faded to a stern ache. Through it all my heart drummed along implacably, on standby for a long night of battle.

There was nothing but heavy breathing in the room for longest time. My johnnie was stained with wet blood, as if finger-painted by the bone tips underneath.

Dr. Sanders surveyed everyone standing around me to determine his or her state. Most eyes were wide. The orderly was assisting a nurse with getting up from the floor. As they came down from the near-hysterical emotions of a minute earlier, they murmured words with a tone of amazement. Monstrous.

Possessed. Special effect? Really? This chest right here, five inches from my face? A parasite?

Once again, no one was talking to me. How could they have missed my agony?

Doctor Sanders recovered enough to order the nurses to inspect my wound site while he studied my chart with renewed interest. When the nurses determined it was safe, the doctors surveyed the reconfigured ridge of bone and gristle and began daubing away the blood and frayed skin.

They were surprised to find I had few bleeding wounds. The skin over the bony mass nearly matched that on my torso, but a very bright pink. The signs of the multiple compound rib fractures I'd had minutes earlier were subsiding.

I let out a sigh of relief. Everyone else in the roomed looked back and forth at each other. No one had anything. I felt embarrassed for them.

"We'll analyze the results, and get back to you," Dr. Sanders said, beginning to back out of the room. Each participant slipped out of my room, many occasionally muttering the stock lie: "you'll be fine."

"I want to see my father," I said to anyone listening. I got no response. I asked if Masako would be on duty that night. That got a response of yes. I was relieved. I knew she'd talk with me.

I was alone for a moment, with someone else's heart sounding the drumbeat of my life. Amplified by the monitor, I heard the heart as if it were a soundtrack.

Still lying down, I felt like I was in combat. My heartbeat had doubled from one moment to the next, and then dropped back to normal. No warning, no build-up. Double the RPMs again. I lay there, rationing my breathing so I wouldn't hyperventilate. It would be better to walk. It would be even better to run. Then I understood: my body needed to keep up with the heart living in it.

I was disoriented from a sleepless night and a long day of tests, punctuated with a waking nightmare, and the unacknowledged desperation the hospital staff was displaying around me. Considering that it had been four days since the transplant, the medical team had become conspicuous by their absence. A team member had visited me every hour—until the bizarre wound had manifested. I had just become a huge liability to the hospital and the doctors still had no idea what was happening.

My heart monitor said I'd been in battle for five minutes, at about one hundred fifty beats per minute. It beat hard, and the medical staff must have monitored the same athletic beat at the nursing station. They all knew my heart had gone run-away, and they had all mentally turned their heads away. I was on an express elevator to hell. They were my unwilling witnesses.

My father returned at last. He had no illusions. Something was clearly very wrong with me, but no one had a good theory to give him.

"You sure don't look like you're dying, Kitten. You look like you just ran a few miles. Not what I was expecting."

"I think it's simple, Daddy. Whoever it was that had this heart before? It turns out they weren't done with it yet. It belongs to someone who only uses it at night. I think they gave me a vampire's heart."

Daddy didn't say anything for quite a while. He was thinking hard. "If that's so, Kitten, maybe it can be exorcised." My father admired Will Rogers.

A beat skipped in my chest. Five beats in a row missed. A stumbling restart, and then the rhythm of battle or exercise resumed. I had an increased enthusiasm for movement. Somewhere the owner of my heart was running down her prey, and there would be no escape. It would be final. I wondered what it would be like to run with her. I had to stay here while they try to change something in my chest. Only problem was, each time I had the thought of getting a human heart, my transplanted heart tightened its grip inside of my ribcage and held on for dear life. The radiating pain of bones about to break from the knotting of that once-trusted organ froze me in place like a bug on a pin. I was learning to not offend my new heart.

CHAPTER 4
DWIGHT

Wednesday Morning

After a refreshing breakfast of Mountain Dew, pork rinds, and pizza, Tanner stretched out on my couch. He said he'd call in to work later. Whenever he'd say that, I'd have my doubts. He never actually left to go to work. I never saw him call anyone. Somehow, he was able to maintain an apartment and a dependable car. He enjoyed being evasive. With everything else about his life, he'd just go ahead and tell me, sometimes with more detail than necessary. But his job—if it really existed—I was not going to hear about.

With the sun risen, I began my quest for Wendy's organs. I was bone-tired but too wound up to back off. Time was working against me on every front. I didn't know how long removed organs lasted or how they're stored and transported. What if her organs had been transplanted already? Four days gone by. They could all be transplanted.

Still, I had to look for them. Wendy's life—or reanimation—depended on it. After seeing the impact of the pump on her, I realized how powerful she might become once she was fully restored. She would be a goddess, standing there at the side of her maker, Roberto.

I was having a hard time with that last bit—saving Wendy to reunite her with Roberto. She might have been somewhat nuts—especially being that she'd become undead—but she was mostly a decent person with freaky tastes. I enjoyed finding the charming parts when she forgot to hide them.

Would I run this scavenger hunt for Wendy, even knowing that she was only using me until Roberto showed up? I hung onto this: Wendy had thought of me first as her way out of her weird-ass situation, and so far, she'd been right about me.

So why would she think—no, how would she know—that I'd be the one who could help her? You see, I take pride in being practical, rational, and reasoned. I'm also principled and a bit of a soft touch. Wendy had to have known about my thing for her. She must have sensed that I'd be willing to help her and that I take on difficult problems. I guess my feelings for her were strong enough to handle her taking advantage of me. She was fortunate to have me. I'd be fortunate to have her. It just wasn't going to be, because... Roberto. But I did what I did because I couldn't bear giving up hope.

From what I'd learned at the hospital, the security protecting transplant organs was weak. Their handling assumes that bureaucracy and obscurity is the best defense. Physical access control, positive identification, written authorizations, etc. didn't appear to be part of their standard. They don't advertise what they have, and they only give it to people they trust. In my case, I had a chance to pick up an organ if I'd only known the name of the transport service and the format for making a request. It could be easier to get than a credit card number.

I didn't know where to go for my information, so the hospital seemed like a good start. I made a double-strength cup of instant coffee and put on my phone headset. I set up shop on my kitchen table, supported by my notebook computer, a spiral binder, and a pen that deposited a useful trail of ink.

The night clerk at the hospital would probably have gone home by then, but I figured that alternative approaches could get me information that would make another visit more useful. After researching the local ambulance and medical courier businesses and downloading a staff directory from the nearby VA hospital, I dialed the number for the thoracic surgery department at Central Hospital, and asked the woman who answered for the transplants director. She said she'd put Dr. Wu on the phone. By then it was 9 a.m.

Dr. Wu picked up and acknowledged that, yes, in the past four days, they'd collected a pair of kidneys, a liver, a pancreas, and a heart. I said I was with the VA hospital and wanted to confirm they'd gotten our requests for those organs. Wendy Allard would have been the preferred donor because of her blood type. Wu laughed.

"Hearts go fast. They are placed right away. This one went from the donor to recipient, going down one floor to the coronary surgical unit."

No heart. I'd been grateful for my good fortune with the aquarium pump trick, but it was only supposed to be stopgap. I'd have to tell Wendy it was in someone else's chest now. I didn't want to do that.

I explained to Wu that I was an administrative assistant at the VA Hospital, and that we had a couple of veterans urgently in need of the kidneys.

"You're a couple of days late on that, too," Wu said. He explained kidneys have a slightly longer shelf life, but both had been transplanted. "Curious..." He didn't continue.

"Dr. Wu?"

"Very odd. Both recipients have had adverse outcomes. We may be retrieving both kidneys."

"Would either recipient be a veteran? If we can't help them out here at the VA, it'd at least be great to have on record that someone got a needed transplant."

"We don't track that. Speak to Vivian in medical records. Nothing happens until the paper travels across her desk to her out box."

Wu wouldn't transfer the phone call for me—probably beneath his pay grade—but he was willing to spell Vivian's full name for me. I was desperate for a way to make progress, so that gave me something. I worried it was all too late.

The Central Hospital switchboard connected me to her direct phone line, but three rings later it forwarded to a receptionist who told me Vivian was in a meeting and was due back any minute. She asked me to call back, but I said it was urgent and asked if I could just stay on hold "so my boss will see I'm doing everything possible."

I was put on hold and ended up listening to 101 Strings' "Tribute to Manilow." I didn't stand a chance. My eyes drifted closed.

DWIGHT
Wednesday Afternoon

I woke up four hours later, slumped across my kitchen table. My headset was still on, but I heard nothing. Vivian must have hung up on me hours earlier. Further inspection revealed that my phone's battery was drained. After reviving it, I found no new messages on my voice mail. Had Vivian been able to retrieve my number, she chose to make no effort to call me back.

I called her extension again. She picked up.

"Dr. Wu gave me your name as the person who could help me organize the information about the available organs from donor Wendy Allard. I'm at the VA, and they're saying we have a priority need for them all."

Vivian was not a member of the Dr. Wu fan club. When she asked why it wasn't the usual person calling from the VA, I answered, "You mean I could have gotten someone else to do this? The politics here are impossible. Please accept my apology. Can you help me then? Who is it that's authorized to call you?"

Without missing a beat, Vivian told me that I was too late getting in touch. All of the organs had been transplanted two to three days earlier. Maybe the kidneys would become available again. Or maybe not, if the pathology department got involved. Out of her hands.

"How about the heart?" I asked. "Is the recipient still in the hospital?"

"You know I can't give out that information—or you should know. They haven't provided you any training for this position, did they?"

"I can bring the forms to your office," I suggested.

"Of course," she answered, "but I won't be able to do it while you wait. I work in a system of priorities."

"I can be there in an hour."

71

"I won't be here at that time. If you must come by, arrive no earlier than 9:30 tomorrow morning."

"There are priorities?" I suggested.

"Precisely."

And I then had my priorities. In Vivian's office, I would find the roadmap to Wendy's organs.

KELLY
Day 4: Wednesday Late Afternoon

Masako dropped in after my dinner to see how I was doing. She hadn't been in the night before, and I wasn't sure if she'd heard about my chest incident.

Nutrition Services had provided me beef broth and yellow gelatin for my dinner. It was late afternoon and the beginning of her evening shift. I mentioned that I was desperate for real food. I wanted a steak, cooked rare if possible. Regret was visible on her face when she said that the dietician had ordered milk soup, broth, and gelatin for at least the next two days. The broth part sounded best.

Then I asked if she knew how the doctors were doing in figuring out my heart's bizarre behavior. She'd heard enough to know that everyone was officially scared witless of what they'd seen happen in my chest. She had an idea. She whispered it to me.

"You've got a kanshaku. It's a demon that lives inside the body. When you have a liver imbalance or a heart imbalance, the kanshaku for that organ moves it around inside."

"You believe this?" I asked. "Or is it a folk tale?"

"Folk tale, for sure." Her smile opened the way for me to laugh. I was shocked how loud I was. It felt good to let out a guffaw, and—even better—discover that my ribcage felt solid again.

"My grandmother told me about them to get me to eat right. 'You eat your oshinko pickles or you'll get a kanshaku.' Anyway, what else explains it better? Stuff moved in your chest, right? It must have been painful."

"True. It hurts like hell. I guess maybe I agree. The explanation must be something fantastic, but I don't know enough about what happened. I'd like to find out where my heart came from. How can I find that out?"

73

"Medical records. Vivian handles all that stuff. She may not be allowed to tell you, but she'll definitely have the information."

"Could I just go see her? I feel incredible now. I've got more energy than I know what to do with." I felt too well to waste time lying in bed.

"It's way too late in the day," Masako said. "Her shift ended at four thirty. Yes, too late now. Anyhow, if I detach you now, someone is going to notice," Masako said, but a knowing smile lifted the corners of her mouth. "Eventually."

KELLY
Wednesday sunset

Wearing a borrowed lab coat and scrub pants to cover my hospital johnnie, I found the door to Vivian's office unlocked. It was almost seven o'clock, so her absence wasn't a surprise, but the unlocked door was. I suspected that direct physical access was a security hole they didn't worry about. I sat down at Vivian's desk, finding myself sitting several inches too high because of her tacky embroidered seat cushion. A cable-knit yellow sweater was draped over the back of her office chair. I turned on her desk lamp and scanned the manila folders piled, filed, or fanned across her desk.

Not knowing my donor's name, I worried I'd have a lot of reading to do. There might not be enough time before someone noticed my absence. Daddy was going to relax in the lounger next to my bed, keep the curtains pulled, and tell the staff I was getting some much-needed sleep. He had a car magazine to read and there was a baseball documentary on the TV, the audio off. I had to promise him I wouldn't leave the hospital grounds.

I started browsing the folders in a vertical separator on the left front edge of Vivian's desk. The most current issues would be close at hand. I took the first and laid it open. I found a death certificate for a man of about forty years facing a photocopy of the back of his driver's license, showing that he was a cornea donor.

"I can't believe my luck," a man's voice said. "How do you do, Vivian?"

In the doorway, I saw a wiry young man, wearing a sweatshirt and baggy blue jeans. In his left hand, he held a small red-and-white cooler, just the size for a six-pack of beer. He had strong features and a confident stance, but he was also given to momentary flashes of distraction, as if he was losing his focus. The bags under his eyes told me he was tired.

"I'm sorry. I'm not Vivian. May I take a message for her?" I picked up a pen and a pad of sticky notes. "And you are?"

"Why, I'd think you'd know my voice by now, Vivian. I certainly know yours. Dwight. Dwight Witken. You were going to help me find out where my girlfriend's organs went, remember? You are going to help me, right?" His red-eyed stare helped me understand I had few choices open to me.

I was worried. I once tried working retail, but it didn't go well. I lasted only two weeks. I demonstrated no reluctance to talk back to unreasonable customers. However, I since learned to take a different approach with angry people since they're—well—angry already.

"Please, take a seat mister…what was it again?" I asked.

"Witken. Dwight Witken. Look, if you remember our phone call, you know that something tragic happened to my girlfriend, and what's worse is they've snipped out all her most marketable organs. She'd left clear written instructions saying to leave her intact. No embalming. No organ donation. She'd prepaid an intimate gathering at Morty Coil's for Tuesday night. So. I'm tracking down what was taken from her. She needs them back."

Scared. How could he just walk in and say aloud what I'd been imagining? I felt butterflies in my stomach. Did he mean it the way he said it? Something about him told me he had few limits. If I was going to get him to go away, I'd have to cooperate with him at least for a while. How would Vivian act? I had no guess. It would be me that talked to him—hiding behind the identity he provided for me.

"No disrespect meant, Mr. Witken," I said, recalling my most frustrating bureaucratic interactions. "Yes, something tragic happened, but let me suggest that she probably can't form an opinion about it anymore."

In the next split second, he was on his feet. He slapped the desk with his hands causing the lamp to pitch over and sending a stack of file folders cascading toward me. I caught the neck of the lamp with one hand and blocked the cascade of paper with the other. I was shocked by my speed, but Dwight continued to demand my attention.

"YOU MAY SUPPOSE THAT WENDY IS DEAD, BUT…"

I raised my hand between us to protect myself. Danger was coming.

"I'm sorry," I said. "I apologize. Please don't shout, okay? I don't do well with shouting." The new heart was beating faster, as it should in a flee-or-fight situation. "Please. If you'll tell me which medical records to check, I'll try to help, okay?" He'd been almost handsome a few moments earlier, but I was frightened by his contorted face, the bloodshot eyes, and his clenched fists. He could explode.

For a moment, he was frozen in his hostile posture. Something finally let him release his tension and take a deep breath. I don't think it was me. I was busy holding my own breath and bracing for a fist coming at me. I was grateful when he composed himself and sat down again.

"Sorry, ma'am. Since Wendy died, my life hasn't been the same. She convinced me that she had to be intact for her funeral, but somehow things have gone horribly wrong. Her heart, pancreas, liver, and kidneys were all removed—here, at this hospital—and her body was sent out for cremation. All against her express written wishes. So, it's my mission to recover her stolen parts… so she can, you know, be at peace. Can you help me?"

"You want me to tell you where the organs are? I can't tell you anything at all unless you have a signed release."

"I'll sign anything," he said, "Just help me get her back together."

"You two weren't married, were you? If not, I'll need to have a release from her next-of-kin." As he got up from his chair, this time with deliberation, he fixed me in his gaze.

"If you have any information about the organs taken from Wendy Allard four days ago, hand it over now." If I'd still had my old heart, fear would have stopped it then and there. My new heart was beating faster, but not so fast as to compound my alarm. Still, violence was standing an arm's length away from me.

"Allard, Wendy." I started thumbing through the folders standing up in the vertical pile in front of me. Wendy. Two nights earlier, Roberto had said to me, "You're not Wendy."

I found the folder right in the center. I opened it out on the desk and focused the lamp on it. Both sides of the folder had anchors for a stack of forms, probably twenty on each side. Each form had three to six examples of mostly illegible handwriting. As a journalist, I'd had some experience reading hand-written notes. I started deciphering.

"Next-of-kin authorized harvesting on Sunday, done later that day. Heart immediately transplanted…in hospital. We got the transplant center authorization." I lifted the page and found a fax from some national clearing center. Its header sheet had more logos than one of Daddy's NASCAR jackets.

The next sheet was the fax itself, authorizing transplantation of the heart to Kelly Williams, but I said nothing. I don't think I gave any hint of my discovery as I paged on through the next dozen sheets. I muttered "pro forma, release, release, pro forma, informational…"

Dwight watched and listened as I pored over the details. He was struggling to look more relaxed. He was too agitated to slow down and read the details from across the desk.

I was still scared. He had been verging on violence two minutes earlier, but he seemed rational for the moment. Still rightfully angry. His love's body had been defiled after her death. Her stolen heart had been transplanted. The heart he was seeking was right here in the room just feet away from him, in my chest, its rhythm solid and insistent.

I'd switched over to reading the papers on the opposite side of the folder. The top sheet had many entries, all with date and time, all in the same handwriting, most likely Vivian's. It was a log showing the dispersal of the organs. Wendy's liver was the second entry on the page. My—her—heart was the first.

"Liver," I said. I flipped a few pages ahead to another multi-logo transplant authorization. "Authorization was issued, payment assured by the Veteran's Administration." I moved back a page and found the log for the organ itself. "Released for transplant—what's the date? Sunday. Same day she was harvested."

"The pancreas…"

"It's still here isn't it," he said. Impatience was putting an edge on his voice.

"Don't know yet." I continued leafing through the right side of the folder. I found the records supporting his statement.

"Yes, it is," I said, attempting to sound impressed. "It was also released for transplant that afternoon. How did you know?"

"Where is the heart? She needs her heart back."

Oh hell. I didn't say that out loud, but worried he'd see a "tell" on me. I knew where the heart was. Oh, dear God, preserve me, I thought. Dwight wants the heart.

"Let me…" I said as I tried to figure someway to send him away. A new distraction thundered in my chest. The heart's rhythm was no longer my own: its former owner was awake and hungry.

"Kidneys," Dwight said. "Tell me about the kidneys."

I was sweating. A trickle had run down my side from each of my armpits. Another stream was tracing a trail down my lower back. I'd been scared like this once before, mistakenly locked in a dark basement as a child. I'd sweated then too. Soon I would smell awful. I shouldn't be allowed to sweat.

My fingers kept working the folder for me, and I found the kidney information two pages later.

"Both were transplanted here on Monday."

"Give me the folder," he said, his face making it clear that compliance was my obvious choice. I flattened the pages, folded it closed, and held it out to him.

"You've been great, Vivian. Let's hope we never have to do this again." He slipped the folder under his arm, holding the cooler on the same side, and let himself out.

I slumped back in Vivian's chair when he went around the corner. My stomach was roiling, trying to pitch acid out through my mouth. I felt lightheaded and confused. That was the most frightening man I'd ever seen up close. I was beginning to believe that I'd guessed right. I'd guessed that, somehow, I'd gotten the heart from a woman named Wendy Allard—and that she wasn't properly dead yet. In fact, she might have been feeding at that moment, judging by the heart's sinuous yet insistent contractions. Was I feeling her pleasure? I shuddered at the thought.

Dwight Witken had not looked how I'd pictured a vampire. I'd been thinking Edwardian coats, tall lace collars, and an alabaster pallor would be standard issue. This guy looked like a cross between a violinmaker and a decathlete. His clothing said geek. But he was clever and athletic too. A vampire would need to be like that to survive if it really drank blood.

I sat a little taller and took a breath. I focused on breathing until I felt a bit better centered. The nausea backed off, but I was still scared.

Whatever Dwight was, he had in that folder the information he needed to find Wendy's heart. Now all he needed to do was to find Kelly Williams, and he could work that all out inside this building. I needed to be as far away from him as possible as soon as possible. If he kills to stay alive, I might be on his menu—and serve as the incubator for the heart he sought. Time to leave.

ROBERTO
Wednesday Evening

The nameplate on her desk said Vivian Randall, but I knew the woman staring at the top of her desk wasn't her. Vivian Randall hadn't called me here—this woman had. Again. No one else would have thought about seeing me, but she looked up from her desk as if she'd known I was there all along.

"There you are again. You're Kelly, right?"

"And there you are again, Roberto. How is Wendy?"

The sound of that name jarred me. I'd forgotten why I'd returned to the hospital. I was diverted by Kelly's summons. How did she do that to me?

"I don't know," I said as I entered the meticulously organized office space. I sat on the straight-backed wooden chair situated opposite Vivian's desk. The inhospitable chair situated directly in her line of sight told me Vivian didn't enjoy getting visitors. "I haven't been able to find her. We were supposed to meet last night, but she wasn't there."

"I'm sorry to hear that. Is that what brings you here?" She asked.

"I found out she'd been in this hospital a few days ago, so I'm looking for any information. For some reason, I came to this office. Call it a hunch, but it was another bad guess. At least I get to see you again."

She was waiting for me to ask her something. I started with the obvious.

"You were in that hospital bed plugged full of wires and tubes three nights ago. It seems just a bit odd to find you at a desk working well after dinner time."

She froze me with her gaze. I held perfectly still, transfixed, frozen in the moment while I watched the subtlest workings of her face. Her mind was racing. And she was welling up with feeling.

"I'm looking for answers," she said. I felt something powerful was going to come from her. I think she was about to tell me her unvarnished truth. I was thrilled by the power I sensed from her.

"Four days ago, I had a heart transplant. It seems like I've recovered a little too quickly. I've asked the doctors for an explanation, and all I get for an answer is, 'there's nothing to worry about, you're fine.' When I ask why I've healed so quickly, the doctors suddenly remember urgent matters elsewhere. So, I'm doing my own research." She was studying my face, intent on my response.

"And what have you found out?"

"Simply put, I have reasons to worry." She looked relieved to be able to say more. "There was a complication with the donor."

"Was she ill? Immune deficiency? Cancer? TB?" I couldn't imagine any of these things would be a problem for her. When I first met her, I sensed how she was wounded by the surgery and a lengthy illness. Now I felt I was in the presence of an athlete.

"I don't know what she had," she said. "I'm fairly sure she wasn't normal, though, because now neither am I."

"That's true. You are very special." Was she surprised? She was hard to read. I felt at a disadvantage. She seemed to have me completely figured out.

"Um, thank you," she said. "Anyway, I was trying to find out about the donor. I was told the records were in this office, so I sneaked out of my room and came down here to read up on it. I found her folder, but then this crazy guy came in and took it."

"What was he looking for?" I asked.

"This is why I think he's crazy, or at least dangerous. He told me his girlfriend died four days ago, and her organs had been taken for transplants.

He thought she wanted to be buried with everything intact, so he's trying to get her organs back. He needed the folder to find out where they'd gone."

"The organs? He's trying to get them back? Why didn't he just call the hospital administration and say there's been a mistake made? I'd think that'd be the appropriate first step—get the people in charge to fix the problem."

She was surprised at my reply. Again, she was assessing me.

Kelly said, "I think that's something the next of kin must have requested, so they'd be the ones to intervene if a mistake had been made. Bottom line is a family member would have signed the authorizations. Dwight is operating on his own."

Why couldn't it have been Kelly who was the one to join me for eternity in my undead existence? She talked right to me, not at me like Wendy did. When Kelly was listening to me, I felt like every fiber of her being was committed to the act. She used more than her hearing, though, and that was unnerving. I'd come to believe there were two ways for people to exist in the world: they were alive or undead. She was something else yet again. The world held at least one other type of supernatural being. Despite her powers, though, she hadn't called me out as a vampire. That much about me was still hidden, or so I hoped.

I felt like I'd made a mistake. Out of the desperation of loneliness, a consequence of the isolation driven by my cowardly attacks on the living to relieve my bloodthirst, I'd accepted Wendy's offer of companionship. "A love through the ages," she'd said, though neither of us had confessed love for the other. I'd spent perhaps seven minutes altogether with Kelly and already I loved her more. Now I wanted to protect her. A crazy man had threatened her. This shouldn't happen. I pointed to her telephone.

"You better protect yourself," I said to her. "You should get the police here. Can you give them a description of this Dwight guy?" I didn't doubt that she could. She didn't miss anything.

"I better start with hospital security. They're right here in the building. They'd need to show the police how to get around in here." Kelly looked around the desk for a moment, and then at the phone. "I don't see anything giving the number for Security. Vivian must have it memorized, or never needs to use it." She picked up the handset and dialed zero. I heard it ring five times.

"Hi. Yes, give me Security please," she said, then pausing to listen. "No, I'm not Vivian. I'm a patient here—Kelly Williams—and I'm being threatened. Yes, I'll hold." I heard a faint trickle of harpsichord music, overlaid with the voice of a woman announcer extolling the virtues of the hospital's orthopedic care unit. A man's voice broke in.

"Security."

"Yes. Hello, this is Kelly Williams. I'm calling because a man came here who is dangerous to me. Yes, I do remember you. No, he's not here now, but I'm sure he'll be back. That's right, I'm in an office. No, he didn't come to my hospital room. I saw him here in this office." She listened for a moment and then looked up at me.

"No," she said, her eyebrows pulling up. "He wasn't the one who came to my room three nights ago." That detail was meant for my ears. "This was someone else. He gave the name Dwight Witken. Yes, I'll stay here." Kelly hung up the phone.

"I'm sorry, Roberto, you better go. When you came to my room three nights ago, I mentioned it to a nurse and she called Security. I told them a stranger had come in, and described you, but I didn't tell them your name."

"Why not?" I asked. For the first time since she'd seen me, she released her hold on me, looking down at the desk for a moment.

"I don't know. I wasn't suspicious of you. Anyway, they err on this side of being thorough, and if I must explain you, it's going to confuse the story about this Dwight creep. They're on their way."

I didn't want to leave. Being with Kelly was as fundamental as breathing. I couldn't imagine doing without it. Among her supernatural powers was a talent for being right, though.

"I understand," I forced myself to say. "This must be frightening for you." In an instant, she had me in the grip of her spell again. Her eyes were holding me in place.

"This is crazier than you can guess," she said. "I should still be in a hospital bed, but I feel like I can run a marathon. The incision on my chest is, is…It's completely healed, bones and all. This heart came from someone incredibly powerful. It feels like it's enough heart for four people. The woman who I got it from? I don't think she's actually dead. Roberto, do you believe in vampires?"

A ding announced an elevator door opening. I heard voices in the corridor. I guessed it was Security. Kelly looked toward the corridor. Deciding that being no-one-here-right-now might not work with the Security people, I made an undignified exit by dropping below desktop level and scurrying around the far side of the cubicle area from the approaching pair of guards. I would have gone sooner if Kelly would have relaxed her hold on me.

I hated hiding under a desk, but my only choice was to wait for the guards to finish their inquiry. The night-to-night existence of a vampire offers none of the glamour of the fanciful novels I've scanned and tossed, though I did owe them some gratitude. Had Wendy not read them, she might not have chosen to join me in this craven and lonely existence. Living in fear of the so-called ministers from CG—not knowing enough about their policies and tactics—hiding became my norm. I kept my focus on my hearing, minimized my breathing, and waited for the young man and woman to complete their interview with Kelly and leave. The man was speaking.

"Miss Williams, do you understand you're in a non-treatment area? That band on your wrist says you're under our care here, so it's mandatory you get back in your room and into bed."

The woman had also been talking to a phone that needed to chirp with each exchange. She had been saying something about needing an orderly. Kelly spoke.

"I understand that the issue at hand is my safety and health, but let me call your attention to the fact that I'm not safe here anymore. The man who just left here is clearly dangerous. He's on a fanatical quest that is going to lead him right to me, sooner or later. And it's clear my health is of no importance whatsoever to him."

I worried that she meant me. Though I have little to fear from any living human being not holding a cross or holy water, if I were spotted and chased, it might divert me from getting to my day lair. I couldn't go there while they had me in sight.

I recall a night when I was pursued by a policeman on a bicycle. He kept up well, taking over an hour to elude. I had to cower, thirsting, among the denizens of a homeless shelter. Trying to feed in their midst, though, would have brought more opposition than undead strength could handle. I was ravenous. My gut grumbled all that night. I climbed out a bathroom window just before dawn and ran in a panic back to my second lair, a boarded-up industrial building on North Springfield's south side.

Kelly was sounding emotional. The security people were discounting her claims of danger.

"His name is Dwight," Kelly said. I heard an angry edge in her voice. "Dwight Witken, he said. He's emotional, erratic, and threatening. I think he's trying to do the Frankenstein thing—re-assemble his girlfriend from her scattered body parts. Anyone who received a transplant organ from her is in immediate danger."

Her statement went right over the security people's heads. They'd already decided they were dealing with a whacko. From there on they stopped listening, missing entirely her competent and detailed description of Dwight. Their focus was getting her out of the chair and onto a gurney. An orderly was rolling one in from down the hallway. Every step was predicted and confirmed by telephone. The chirping and the distorted voices were deeply grating to my ear.

Kelly's pull on me hadn't stopped for even a second while the security people were interviewing her. She resisted leaving the area, rejecting all offers to assist her getting on the gurney. She backed up to it, put her hands back, lifted herself to a seated position, and then pivoted as if she was going to lie back. Instead, she sat cross-legged, her arms folded on her chest. She refused to lie back. The gurney's wheels rattled as it crossed the threshold of the cubicle area, as the officers and the orderly took her back down the corridor.

I was holding the legs of the desk that sheltered me to keep myself from running to her aid. She would be safer with the hospital staff. I clenched my fists and bit through my lip as I fought to stay out of it.

"No! No!" Kelly was saying. "You don't understand. He was just here. Check your surveillance. He's going to come back. He's going to take my heart back. Please. Why won't you listen to me?" The conversation cut off as an elevator door closed.

I left the hospital. I needed to contact one of Wendy's friends if I was going to make progress finding her. If I stayed at the hospital any longer, I'd be drawn back to Kelly.

DWIGHT
Day 4: Wednesday Night

I parked my Le Mans in the carport next to my townhouse and hustled inside, folder in hand. Vivian had given me the roadmap to my task with that folder. I thought it would be the easiest to go after the kidneys first. I only needed one of the two to fix Wendy up, assuming her physiology still had some basis on her previously human condition. So, I was back to my scavenger hunt. The hard part would be the heart. No idea where the heart was. At least the pump we'd put in her was keeping her going. We were still having some leakage issues at that time. It was time to coordinate.

"Tanner? Hey man, where are you? Hey! Tanner?"

"Down here, Dwight." He didn't sound right, maybe like he'd been drinking. I scrambled down the stairs to the basement. He and Wendy were sitting next to each other on the basement floor, leaning back on the wall next to the washer and dryer. She was working Tanner's arm like it was corn on the cob. His eyes were closed.

"Let him go!" I yelled. I startled them both awake, but Tanner's eyes opened more slowly. Wendy looked disappointed, like a kid whose lollypop had just fallen into the dirt.

"It's okay, dude," Tanner said. It sounded like he was stoned, though I'd never known him to do that before. "S'all good."

Wendy looked beautiful. She'd somehow shed the burns, scales, and scabs gained during her aborted cremation. Her skin looked sort of gray, but it was smooth and unblemished. Something still smelled bad, and I was pretty sure it was her, but now it was more like a men's locker room than an incinerated steak.

"Step into my office, will you," I said to Tanner. I held out my hand to help him up. "Be right back," I said to Wendy. Tanner managed the stairs on his own and I followed him up. We stepped out through the kitchen door to the carport.

"What the hell do you think you're doing?" I asked. I was worried we were indulging her too much, but it also bothered me that the scene I'd walked in on looked intimate, like they were making out.

"Damn it, Dwight. Give me a break." Tanner pushed past me and turned to stare me down. "I should be grateful for you bringing such exciting new elements into my otherwise pedestrian existence, but honestly." His face relaxed a little. "It's actually kind of nice after the initial bite—very relaxing. And it is more like she's a baby sucking at her bottle than a Dracula type when she's feeding. She sips and licks, and it sort of tickles. I nearly dozed off before, but she was all pepped up and had me put on some music. She would be a great dancer if she could just stand up straight, but her belly is messed up. I haven't quite figured out how that gets fixed."

That was exactly the kind of exposition Tanner was prone to while trying to distract me, but he had a point. She needed a substantial upgrade. I sat down at the table and opened Wendy's donor folder.

What's this? Her dental records?" Tanner pivoted the folder on the table to read the label.

"Oh man, Dwight, this is serious stuff. Or do they even have a crime for organ theft? Oh, wait."

"Wait for what?" I asked.

"You're going to actually go on with this?"

"What?" I was deep in thought already. "The kidneys, I guess. She smells like low tide meets a urinal."

An hour of studying various Internet resources gave me the fact that made the crime I was planning slightly less distasteful. Most kidney patients keep their old asleep-at-the-wheel kidneys and have the new carry-the-load kidney installed just downstream. No special skill would be needed to find it. If you see an incision in the side of the abdomen, just follow the wound and there's your kidney. The first abdomen I was going to look at was back at the hospital.

KELLY
Wednesday Night

Daddy agreed to let them medicate me. He didn't come in to see me: he took their word for it that I needed it. Their justification for doping me up was my agitated state and unpredictable heart rate. They injected something into my IV that made me muzzy-headed, and about ten minutes later, Masako coaxed me into swallowing a couple small white pills. I was peeved with being so relaxed. They were trying to distract me from something. Something like Dwight coming to take back the heart and reinstall it in Wendy's corpse. I fought off the drowsiness and reminded Masako that I needed to leave so I could save my own life. That wasn't what hospital staff wanted to hear about my recovery.

When they had me sufficiently stupid, Masako brought Daddy in to see me. I had started explaining that I was in danger from Dwight when my surgeon, Doctor Sanders, and his entourage came in. I tried to engage them, but they recharacterized my fright by saying, "patient presenting with anxious demeanor." Just another symptom. They were intent on giving me a physical once-over while trying to figure out what I was really going on about. Daddy stepped back and looked away.

The exam proceeded normally until they got to the main point of interest. Doctor Sanders inspected the wound site first. Though the scar had faded to light pink, the rearrangement of bone in my chest gave me some odd bumps and valleys. A couple protrusions looked like they might break through, but I felt no discomfort. Dr. Sanders recited a list of medical observations, a jargon I've never mastered, and then let Dr. Harper, the head of transplant medicine, have a look. Another man he introduced as Dr. Morgan joined them.

"I see what you mean," Dr. Harper said. He'd been quiet for the first fifteen seconds of his inspection. "Kelly—is that your name? How long ago was your surgery?"

Someone was speaking to me directly. I was caught off guard. I wanted to say that Dwight wants to take my heart back and put it in his dead girlfriend. Instead, I said, "Four days ago."

"Do you usually heal so quickly?"

"It seems unusually fast to me, but it's my first heart transplant." Masako snickered and Daddy grinned. The entourage kept straight faces.

"Look," I said to Dr. Harper, "something very unusual has happened here, right? This is not an ordinary heart. And there's someone who is out to get it and the other organs from the donor so he can restore them to his dead girlfriend. If she was dead. This guy Dwight is going to find out who's got the heart and come try to get it back. He's got the donor files, and he's going to find my name is in there. I need to get out of here." As I spoke, a woman's voice on the PA system called for Dr. Morgan, asking him to call urology.

"Is it that kidney transplant again?" Dr. Harper asked the latest doctor inspecting my disarrayed ribcage.

Dr. Morgan answered, "Yes, but which one? Probably the older man again—he's not doing so well. I thought he'd settled down this morning, but tonight, he's micturating like a racehorse again. He's probably dehydrated too. It's going to have to come out. You should come along. I need a consult. Another baffling case." They left the room.

"I'm sorry, Kelly," Masako said. "If it's any consolation, they're the hospital's best team. They've got something urgent to look after, but I'm sure they'll come back when they can."

"I think you don't believe me either," I said to her. She looked trapped.

"I believe you. I just don't know what to do."

"It's simple. Help me leave."

"It's not that simple," Masako said. "I can't sign you out. Only Dr. Sanders has that authority."

"I can just walk out, if you promise not to notice."

"No," she said. "If your monitoring is interrupted, it signals the nurse's station. It's now configured to also page Dr. Sanders. Look, I should get back to the station. I'll sit where I can keep an eye on your door, okay?"

"Okay," I said. Masako left. "Daddy?"

"Kitten?"

"Do you believe me? I need to leave now," I said. Daddy frowned.

"They're going to be resistant," he said. I was so grateful to hear that. He was starting to see it the same way I did.

"I guess I can see why, but they're leaving me at risk from that whacko. Can we put together a list of what I will need to leave? Will you help me? I need to leave as soon as possible."

Daddy's yes was conditional. He simply had to go through channels one more time. He marched his way up through the available administrative hierarchy, finding them almost all working past 9 p.m. Each bureaucratic level quickly explained to him the next level he'd need to petition. It quickly ended at the hospital president's office.

"His secretary said 'he's not in,'" Daddy said, "but the lights were on in his office. She wouldn't look me in the eye." He'd explained there was an urgent issue with his daughter's safety, emphasizing I was a heart transplant patient there.

According to Daddy, the admin had said, "that's all he's been dealing with the last two days. Several transplants haven't gone so well." Daddy asked for more information, but she clammed up.

It was all the stonewalling that convinced Daddy. He stopped by my room on his way to collect some of the items from my list. He already had my bag of release-day clothing waiting in the back seat of his car. That sweet man had believed all along I would be coming home. He was my rock when my heart was failing.

KELLY
Thursday, Early Morning

We were forced to test out nurse Masako for her sensitivity to my exit. I didn't want it to hurt her professionally.

"You and Umakan want to run away, right?" Masako had figured out what we were up against.

"Who is Umakan?" I asked her.

"That's the name for the kanshaku spirit for the heart. I'm trying not to be superstitious, but something strange is going on there. The doctors are clueless, and there has been an ongoing stream of transplant emergencies the past two days. I think they may be a little frightened. You're the only transplant recipient that seems to be doing well at this point. Three others— maybe four—are quite ill. Top staff are totally focused on this, which is why it's hard to get their attention. I wish I could sign the release forms for you."

"And if I just leave?" I asked. "The alarms go off?"

"Yes. You're under continuous monitoring. Betsy is covering for me while I'm making this personal appearance."

"Can you perhaps let me know when you go on break? Call?"

"Should it be a long break?"

I started to change clothes, but the johnnie revealed the electrodes and sensors that completed my prison. Masako explained what we needed to do. She returned to the nurse's station.

About ten minutes later, the phone rang. Masako's voice was clear and maybe too convivial.

"Okay, Marjorie," she said. "I'm on the way to the cafeteria. Don't forget a deck of cards." An instant before she hung up, she whispered, "Good luck, Kelly."

KELLY

Thursday, early morning

"You look like the Bride, Kitten," Daddy said.

"You mean *like* a bride?" I asked.

"No. That yellow tracksuit—if your hair was a little blonder, you'd be the swordswoman from that Tarantino flick."

"Except that I don't have a sword. Look, I've got to go now." I kissed him on the cheek. I'm certain his heart rate went up. "See you in a couple of hours." That would give me time to get away and at the same time stretch my legs. I needed to run.

Though the heart was beating with a tranquil roll to its rhythm, I had power enough to send myself dashing down the sidewalks. I was moving. I no longer had to resist the surge of energy I got after sunset.

Daddy and I had planned to meet at the I-Way truck stop out in the northwest corner of the city. He insisted I take the twenty-dollar bill he had on him, and Masako lent what cash she could. I had Daddy's cell phone, as mine was still home on the charger. I took a bottle of water, slipped out of my room and down the hall to a stairway.

I was liberated. I had transformed from deathbed invalid to world-class runner in four days.

I learned later that they discovered Daddy in the lounger next to my hospital bed reading a magazine. The heart, oxygen, and blood pressure readings had been coming from him for almost ninety minutes without the staff noticing the impressively normal pattern on the vitals monitor. Masako finally decided to notice something out of the ordinary and followed protocol from there on. Hospital security took charge of Daddy.

By the time they'd sorted out what had happened, I was ten miles away, running. My leg, hip, and back muscles emphatically protested being put to the unnatural task of exercise. However, they were not short-changed for oxygen. I had energy to spare. It was dark out, but the cool air in my face was invigorating. It felt like the occasional breezes that came as a relief while running cross-country races. It was magic.

At one point, I was running through a well-to-do neighborhood and hopped up to run along the stone block wall enclosing someone's estate. I came to the driveway, where a pillar supported the iron gateway protecting the driveway. I stood on the pillar, took a standing leap, and landed on the pillar on the opposite side. I ran along the wall again, even faster.

When the wall ran out, I returned to sidewalk running and came tearing up to an intersection. The light in my direction turned yellow. I took two bigger steps and leaped, crossing the street and landing on the far sidewalk. The light finished turning red as I stuck the landing. There were no cars at the intersection to witness my feat.

My new heart was beating in a variety of ways, none of which had any relationship to my exertion. At one point, its rhythm was shallow and thready. I dashed along unimpaired. For about ten minutes, it thrummed in my chest like it was in ecstasy. This was followed with a metronome-like pulsation that insisted it was time to dance. It felt odd identifying that feeling since I never had an aptitude for dance.

I worried that I might not last that long, but I made it all the way to the I-Way truck stop, ten miles away from the hospital. I arrived walking at a brisk pace. Sun rise was coming soon. Would control of the heart be returned to me then?

Daddy and I agreed our house might come under surveillance, if not by the hospital or the police, then maybe by Dwight. At that time, Daddy might have still been in custody of the hospital authorities or the police. Was it protective custody? Then he would be asking them the obvious question,

"Protecting me from what? Protect me from helping my daughter?" He'd have the police exasperated within five minutes—ten at the longest.

Daddy had suggested the truck stop for their reliable food, reasonable prices, and for their small rooms with showers. Cash was accepted. I was finally going to have a meal of genuine solid food while I waited for him. He planned to meet me there after he was done at the hospital.

The lobby clock said it was five-twenty in the morning. I'd been running or walking for almost two hours. The heart gave me more than enough energy to get there.

I sat down in a booth and closed my eyes for a second. It was the most privacy I'd had in weeks.

"Shouldn't be driving if you're that tired, Hon," a woman's voice said. I opened my eyes to see a waitress of about the same age my mom would have been.

"I'm okay, thanks. Or I'd like to think I will be soon." As I said that, I realized I had no certainty I'd ever be okay the way I was before my birth heart died.

"Sorry," I said. "Can I get a cup of coffee and a cake donut, please—and a glass of water, no ice?" I said, turning down the offered menu. I wanted to wait for Daddy to join me.

About then I began asking myself, who would have had such a powerful heart? Why would it be needed? How could someone die with such a tenacious cardiac muscle? I tried to imagine the body where the heart had been born, where it fit in and belonged, but didn't come up with the mental image.

Anyway, it was the behaviors implied by my heart's various rhythms that concerned me most. Why would someone need to be this ready, this intense, all the time? When the heart rate doubles, the violence must be unimaginable. This heart had to belong to something no longer human, something that must avoid the day. Again, I thought vampire. If there was such a thing, how would it live without a heart? I knew I couldn't. If this was Wendy's heart—and somehow, she's still alive—I imagined she might want it back.

Things looked bleak. It would be so bad if the monster that once owned this heart came back for it. Could it find me through our heart connection? Would she be coming closer every night? Every minute? How would she take it back?

While waiting for my coffee and donut, I let my eyes close again. I saw Wendy standing over me, faceless yet monstrous, tearing open her blouse to reveal her scarred chest—one like mine. Bony fingers dig into the ridge and she pulls and struggles and stretches the seam open, revealing a noisy metal egg, its shiny housing streaked with blood, jiggering back and forth, a substitute for her missing heart.

She speaks. "Return to me!" My chest swings open, like the doors on a wild west saloon. My heart squirms and writhes, breaking free of its connections to me. Disconnecting from my last weakly spurting artery, the heart knots itself and then swells, leaping from my chest to the monster's ribcage, propelled on a jet of my blood. The motor falls away from her chest as the heart returns to its home and the bones slam shut behind it, embracing the prodigal organ. Twisting stubs of bone and quivering ridges of gristle coil across her chest, sealing the vault. The heart will not be coming out again.

No heart means no blood to the brain. Impaired in 20 seconds, dead in 360. I'd be dying. "Maybe it's not so painful," I thought.

A white light appears in front of me. I hear the voices of friends, of family departed calling to me. Is that my mother waiting for me, her arms open to embrace me? And I hear Wendy saying, "See, you're still alive. Must be a few good swallows left in you before you go bad. Thanks so much for taking care of my heart. You ought to get one for yourself...real soon would be an excellent plan, seeing that blood trickling out of your chest." She picks up the egg pump and tosses it to me, saying, "You might give that a try." I fumble the catch as she comes towards me. She's going to bite my throat.

No. She's saying, "Here's your coffee and donut. Water, no ice. Ready to order?" It was my waitress. I'd dozed off.

"Look," she said, "don't take any chances, okay, Hon? You've only got one life to give. You let me know if I can help, okay? You can be safe in one of the roomettes."

That fantasy grew out of my fear and panic. No one had given me a better theory of what was happening. In fact, no one was even admitting something was going on. Meanwhile, I was on the run.

I still wasn't certain I was doing the right thing by running. But it seemed clear that Dwight's intent outweighed the hospital's inattention. Also, I needed to be able to move, at least at night. There was no sleeping while my heart beat out the rhythm of my donor's life. Daytime, when the heart was mine, would be when I would sleep and recover from hyperactive nights.

Of course, there was the matter of paranoia. I'd wondered if someone from the hospital would come looking for me. I didn't know whether I was required to obey, but I'd already decided I wouldn't. There might have been something in that pile of waivers I signed at the hospital that would allow them to take away my rights. Was that a bad idea? I worried I was ignorant of some never-fails top level hospital protocol for dealing with extreme cases, some proven process that would straighten out any problem if allowed sufficient time and supported by my unquestioning compliance. I don't think they'd go as far as a situation like mine. I wasn't going to ask the hospital about it—they probably wouldn't have an unbiased opinion.

Then I thought, might they have the police looking for me? My skill at paranoia was increasing with practice.

I decided that I had been equally paranoid at the hospital, but now I was feeling much better. "I can work this out—as soon as I've eaten," I assured myself.

I was ravenous—that was a bit discomforting. The waitress offered me more coffee, which I turned down, asking instead for a menu that I really didn't need. I knew all along what I wanted: a steak—bloody. I'd been craving that for three days. The context of my heart health made the thought just a bit creepy. I ordered it anyway. Daddy would understand that I couldn't wait any longer.

The steak was delicious. I loaded up on gravy mashed potatoes, mac and cheese, and broccoli. I'd hoped Daddy would come soon. I'd been out of the hospital for over four hours and had been there at the truck stop for half that time. I had a slice of apple pie and more coffee while I waited. Another half hour passed, but he didn't arrive. I had his cell phone—mine was still on the charger back at our house. We agreed I'd move back in with him after the transplant. I called the hospital and asked for Masako in the cardiac care unit.

"Fifth Austin North." It was Masako. I reassured her I was okay. I asked about Daddy and why she was there so far beyond the end of the night shift.

"They're still speaking with Mr. Williams," she said, "and they have a few more questions for me. The medications nurse was just a little distressed to find your father sitting in the easy chair wearing your electrodes, blood pressure monitor, and oxygen sensor. I didn't admit I'd helped, but Security is very suspicious. Dr. Sanders is a bit disappointed no one noticed the difference in the signals at the monitoring console." She sounded amused. "They're conducting interviews with everyone on duty before you disappeared. It looks like they're saving me for last."

After reassuring her I was fine—great even—Masako let me know that Daddy wouldn't be leaving any time soon.

"It's obvious he's involved with your disappearance," she said, "and the doctors are quite distressed. They say they're worried about you, but I think their biggest worry is you'll go to another hospital where they'll figure out what we couldn't diagnose here. They're stonewalling the story about you and all the other bizarre transplant outcomes."

"I don't know if you can talk to him, Masako, but if you can, tell Daddy I'm staying with our plan."

"I'm glad I don't know what it is. Safest that way, I'm thinking. Has the kanshaku moved?"

"Nope, nothing like that. I feel really good. Great, really. Are they giving my father a hard time?"

"He seems okay. He's being polite but firm. I can see he'd like to leave, but he's respecting authority."

"Though he may not be doing what they're asking…" I added.

She wished me luck, reassured me she had no regrets for her role in my exit from the hospital, and then disconnected.

Daddy had given me what cash he had. Masako gave me a loan too, but it wasn't much all put together. Our main goal was to get me away from the hospital before Dwight showed up. Money for food and cab fare. We'd all felt defenseless with Security having decided that I was the real problem—I'd cried "wolf" twice, the way they saw it. Masako couldn't spend the night in the room with us, and neither Daddy nor I am passive enough to wait for trouble to come to us. He taught me not to get caught up playing someone else's game. This was particularly wise as it might be a vampire's game being played. So, I waited for Daddy to get away and come for me.

As there was nothing else to do but sip coffee and wait, I had time to notice my heart again. It was appropriate and consistent. Something exciting was soon going to take place, though. Was it Dwight's girlfriend Wendy who controlled it? I wondered what she was anticipating.

Guessing it would be a while, and being done with both coffee and bloody steaks, I decided to release my only twenty-dollar bill to the rental of a roomette. It offered a place out of sight to nap and even take a shower. Once I went in and closed the door, though, I had no choice. I needed sleep.

I set the alarm for noon. That would give Daddy enough time to disengage and then come collect me. I went to sleep enjoying the perfect rhythm—my own—of my new heart.

KELLY
Thursday Afternoon

When the alarm brought me back, I went out to look for Daddy in the restaurant. There was no sign of him.

I dialed the hospital with his cell phone. Fortunately, it still had some charge left on it. I made two calls to the hospital. Connecting to the number that Masako had answered early that morning, I was still unable to get any more information about Daddy. On the second call, about twenty minutes later, an authoritative male voice asked if I was Kelly. I hung up right away, as I knew that they might be able to identify my location in a few minutes. They might have figured out I was using Daddy's cell phone and would try to determine which cell tower was nearest my location.

The voice on the phone was unfamiliar. I knew it wasn't my surgeon, Dr. Sanders. I considered the possibility that I was being unreasonably paranoid, but then why wasn't Daddy calling me?

The cell phone rang, and I answered. The same male voice said, "Kelly. You need to come back to the hospital. You may be contagious and dangerous to the public, so we're asking you to cooperate and tell us where you are. We'll send a team to pick you up so that we can minimize public exposure. Where are you right now?"

"Outbreak of what? What are you saying is wrong with me? And while we're at it, who are you?"

"I'm Dr. Garrison, and I'm responsible for infection control. So—in answer to your question—we are trying to work that out. But it must be clear that we can't make optimum progress without you here." I was getting the sense someone else was listening in, maybe coaching him on how to spin out the conversation while they triangulated on my phone.

"Let me speak to my father," I said. Dr. Garrison was quiet for about fifteen seconds. Too long.

"He is currently cooperating with our security people. He's doing fine, and he hopes you'll come back here soon so we can take care of that infection."

"And what kind of infection is similar to what I'm experiencing?"

"Well, actually, Kelly, there is a range of possibilities," he began. "Superficially, it may be difficult to sort them out." It sounded like he was relaxing into a professorial mode. He would spin things out for quite a while if my instinct was correct. I could just sit here, mesmerized by the patronizing but mellifluous tone of his lecture, while his infection control squad converged on me. I disconnected the call and powered off the phone before I walked out the truck stop's door. Every time my phone connected, they'd have another data point about my location. I started jogging toward the center of the city.

After less than a hundred steps across the parking lot, I discovered that the gift of unlimited energy had expired at sunrise. I warmed up quickly and was panting from the exertion, like any normal person. Whatever it was that made me so vigorous at night was no longer available. It took me almost an hour to get to my next destination. I think it would've taken me only twenty minutes if it had been nighttime.

Who do you trust when you don't even know what you're up against? Where do you go when you don't trust the people who know where you live? I had no faith in the Hospital's medical staff, and they'd proven they were unwilling to pay attention to my claims about Dwight. And what about Daddy? If he felt they were trustworthy, he would be calling me on the cell phone. I had two priorities. First, to not be captured, and—second—to find out what I was up against. That meant I needed to understand Wendy Allard.

KELLY
Thursday afternoon

Libraries are the most uplifting service government can provide citizenry. The contrast of a library's order and accessibility compared to the chaos of the popular media had been obvious at I-Way's restaurant. The TV monitors in the truck-stop's restaurant displayed national news and national weather, of little use to anyone locally. The nationwide paper I found in my booth failed to provide more than a single blurb per state, let alone any regional detail. It amounted to organized noise provided as a substitute for information and knowledge.

In Springfield's time-worn public library, I was able to fill in some of the gaps in my understanding of my puzzling connection to Wendy Allard. She had died five days earlier—I already knew this about my donor, but I hadn't known her name until the preceding evening. I was able to learn more about the circumstances of her demise. It was through back copies of the *Springfield Free Press*—the newspaper that had employed me until my heart problem laid me low—that I found my clues.

No obituary had been published. I found it odd that the only reference in print was the call in the police log. A 911 call had come in from 933 E. Highland on Sunday. A young woman, Wendy Allard, had been found unconscious and unresponsive. Taken by ambulance to Central County General, she was declared dead on arrival.

I calculated that six hours after the 911 call, her heart had been transplanted into my chest. The caller who reported Wendy's condition was Leticia Clark, also of 933 E. Highland Avenue. A hard-copy local phonebook revealed that there was a Walter and Angela Clark resident at that address. Much to my relief, the library had a working pay phone in the basement. Even better, I had enough change to make the call. It rang a half-dozen times before it apparently forwarded to another phone: the ring tone had changed.

"Hello?" said a woman's voice.

"Hi, this is Kelly Williams with the *Springfield Free Press*. Is this Leticia Clark?"

"It is."

"I'm calling to update the record about Wendy Allard. Can you spare a few minutes?"

"Okay." I'd expected her to sound either irritated or depressed, but what I heard was a tone of indifference. Having heard four words so far, I had little to go on, but the impression proved out.

Leticia had found Wendy unresponsive in the basement rec room of their house. She had bloody wounds inside her elbows and her inner thighs. With Wendy's mother and stepfather out of the country, it was older stepsister Leticia's duty to deal with Wendy's situation. Leticia had her parents' power of attorney in their absence and a health-care proxy for Wendy. With the supporting documentation on hand, Leticia acted swiftly when the hospital proposed harvesting Wendy's organs.

"Will there be a memorial service?" I asked.

"She'd actually left a note saying she'd planned to have her funeral at Morty Coil's, that weird funeral chain that had the gall to open a franchise in town. I had her remains sent there, but the staff said there were signs she had an undefined infection and recommended she be cremated right away. It was a public safety concern, they explained. Some of her friends have called, and they were kind of hysterical—particularly this one motormouth named Rose. I'm waiting for Dad and New Wife to get home from vacation before scheduling the memorial service. They're due back next week."

"I know this must be hard for you. Do you recall the name of the *Springfield Free Press* reporter who first covered this story? I can review the details they've got on file so far and then call you back to fill in any gaps."

"Well, actually, no one has called, but it would be a huge help if you did get something in print. Her goth friends are a real pain. They were acting like the Morty Coil's funeral she wanted was a matter of life or death."

"I'll check the file, make a few calls, and then get back to you. Again, I'm sorry if this is disturbing. If so, please say so and we'll cover it at another time."

"No problem." I didn't detect any concern or commitment.

"Where was she sent for cremation?" I asked. "And how will her remains be disposed?"

"Again, no problem. I've got the notice right here. Came in today's mail. Hold on. Yes, this is it. She was sent to Modern Memorials. The ashes are going to be put in a cut-crystal skull. It was an ancient Aztec design I thought she might have liked. I paid for it out of the refund for the cancelled funeral. I have no guess what we'll do with the ashes, but Dad and New Wife can work that out."

Now that was strange.

"You said there were already funeral arrangements?" I asked.

"Yes, she'd reserved it on a credit card a week ago. Her dying was no surprise to me either. New Wife says Wendy's been depressed since her father died four years ago."

"She was planning to die?"

"It was no surprise to me. She was always threatening suicide. The only problem the coroner had with that—hey, don't print this part, okay? Just say 'blood-borne disease' or something—was that there wasn't much blood around." Her matter-of-fact tone spoke volumes about her history with Wendy. It's hard to get close to someone so despondent and resentful.

"Okay, nothing about diseases or suicide. For the story, Miss Clark, can you give me your profession and employer?"

"Sure, thanks for asking. I'm a financial planner. I work for Schwartz and Clark—my father's firm—at the office at Commerce Tower."

"Are you handling Wendy's estate?"

"I'm acting executrix for what there is of an estate. Her dad left her a small trust fund and she had an insurance policy through the state college. Not even a hundred grand altogether."

"Any other brothers, sisters, cousins?" I asked.

"She was the only child of two only-children. She has a surviving grandfather in Connecticut. New Wife's father is in a nursing home."

"Any notable achievements? Academic awards, arts, civic activities, volunteer work?"

"Well, she swore off shoplifting, and got a most-improved award in her third week at rehab. I think she also moderated a chat room at a goth singles website. Oh, and she wrote poetry. Doggerel I think is what you call it. Well, if you'll excuse me, I'm picking up my new car this afternoon. My new BMW is the one thing I can thank Wendy for."

"Why is that?"

"My income as her executrix will cover the down payment, and the estate will pay off the balance once we're through probate."

I got off the phone, my conviction about vampires growing. If someone alive like Leticia lived off the dead, maybe the opposite was equally true.

I considered my next steps. Tracking Wendy might lead to a dead end if she'd been sent out for cremation. Morty Coil's might yield information about that, and maybe financial parasitism too.

Then there was the matter of Daddy. It had been the better part of a day since I left him behind at the hospital. They must have let him go by now. I tried our home number from the library's payphone. The phone picked up right away.

"Daddy?"

"Hi, Kitten. Are you okay? Sorry I wasn't there to meet you. Something came up."

"Hi, Daddy!" I was relieved to hear his voice. "I'm sorry too. I waited as long as I dared, but I worried they might track me using your cell. Are they looking for me?"

"Yes. Yes, they very much are," he said. "Two reporters are hanging around the hospital, looking into the rumors of transplant problems. One of them tried to engage me on the way out, but I didn't say anything. You shouldn't stay on this call too long either. I don't think they mean you harm, but I can't see how they can do you any good. Look…"

His tone changed. I don't know if anyone else would know, but I'd been listening to him for over two decades. He was saying something that only I should get.

"Pumpkin, I need to get my Oldsmobile to the shop before they close. It's got a carburetor problem. Wastes enough gas as it is, you know. Can you call me back later?"

"Sure thing, Dad. Okay, bye." Who was Pumpkin?

I had to sort out his hidden message. The Oldsmobile had been running perfectly. It was a 70's station wagon about a city block long, featuring a raised-up roof over the backseat and cargo area with narrow windows facing forward. This car was Daddy's favorite automotive project. He'd installed the biggest possible engine that fit under the hood, and that was indeed a large space. Carburetor? Was that the clue? Then I got it. I'd been along for the ride when Daddy had purchased a fuel-injection system for the Oldsmobile. The carburetors had been replaced. I took this to mean he would be leaving the car somewhere for me to use. There was only one service place he used, which was for oil changes. He started taking it to Spiffy Lube after I scolded him for dumping changed-out oil down the storm drain. I'd find the Oldsmobile at Spiffy Lube.

I wanted to run out, get the car, and go see him—but he was acting as though he was being monitored. Better give him some time.

Upstairs in the library I took a seat in a comfy chair and killed some time scanning the day's issue of the Free Press. I made the mistake of reading an article about an annual dinner for a lady's auxiliary group. My eyelids must have made a noise when they dropped closed.

A librarian lured me back to wakefulness. The shadows in the reading room had moved. "We'll be closing in thirty minutes, miss. I'm glad you find it comfortable here, but I'll have to ask you to conclude your business soon." The sun was setting outside.

"Thanks. Sorry." As I refolded the newspaper so it would hang properly on the rack, I saw a headline I hadn't noticed before:

"Arson Ruled Out in Crematorium Blaze."

CHAPTER 5
DWIGHT

Thursday Afternoon

After studying Vivian's folder, I set my course back to Central County General Hospital, with a stop-off at a fabric store. As I was about to up my game as a meatball surgeon, I needed needles and thread. That same part of the store yielded a wonderful strategy for repairing my undead patient. I found a heavy-duty plastic zipper ("Water Resistant and Rustproof!") that looked long enough. I added that to my purchases and resumed my journey.

It was clear to me that I would find the kidneys. I figured I would keep working someone's morphine drip until they conked out, and then snip the kidney out with scissors and forceps. They must have those around the hospital somewhere. I studied the floor plan of the hospital, graciously posted online by their facilities department. The area I'd visited for the organ pickup was one floor away from the intensive care unit. Whether the organs were inside or outside of the recipient, I'd be close.

I had a couple of ploys in mind. The one that felt most comfortable had me claiming I'm there to look in on my dear old uncle Jurgen. Or was it "Your gun"? Since I had to guess the pronunciation of his first name, I wasn't going to take a chance with Sonnenschein, either. So, I decided I was there to see dear Aunt Surya. I could spell Srinivasan, but I didn't dare try saying it. The answer to your question is, she'd be my maternal uncle's sister-in-law. Probably.

A quick stop at the sporting goods megastore got me a small flip-top cooler—about big enough for a six-pack—and a backpack for carrying it all in. When I got back to the car, I added the boning knife and salad tongs I took from my kitchen. I had a change of clothes in a drawstring trash bag. I stuffed that into the backpack too.

I wanted to park in the hospital's lot, but it was full. As it was late morning, that was no surprise. I parked on a side street a few blocks away, accepting the possibility that a chestnut pod falling from the tree next to it might pockmark the roof of my trusty old Le Mans.

At the reception area, my request for Aunt Surya raised no concern with a volunteer who wore a nametag proclaiming, "Hi, I'm Randi. CCG Volunteers Assoc." I simply spelled Srinivasan, and she gave me directions to the third-floor intensive care waiting area. There were about ten people waiting in a room with room for twenty. The two women wearing saris had to be there to see Aunt Surya too. I had no guess whether she would be the sister, mother, or daughter of either of the women waiting, as I couldn't guess the ages of Asian women any more closely than two decades. In any case, it would be clear that I wasn't with them. Still, I sat near them. Maybe news would come to them that I might overhear.

I tucked my backpack under my legs and leaned back in a plastic-covered recliner and watched the "Your Personal Health Advisor" program on the TV. We were all benefiting by a lecture about hand washing.

About ten minutes later, a young woman in blue scrubs with white flowers came into the waiting area. She surveyed the room and then walked over to me. Her nametag read Beverly.

"We haven't seen you here before," she said.

"I'm here about my uncle. He had a kidney transplant a couple of days ago. Some sort of problem…" I didn't dare say "Aunt Surya" with her likely family members sitting five feet away. I'd switched allegiance to Uncle Jurgen, hoping none of his family was any closer.

"Oh, Yoor Genn is your uncle?" That's how it was pronounced.

"Yes," I said and nodded. "Is it correct there's been a complication?"

"Could we speak out in the hallway, mister…?"

"Wagner," I answered. "David Wagner." I followed her into the hallway.

"I'm surprised you don't say Vogg Nurr, what with your uncle being so German," Beverly said.

"Mother's side," was my answer. That embraced a lot of ambiguity. We stopped about three yards from the waiting room door.

"It's good to have someone here for him. They're removing the transplant," she said plainly. She was watching for my reaction. I stood there blank-faced, unable to guess what a suitable reaction might be.

"And that's related to the symptoms?" I asked.

"Well, it's unprecedented, but his kidney is overachieving. He's dehydrating as fast as we can pump saline into him. He's passing urine at an incredible rate, and he's extremely anxious."

"That is very unusual, isn't it? What causes that?" I asked.

"We've never seen anything like it before honestly, and we actually have two instances of it going on now. Another kidney went to a woman who had a similar reaction. They've already removed hers."

"Wow," I said. "Now what happens? How do they survive?" Was it going to turn out I might get one of the kidneys, or even both?

"They'll both have to go back on dialysis, unfortunately. The surgeon will be out to see you and your…?" She wanted me to state a relationship with

116

someone or some group in the waiting room who I was unaware of. I had no idea how many people that might be, but it was at least one. But male, female?

"Brother-in-law," I said. I was ready with my follow-up.

"You're Mr. Stendahl's brother-in-law is what you're saying?"

"Right." I'd never heard of Stendahl. "Sorry. Pre-occupied. How much longer? Minutes, hours?"

"He's our highest priority right now. He should be in recovery no later than one." That was less than an hour. That kidney might be liberated already. Both kidneys might be back in the organ trading room.

Beverly was more than done with me, and she started to move on when my questioning lapsed. Then I realized I had one more question to ask.

"Can you tell me, did those kidneys come from the same donor?"

"Yes," she said. "There've been issues with every organ transplanted from the donor. A lot of interesting theories to be considered."

I returned to the waiting room and collected my backpack. I left without saying goodbye to either of my borrowed families. From my study of the hospital's floorplan, I identified a stairway halfway down the corridor that would drop me close to the organ emporium.

As I emerged one floor down, I felt I might pass visually for a medical courier, but a lack of certainty compelled me to look for ways to sharpen my impression. I saw a set of doors swing inwards as I passed them in the corridor. The scrub area of a surgical suite was revealed. No one was there, so I darted in and grabbed a full set of scrubs, a mask, cap, facemask, and matching booties. I stuffed the goods in my backpack and returned to the corridor, relieved that there was no one nearby.

In the restroom across the hall, I examined my haul and decided it might be useful, but not immediately. So, I extracted the cooler, repacking the backpack to be less bulky, and made my way to the organ emporium.

Going down the hallway to third Parker, I recognized the service window where I'd visited Devin hours earlier. This time I was there during business hours, so a receptionist opened her glass partition to ask my business.

"Action Medical Transfer, here for the two retrieved kidneys." I had the cooler in my left hand. What did I have to lose by asking? I wasn't going to just pull open the door and walk in.

She looked at a sheet of paper on her desk for a few seconds, tapped three of her very ornate fingernails on the desk, and looked back up at me. "There's nothing going out." Her face said, "What are you going to do about that?"

"Is Dr. DeSaul here?" I asked, remembering his name given by the receptionist on my first visit. If I was going to be turned down, it would be by the man in charge. "They told me to have him call Dr. Butler in urology if there was any delay. These need to be looked at by experts now."

"He's not here," she said. She'd looked up at me several times, showing signs of increased interest in my emerging story. "You want to have a seat?"

"Time is wasting," I said. "Please call them." I wanted to bang on her desk like I did Vivian's, but that might draw the security guards. I needed kidneys, not opponents.

"He's in a meeting. He can't be interrupted."

"It's about the kidneys, right?" Receptionist nodded agreement. "They're not talking to anyone because they first need to get some answers. Our team does that."

"I don't know..." she said. I acted while she hesitated. I pulled the door open and walked in. Ahead was a heavy white door with a porthole. It looked cold back there. Before closing the door, I said to the flustered receptionist, "Call them! I'll get started." I hoped that the prohibition against calling would cancel out my order to call, leaving her frozen in indecision.

I went through the white door and saw the objects of my quest immediately. I also saw my breath. The room was very cold. A wall thermometer indicated −2° Celsius.

I saw two stainless steel pans, each holding a thick plastic sliding-closure pouch with a single kidney and pinkish liquid. There was a stick-on label on the first pan I came to. In pen was written "Sonnenschein." The other pan was labeled "Srinivasan." I noticed an office phone on the wall behind the organs. None of the lines were lit. She hadn't called.

I opened my cooler, placed the organ pouches inside, and exited through the swinging door. I brought along a second cooler I found in the cold room and stuffed my loaded one into my backpack. At the entrance, I saw the receptionist dialing. She hadn't seen me. I tapped on her window, startling her.

"Are you calling them?" I had to speak loudly because of the glass between us.

She startled and slapped her hand on the cradle button.

"Yes, I am," she said. She started dialing again.

"Great," I said. My conviction was growing that she was calling Security. "I'll leave this here with you, okay? Be back in ten." I offered her the decoy cooler. She was forced to open her glass partition to accept it.

"Be right back for it," I said. "Last chance to go for a while."

I turned, walked out, and went back to the stairwell that had gotten me there from the waiting room one floor up. I went two floors down to a half-flight ending at a door to the outside. Despite a warning sign saying an alarm would sound, the door was propped open with a brick. As I approached, I caught a whiff of cigarette smoke. This must be the nurses' secret break spot. I pushed out through the doorway. I saw a man in scrubs, having a smoke, looking back at me from a dozen yards away. He was far enough off he wouldn't get a good look at me. I walked briskly back to my car.

A handful of chestnut pods were distributed over the roof, hood, and trunk of my Le Mans. One found its mark on thin metal over my left front wheel, punching a knuckle-sized hole and lodging in it. It seems there was still plenty of rust under the gray primer paint on my handsome old Pontiac. My Le Mans was every bit as powerful as its brand-mate, the GTO made in the same year, but the Le Mans was looked down on because it didn't have the GTO badge. I'd hoped to restore it one day, but the chestnut put a dent in that dream. I hadn't realized how much rust was under there. A lot of the best things in my life were not in the best of shape.

DWIGHT
Thursday afternoon

Tanner pressed the cover release button on the side of the cooler while I switched on the kitchen's overhead light. The last beams of daylight were shining in, but at too low an angle to help view the goods.

He flipped the cover to the side. The momentum of the top threw the cooler off balance. Tanner grabbed for it but hit it too hard. Two bagged-up kidneys tumbled out onto the kitchenette table, catching the rays of late-afternoon sunlight shining through the window over my kitchen sink.

The thick plastic pouches ballooned up, filled with steam, and popped open, spraying hot pink liquid across the tabletop. I tasted brine.

Steam began rising from each kidney. Fwump. Fwump. It was the sound of burners lighting on a gas stove. The kidneys both had bluish flames on them.

"Oh my god, holy shit, put them out put them out put them out!" Tanner said. The flames brightened to orange, surrounding each organ on all sides. They hissed and crackled as I ran to the faucet to fill a glass with water. As I poured a half-empty glass of water over one kidney, Tanner attempted to cover the other one with the inverted cooler. His coverage appeared complete, but the hissing from underneath continued. The water I poured over the other kidney went up in steam.

I clawed the cups, plates, and silverware out of my dishpan and set it with all its benign soapiness on the table next to the balls of flame. Using two spoons as tongs, I scooped up one sizzling organ and then the other, dropping them into the dishwater. The water didn't cover them completely, so I tilted the dishpan up until I had the bubbling spheres covered at the lowered end. Getting my body between the window and the dishpan helped somewhat, but the water fizzed and hissed for another ten seconds even after the flames were covered.

Outside, purple clouds glowed above the horizon. The sun was down. I still drew the blinds closed. I had a newfound respect for the threat sunlight offers to a vampire.

I looked in the dishpan for cooked kidneys. I found two black meatballs. The twin fireballs had left black bubble marks in the plastic finish on my table.

"What are you two cretins up to?" The Wendy I'd always remembered was at the top of the basement stairs, using a hockey stick like a crutch to hold herself up, a couple of loops of her yellow extension cord in the other hand. She looked amazingly better. The skin on her face was completely healed and her hair had grown back. Her hands looked better also, but the bones were sticking out of the flesh of the fingertips of the three longest fingers on her left hand. The karate jacket hung open to her waist, revealing the duct tape seam running down the middle of her chest.

"Top o' the evenin' to you," Tanner said. "How's sleeping beauty?"

I had been about to explain our boneheaded error, but Tanner's banter was buying us time. My mind was frenzied but directionless. I had no guess what to do next.

"I'm feeling okay, now that I'm switched on," she said, jiggling her power cord back and forth. "So, who wants to be breakfast first?" She was looking at Tanner.

KELLY
Thursday late afternoon

My dad proved to be a brilliant schemer. His Oldsmobile wagon was in the customer pickup area at Spiffy Lube, and the key was in a little magnetic box inside the front bumper, a huge chromed-steel mass that might weigh more than most Fiats. Daddy so loathed those vehicles. "Artsy but flimsy," he'd say.

I found a blue NASCAR Racing jacket on the passenger seat, and I put it on right away to cover my Kill Bill tracksuit top. I was still stuck with yellow legs, though. The Oldsmobile started up right away, the engine rocking the vehicle with its deep rumble. I think it did show up on a seismograph somewhere.

Daddy had anticipated my situation well. The gas tank was full. At nine miles per gallon, I could drive about 180 miles before being bankrupted by the next fill-up. Time to get on with my investigation.

In the glove box, I found a GPS. Even better, it was charged up. I keyed in the address for Modern Memorials and configured it for a male voice so I'd feel comfortable talking back to it. I decided to pause my route, though, because I'd pass Morty Coil's, the destination funeral home. I thought I might find some information there about how Wendy was declared "contaminated," and learn more about the nature of that contamination.

I got to Morty Coil's a little before sunset. I was still tired despite my library nap, and I wondered if there'd be another energy boost come sunset.

As I walked from the visitor's parking lot to the entrance of Morty Coil's, I was angered by the sight of what I thought was a delivery van parked in the only handicap space available in front of the building. The van's brown coloring seemed familiar, but I didn't recall the gold logo on the side of the van before—a map of the North American continent composited out of tiny squares, surrounded by a circle. I know I'd seen the name Continental Grid somewhere before but didn't recall anything about them. If I came across the driver, I was going to give him a piece of my mind for his inconsiderate parking.

The front entrance to Morty Coil's was simple yet imposing because of its scale. The pair of two-story-tall brushed-steel doors had no doorknobs or obvious motion sensors, but they opened inward at my touch. Once inside I saw how this enterprise came to have the nickname DDD: Disney Does Death. Though they advertise it as a multi-personality funeral space, it doesn't serve all possible purposes equally well. The presence of ironwork, though simple and elegant, added to the soaring columns and the occasional velvet drape, leads one to the conclusion that they do goth particularly well. Sports themes appeared to be the other common choice, accomplished with the liberal use of projected video.

Once inside the massive doors, one arrives in the grand foyer. Ahead of me and to both sides, I saw receiving podiums at the front of each of three sets of large doors. The one to my right was lit up. A video monitor over the area announced the deceased's name: Siggy Andersen. The doors behind the receiving area were open, giving me a view into a funerary area decorated with a sports theme. Syracuse Orange figured heavily into the room's decoration. A small group of adults were gathered around a closed coffin at the far end of the room, engaged in what looked to be friendly chat.

From where I'd entered, the suite in front of me had a monitor proclaiming Amanda Bergen. This was a more inviting direction to me than trying to weave through a grieving pack of football fans to find a Morty Coil's staff member. However, the doors to Amanda Bergen's area were closed. The third suite was also closed, dark and unlabeled, so I turned and went back to the front door. When I'd first entered, I'd gone right past a door marked "Offices." I knocked on the door with some vigor. After counting to twenty I tried the door handle and let myself in. The receptionist's desk was unoccu-pied, as was the glass-windowed conference room behind it. I continued past another door on my right, walked past another unlabeled door on the left, and stopped in front of the elevator. The legend to the right of its call button indicated there were three lower levels. The upper basement offered "techni-cal services," and the middle basement was labeled "records." The lowest one had nothing listed. I pressed the down button and it opened immediately.

Once inside I tried the buttons for the upper level, "technical services." I was able to access the middle level, but not the lowest. Next to the unlabeled button was a key slot and a pack-of-gum sized red glass window.

The elevator doors opened, revealing a corridor running off to the right, probably ending underneath the three funeral areas I saw above. About ten steps in I came to glass doors on the right. Inside at the far end, I saw three people speaking. The space on either side of them was packed with small metallic doors. An open one had a long sliding drawer with a sheet-covered human form on it. I decided that I'd found their morgue.

The glass doors pivoted open automatically as I approached. There was a young man and a young woman, both dressed in white lab coats over dark trousers, speaking with a powerful-looking older man in deliveryman's gabardines. The young man in the lab coat glanced in my direction as the woman and the older man continued a heated discussion.

The deliveryman had a name patch on his matching shirt, right next to the Continental Grid logo. It read Black. There was a peculiar V-shaped pocket, stitched on like on painters' pants, about mid-thigh on his right leg. Whatever tool was in there had a white knob at the top. Silver hair peeked out around the edge of his cap, but he carried himself like a football team's defensive tackle. He was saying something about someone named Allard.

The young woman responded, "Listen Mr. Black, it's all in the report you're holding in your hand. You brought it here with you, so it seems likely you've read it. So then, instead of going through this step by painful step, why don't you just ask us about the parts you don't understand?"

"Think back to your Hygiene Outreach Committee training. What was the escalation protocol? I'll tell you—it's to 'assist in all ways any senior staff brought in for extended case management'. I am senior staff. You, as yet, are not. And you are not assisting. Let me give you another opportunity to do so." Mr. Black looked toward me, and then back to the young woman in the lab coat. "Deal with this quickly."

The young woman turned toward me and took a couple steps. "Yes? How can we help you?" Mr. Black watched me while the young man in the lab coat busied himself with his clipboard. Black looked up at me again, suddenly looked concerned. I went ahead speaking with the young woman.

"Hi! I'm Kelly Williams from the *Free Press*, and I'm looking for some information for an obituary. Nothing front page I can assure you, just pro forma stuff for the back of the Metro section. With a little luck I can be out of here in two minutes. I'm inquiring after Wendy Allard, died last Sunday morning."

"Just one minute," Mr. Black said. "You should step aside." That was directed to the young woman.

Mr. Black was face-to-face with me in three quick steps. "You don't look like a reporter." I glanced down and rediscovered the blue NASCAR jacket over my yellow Kill Bill track suit but got my eyes right back to meet his. His speed and physical presence unnerved me.

"I sometimes do undercover work," I said. "I left my press ID in my car. If you like, I'll go back and get it." Or I might just drive away.

"Yes," he said, but not in response to what I was saying. "Passing as a human," he said to himself. He was looking at me hard, like he sensed something off about me. Stepping back, he reached into his special trouser pocket, pulled out an ivory-white cross, and held it right in front of my face. It looked to be made of machined wood, painted glossy white.

After a few seconds of staring at and then around it, I locked eyes with him. His eyebrows raised. Then he looked down at the floor and withdrew the cross. I hadn't flinched.

"Sorry!" he said, taking a step back from me. He put the cross in its pocket, taking a moment to study it first. "That was rude, wasn't it? My mother was Romanian. She was always doing that—got it from her." He smiled as if it was vitally important that I understand and forgive him.

"That's how you ward off interrogating women?" I asked. I attempted a smile.

The young woman in the lab coat said, "Say, that was kind of random, Mr. Black," Mr. Black was watching me again. He looked much less sure of himself. I started to think he was intimidated. Physically, he looked prepared and quite capable of fighting, but his face said he thought himself outmatched. He was waiting for me to make a move—and hoping I wouldn't.

I stayed on purpose. "Wendy Allard?" I said to the young woman. "Received here Tuesday from Central Hospital. Can you give me the details?"

The young man with the clipboard came a few steps closer to me, showing no sign of Mr. Black's hesitancy. His nametag read Basil.

Basil said, "Well, we were just discussing that, and…"

"Please come back and inquire at the business office during regular working hours." The young woman placed herself next of Basil. Her name tag said Annie.

"They'd have information that you don't have?" I asked.

"No, I have pretty much everything right here," Basil said, studying his clipboard. "Let's get her on her way, Annie. 'We Serve the Departed—and those touched by their loss,' right? Yes, we had Miss Allard here."

I'm not certain it was simultaneous, but I caught Annie rolling her eyes and thought I saw the same happening with a slightly less tense Mr. Black. He was still watching my every move.

"The official time of death?" I asked.

"10 a.m. on Sunday," Basil replied.

"Cause of death?"

"It was classified as a cardiac event, resulting from a catastrophic drop in blood pressure caused by fluid depletion. Ms. Williams? Would it help you to have this form? I can always print out another copy."

"Yes, that would save us both a lot of time. Thank you."

As Basil surrendered the sheet on his clipboard, I asked, "How's this been for the family?" Mr. Black hadn't moved. He was completely focused on me.

"The family has been very straightforward to deal with," Basil said, "but this client has a half-dozen friends that have been completely hysterical about canceling her funeral. They've been calling every phone extension in the building trying to get us to put it back on."

"Do you have any contact information for any of her friends?" I asked.

Basil handed me a telephone message slip, retrieved from a lower sedimentary layer of his clipboard. "This is her friend Rose. She's made eighty percent of the calls. She could give you more of Miss Allard's back story."

Because of Basil's graciousness—or perhaps despite it—there was as much tension in the room as when I walked in. It felt like the right time to leave, but the reporter in me still had questions.

I paused. My heart had begun beating with the pulse of someone dancing. A second earlier I thought of the three people around me as a threat, particularly the wrestler in the deliveryman's jacket. Now, while Wendy was dancing somewhere else, I was experiencing the power that had intimidated Mr. Black. What he didn't know was that the essence he sensed wasn't mine. Somehow my heart was channeling Wendy.

I don't know for how long I was distracted, but Annie was prompted to say, "Ms. Williams?" That snapped me back. I gave her my attention.

"What is the issue you had with Miss Allard?" I asked, putting on my best open-and-accepting expression. I watched her as her eyes darted up to the overhead lighting. Whatever she was going to say would be something short of the truth.

"Based upon a thorough field examination, it was determined that cremation was the most effective resolution for her remains. Mr. Black, here," she said, nodding her head toward the big man, "is just checking up to see that the transfer went through properly."

"What did this field examination reveal that would make cremation an appropriate choice?" I asked.

My focus wavered as I waited for her answer. I sensed Wendy's music again.

She briefly examined another light fixture overhead. "It's not one thing, you see. There's this checklist we go through, and when you're done, you tally the entries for the various categories and check it against the grid. Miss Allard fell in the unfavorable quadrant apparently. There's nothing to be embarrassed about, really."

More than I expected. "What's the problem in that wrong quadrant you most worried about?" Again, I provided a pleasant and expectant face, mostly ignoring the sense of distant music driving my heart.

"Once the client is deceased, the immune system no longer responds to forces of corruption. If the risk of corruption is high, it usually corresponds to the fourth quadrant." It sounded like she was reciting from memory.

"What kind of corruption?" I kept my eyes on Annie. She wasn't going to speak.

"Revenants," said Basil. Nice of him to yield to the pressure I put on Annie. Mr. Black stiffened, but stayed quiet. Carefully monitoring the distance between him and me, he seemed less concerned about the danger I presented to Annie or Basil. I started thinking I could take him.

"Vampires?" I asked.

"We believe it's possible," said Basil. "It's our job to be the first line of detection." He nodded toward Annie.

"So, you had Wendy Allard sent out for cremation, is that correct?" Both Annie and Basil nodded yes. "And Mr. Black is here to confirm you did your job?" Two more nods.

Mr. Black had to break into the conversation. "I think that might be more than you'd want to put in print, Ms. Williams. These two are relatively young for having spent so much time among the remains of the deceased, and you should consider the damage to your paper's credibility with a wild speculation of this type. They may be having fun at your expense." He leaned just slightly toward me as he spoke. He might not have wanted conflict, but he was ready for it.

"No worries. I'll be going," I said. "Thanks to both of you for your help. Good evening, Mr. Black." I started turning toward the door, taking half a step but then turning back. "Was there anything unusual about her body?"

"Well, besides the checklist correspondences of course," said Basil, "we were surprised that her organs had been harvested. Her pre-order had specified no embalming."

I thanked them again and was about to be on my way, when I remembered what I'd seen outside the building.

"Mr. Black? Is that your Continental Grid van in front of the building? Brown, with a gold logo?" We locked eyes and he tensed up. I really did bother him.

"Yes?"

"Don't park in handicapped spaces!"

Mr. Black took a step back. "Sorry!" He said, and looked side to side as if seeking the quickest exit.

I strode out the door and took the elevator back up, relieved to be away from the tension and possible danger, but also distracted by the rhythmic pulsation of my heart. I imagined it was Wendy dancing to some favorite music.

Getting back into Daddy's big car, I turned on the radio and the song was so good it made me turn the volume up. This was the rhythm my heart had been beating to, a funk oldie called...

DWIGHT
Thursday Night

"Stand" by Sly and the Family Stone was on again. Wendy was playing it over and over on my turntable, wiggling on the sofa and banging her heels on the floor like it was a drum. An hour earlier, I loved that song. Now I only loved the girl that was wriggling to it.

We decided to wait until after we'd fed Wendy to break the news about her kidneys. We each let her take fifteen swallows. Tanner had become worried about blood-borne infections—I guessed he meant between him and me—and insisted we all swab our arms with alcohol first.

It was scary work, but we managed to keep her focused while she fed from my arm again. Tanner counted out loud. What a sport he turned out to be. He allowed her to do the same, and she stopped when I said "fifteen." We were all seated around my dinette set. With all the blood spilling and improvised surgery, the area looked like a slaughterhouse—and not in a good way.

"Okay, I'm feeling better now," she said. That was a huge relief. We never saw her drink her fill, so we feared that she would drain either, or maybe both, of us. After the feeding, I felt a little light-headed, but Tanner said he was okay. Having been her second and third meal, I'd lost enough blood to notice a difference. I'd given one more time than Tanner had.

"I need to eat a steak or two," I said. "You too, Tanner. We probably should load up on vitamins and minerals, especially iron."

"Listen, Dwight. Thank you," Wendy said. "You too, Tanner. You guys are lifesavers. I need to be moving along though. I'm a little late starting eternity with Roberto. I want to get started now, so can we finish putting me back together? You got the rest of my parts back?"

"Well, yeah, mostly," I said. Her eyes narrowed. The grateful goth had been replaced by a demon poised for attack. I carried on matter-of-factly. "I got your kidneys back this afternoon, but there was a small accident. They got—err—sunburned."

The transformation to undead amplifies emotions. Her face played fear, then anger, and then despair. Each expression pulled her face in an exaggerated new direction, like we were watching her through a fish-eye lens. I saw on Tanner's face that he was intimidated. There we were, nurse-maiding a creature that could kill us both in seconds. We were both on good behavior. I was in love—and afraid for my life.

"Wendy, we're sorry," Tanner said. "It was an accident. We don't have any experience with this sort of thing. We're both technology geeks."

I picked up the story. "Until I picked you up from Modern Memorials I didn't believe in vampires or anything supernatural. It's kind of cool, actually. But we're lacking for guidance here. It's not like you came with an owner's manual." She didn't respond.

"But we're going to try," I said. "We've gotten you this far, right?" Still no answer, but no attack either. Sobered by the painful glare she had directed at me, and embarrassed by our collective silence, Tanner and I sat down at the table with pencils and donut shop napkins to write up a plan.

Taking advantage of Tanner's tinkering skills, we improvised a kidney system. Because of the scorched meatball situation, we didn't have much to work with. My contribution to the workaround was to insert the kidney remnants into a couple hard plastic aquarium filter housings, orienting the organ's output horn toward the edge of the tube. I drilled an exit hole there, jammed in a piece of surgical tubing, and sealed the junction with bathtub caulk. We attached the exit hoses to the tubes running to her bladder and routed her arteries through the filter housing so the kidneys would be bathed in blood. That last was nasty messy work. We quickly learned to turn off her heart pump: it was our own recently donated blood being squirted around the kitchen. A tiny goldfish bowl pump between the kidney output horn and her ureters pushed waste fluids to the nearest appropriate exit. We finished securing it all with cable ties, double-checked for leaks, duct-taped her closed and plugged her back in.

It worked immediately. Before she smelled like toxic waste dumped in a men's locker room. In less than ten minutes, the salty acidic edge was gone. Now her breath stank like she'd been gargling kerosene. It had to be the lack of the other organs that was causing other imbalances.

I concluded our surgical procedure with the installation of the zipper. Hand stitching was not my strong suit, and she was not all that pleased with the idea, but I argued we'd come up with a better solution once we'd recovered the rest of her missing parts. At that point, we needed to stop wasting blood—half of what she'd drunk from us had sprayed out while we worked on her, even with the pump turned off. The blood going to waste was Tanner's and mine.

"I want to stand, dammit," Wendy said after I'd lifted the needle off the old vinyl LP record. "It'll be good to get my parts back, but it's going to suck if I can't stand up without using a hockey stick or crutches. You geniuses wouldn't have any ideas about that, would you?"

Tanner and I had already discussed this on our own, but we had temporarily exhausted our allotment of workable weird ideas. We would have to move on to the domain of difficult weird ideas.

About a half an hour earlier, I had announced my plan to go back to the hospital and collect the rest of Wendy's missing parts. According to

Vivian's folder, I still needed to find Frank Pierpoint, Johnson Cooper, and Kelly Williams.

I was running out of excuses for not leaving. Part of my reluctance was Wendy's thirst for Tanner, and his willingness to be seduced into satisfying it. Feeling jealous, I tried to assert some order on my way out into the night.

"My good friend Tanner here excels at 'thinking outside of the box.' If you can avoid killing him before I get back—maybe don't drink him at all, okay? I'm betting he'll come up with something. Can you try to do that?" I hated having to be stern with her. It felt like a losing strategy. She's waiting to get back to Roberto, while enjoying the use and devotion of Tanner. I get to come off as the taskmaster.

"Okay," she said, her eyes finding mine for an instant where I imagined I saw a flash of connection. Or maybe a flash of recognition. Somehow, I had touched her. The possibility suggested in that instant—her eyes telling me there's a chance that she might feel something for me—readied me for my task. It may have been an illusion, but I picked up the insulated cooler and my backpack and marched out to my Le Mans.

ROBERTO
Thursday Night

This evening was the first night since I transitioned Wendy that I hadn't felt blood drunk. My thirst would return just before sunrise.

As a full-time creature of the night, it's hard to find gainful employment. I've often wondered if other free-range vampires were destitute as well. They probably couldn't keep a steady night job because they'd take time off to hunt.

The night I woke up undead, I snapped the chains binding me to the pipes in the desolate basement where Jack Murphy had finished me off. I returned to where he and I had last worked together, at a road construction site. Jack wasn't there, and my newborn hunger for blood drove me to attack my buddy, Walt, who made the mistake of noticing me and calling out to me. I didn't take that much blood, but he went into shock. No, I didn't kill him, but I left him shattered and terrified.

After three nights missing from my road-crew work, I'd come back and attacked a co-worker. Obviously, I wouldn't be working there again. With the likelihood that the police had a warrant out for me, I wouldn't be working nights in Springfield again.

Leaving Springfield was a logistical problem. In the Midwest, the big cities are eight or ten hours apart. Between stealing a car, getting it to another city, and then finding a haven—to do that all before sunrise didn't feel possible. It was too risky.

I was already behind on my financial responsibilities when Murphy took me down. My new status made for my greatest failing yet. I was dead but failed to leave a corpse behind. There was no evidence to authorize life insurance payments or death benefits to my family. I had no way to support them, except for the few times I left them envelopes of the cash I'd taken from victims. It pained me to leave no note with the money, but they needed to believe that I was dead so that, someday—maybe years later—they would finally collect on my death benefits. At least I didn't cause them a funeral expense.

I thought it would be much easier to find Wendy, but both our plan and my instincts were off the mark. I didn't have useful intuitions about where she might be or what she'd be doing. It was time to go directly to her friends—and maybe her family if necessary—to make good on my promise to be there for her.

I found a possibly working pay phone at the corner of a strip mall, just outside a laundromat. I paused, realizing that my small handful of change was going into a gadget that might fail to make a phone call. A flickering fluorescent fixture overhead highlighted the armored cable to the handset. The phone's housing was pockmarked with wads of chewing gum.

The undead fear few things, but I feared this phone. I dropped in the sequence of coins.

Rose's phone rang for me. Her snappy hello was a relief to hear, an unexpected bit of grace visited upon the divine's unwanted servant.

"Rose, it's Roberto. Do you know what's happened to Wendy? I haven't been able to find her."

"This is so incredibly amazing talking to you, Roberto! You guys really did it. I mean I heard she was no doubt about it dead and then her bitch of a sister canceled the funeral. Or was there going to be a wedding too, hmm? You guys never said. But then Wendy calls me last night and says she's hiding out somewhere, and she's got a sort of problem and getting help from some good old friend but won't say who. And then she says, oh yeah, I'm dead and I'm a vampire. So like you really did it! You ingratiated her."

"I transitioned her. Sounds clinical, doesn't it? Please, where is she?"

"She says that she wants to meet you at Worship tomorrow night."

"Please deposit one dollar for another two minutes," a mechanized voice said. "Twenty seconds remaining."

"Where is that?" I asked after the message exited.

"Worship is so amazing! It happens at various places, you see, but this week it happens at Schlock House Funk." I had no idea where that was.

I was running out of seconds. "Rose, quick—tell me, where are you?"

"We're going to have a vigil for her at Modern Memorials. It's so great…"

Again, the mechanized voice interrupted. "Please deposit one dollar in the next fifteen seconds or your call will be disconnected." A recorded tick-tock sound consumed my remaining seconds—I had no coins to buy more time. I received two more warnings, followed by the voice saying, "disconnecting." The line went dead.

Rose had said Modern Memorials. That was someplace I knew. I'd be there in thirty minutes, avoiding attention by running half my top speed. I was excited by the idea of seeing Wendy again. As intriguing as I found Kelly, I'd committed to being with Wendy, and I'm the kind of man that tries to do what he says he'll do.

I set off at an easy jog. Whenever I found an unlit street or crossed through an alley, though, I stretched out my legs. I love how the air roars past my ears. I'd believed I could run over forty miles per hour, since I kept up with traffic on University Avenue. It's not wise to do much of that because it's so conspicuous. And there was a consciousness issue too. I couldn't run forty miles per hour and also be nobody-here-right-now.

Traffic was sparse when I crossed County 203 and turned onto the frontage road where I recalled Modern Memorials being. Lush green lawns, tall dense hedges, and an occasional birch tree now improved what was once a bare dirt and rock industrial park. A few hundred yards down the frontage road, I saw a flashing blue light. It proved to be a police car just inside the parking lot entrance.

I got closer, ready to roll up against the base of the hedge if I needed to hide. The police car turned out from the driveway, coming toward me. I slipped my hands into my pockets and slowed to a stroll, becoming nobody-here-right-now. By the time the car rolled past me, there was no one who needed to be seen.

Just after the police car had passed, I was startled by something I felt in my heart. It was like the sense of connection that I felt at the hospital with Kelly. I guessed I was about to be reunited with Wendy.

I turned the corner into the parking lot of Modern Memorials. The lot was empty except for three cars and a cluster of youths all dressed in black. With them was a woman in blue and yellow. They were near the loading dock. Four tall poles lit the area with coppery light.

The building had a loading dock with a business entrance to the left. The two bay doors were both charred black and were marked off by a web of yellow and black emergency tape. The roof of the building looked to be seriously damaged. Brick and concrete had fallen from the upper edges onto the pavement below.

My heart led me right to the group. I remembered to be visible. All heads turned in my direction at once. I recognized everyone there, including the odd woman out.

My heart had been right. There was Kelly. She was speaking to Rose. The others—seven of them I counted—had their suspicions. I had to go right up to her.

"Kelly," I said. My eyes found hers waiting.

"Hello, Roberto," she said. I saw the hint of a smile.

"What brings you out to this gloomy location?" I asked. "I recall you were in the hospital yesterday."

"My HMO pushed for an early release," she said. "I'm a reporter. I'm working on an obituary. Does your presence here tell me it's your Wendy we are here about?"

It bothered me that she was right. Yes, it was true I was here about Wendy, but I had forgotten all about her when I realized Kelly was there.

"True," I said. "So, you're okay then? I worried about leaving you there." Rose started paying closer attention to our conversation.

"I was not enjoying myself as much as you'd think," Kelly said. "It became clear I should get out of there. So let me ask you this. Was it Wendy Allard you were looking for at the hospital?"

"Yes, it was." Again, I was subject to that power of hers to completely engage me.

"She died five days ago, right?" She asked.

"Yes, that's right."

"And these people here are gathered because they are expecting to see her again?"

"You are correct yet again," I said.

"Why would they expect this to happen?"

"She wasn't exactly dead."

Rose shrieked. "Oh, my God, I knew it. You see, guys? That's what is going on. Now you've heard it from them. You, reporter girl, how do you know Roberto?"

"You can call me 'Miss Williams'—or 'Kelly'," she said, looking back to me. "We've met by chance a couple of times over the past few days."

Rose looked at Kelly and then me with suspicion. "And the third time is the charm?" That came with a hard look. "What about Wendy?"

Is it a lie if you don't know, until you've said something out loud, that it's no longer the truth?

"Nothing has changed," I said. I knew right away that everything had changed, but I kept going. "I need to find her. She needs me. I know what she's experiencing, and what it's like to go through it alone. Rose, you said Wendy was coming to something called Worship tomorrow night. Where is she? She must really need me." Try to do the right thing, I thought.

Rose looked slightly appeased. "She wouldn't say. Yes, she thinks it's important to see you too because she says some stuff happened to her that she didn't expect and some friends were helping her so she figured if she set a place and time and put the word out so that everyone might get together and now it's working because you know."

"Rose. Stop. Please stop. Can you tell me again? Where is Worship?"

"Like I said it's at Schlock House Funk this week. They mostly do industrial and hard rock, but every month or so they host us creatures of the night." Rose looked apologetic. "Or us wannabes, anyhow. It's such a cool place. It used to be a warehouse."

"So, let me get this straight," Kelly said. Again, she had my attention. "You're a vampire. You made Wendy into a vampire too, lost track of her, and now you're trying to find her?"

I had come to believe that one of the skills of the undead was to misdirect and deceive, but I couldn't make it work with Kelly. She was like truth serum and a lie detector operating as one.

"There are some things about this that might take some time to explain," I said.

At that moment, a delivery van pulled into the parking lot, stopping about a dozen yards from where we were gathered. The van's passenger side was toward us. The driver climbed out the passenger side door and approached us. He appeared to be a deliveryman, probably looking for directions. He stopped halfway and unfolded his cell phone. We all watched him.

"Dion," he said to the phone. "Acquiring target. Wait for my go." He aimed his cell phone toward Kelly and started walking toward us. He was a powerful looking man despite some age, but he slowed, stopping a few steps short of handshake distance from her.

"Hello again, Ms. Williams," he said. She said nothing.

A moment later he saw me. I was a few steps behind her. He turned pale. He saw what I was. Even that far away, I felt his skin temperature cooling. He looked ill.

"Dion," he said into his phone. "New target. Primary candidate is an OTG Caucasian male, maybe Hispanic, six feet one, one-seventy-five, dark shoulder-length hair. Let's bring him in. I'm posting the override with Westborough. This is your go." He aimed the cell phone toward me, probably taking a picture.

The side door of the delivery van slid open. A man dressed like a priest stepped out and came jogging toward us. He was moving much too fast, though—as fast as I could. Despite his gaining the initiative, he didn't make it all the way to me—I was in the middle of Wendy's cluster of friends. He stopped short.

"Please step back," he said. His baritone voice was calm and compelling. The group shuffled a few steps backward, leaving me and Kelly exposed. The deliveryman was standing just to my right. The priest took another step toward me and stopped a yard away from me, his arms folded flat, crossed over his chest. Each hands' fingertips rested on the opposite shoulder.

Dion. No heat came from him. He was statue-like, wavy long black hair framing a beautiful face, like the guy on the cover of a romance novel. He was so close I could reach out and touch his slim perfect nose.

If his heart was beating, the sound of it was masked by my connection to Kelly's heart. I sensed things he had in common with Jack Murphy. This was another vampire, the first I'd seen since becoming one myself. He was watching me very closely. He looked very relaxed. He shimmered copper under the industrial light.

"It's time to come home, brother," Dion said.

A moment earlier I thought I might be fighting him, but then I started feeling confused. Had we met before? How was he my brother?

"It's been a struggle being on your own, hasn't it? It doesn't have to be," he said.

Yes, it was hard. It doesn't have to be.

"Come, brother," he said. "Let's go where we both belong."

We were going where we both belonged. My body began to take a step.

"Not a good idea, Roberto," Kelly said. Her urgent words made something happen with my heart. Dion's suggestions evaporated. My step toward him became a step back. Except for my hands being down, I ended up in a good boxing stance. This creature wanted me to come along with him. I was no longer willing.

Bang! My fist connected with Dion's chin. Only then had I realized he'd attacked me. My body had reacted before I was conscious of it. I didn't know I was that fast. I was grateful for the advantage, seeing Dion stagger several steps backward. It took him only an instant to regain his footing, though. He straightened up, massaging his chin. He shook his hands and shoulders to loosen up and smiled at me, as if telling me he was looking forward to a ruckus. I needed to hit him again. I took two steps toward him.

Expecting my greater speed to prevail, I exploded a punch at his exquisite nose. His two opened hands intercepted my incoming arm, redirecting my punch down and toward my feet. I was rolling over and slammed down flat on my back, my arm still trapped between his hands. I resisted my urge to pull my arm out, instead rotating my shoulder forward to restart the punch he'd interrupted. I connected. He stepped back away from me as he raised his hands to his nose. I got back on my feet.

If this vampire was anything like me, he felt pain. As I'd reanimated, though, pain was less important. I felt it as deeply as when I was alive, but I no longer panicked. It's not like you'd die from it. In any case, I'd succeeded at hitting him in the middle of his vanity.

I saw lines over Dion's eyes as emotion took root in his face. His martial arts move had spared me pain and I had spared him none. He looked ready to pay me back.

KELLY
Thursday Night

It sounded like a gunshot when Roberto's fist found Dion's chin. Roberto threw another punch but Dion gently intercepted it, leading Roberto by his arm into a summersault that left him flat on his back. While still essentially horizontal, Roberto somehow managed to connect again with Dion's face, sending him staggering back a few steps. They moved so fast I almost didn't follow it, but—aside from seeing Dion walk into two of his punches—Roberto looked outmatched. Dion had moves like a martial arts master. He'd used restraint.

I was suffering stomach butterflies when I'd realized how this all worked. Roberto was the vampire, and he'd made Wendy into one too. She was apparently alive and planning on meeting Roberto the next night, despite her heart being in my chest. Somehow, she was okay. My truck stop nightmare about my chest came back to me for an unpleasant instant. The heart clenched in my chest. It didn't care for the thought either.

Roberto still looked like the best friend I had there. Mr. Black and Dion had come to take me away, but had become more interested in Roberto, who'd just admitted he was a vampire. Dion appeared to be one also. With Dion and Mr. Black coming after me next, it was in my best interest to help Roberto.

Mr. Black was focused on the two combatants. He was only an arm's length away from me. I snatched the white cross from his leg pocket and started toward the two vampires, holding it out in front of me. Roberto's back was toward me, but he seemed aware I was approaching because he took a couple of steps to the side. I continued walking toward Dion.

"This would be a good time for you to get back in the van," I said. I wasn't certain Dion was going to move, but I kept advancing. With only a few steps remaining between us, he did a rapid shuffle backward, over halfway back to the van.

The cross was working. I was impressed, but more important—I was relieved.

I looked toward Roberto, but my attention caused him to flinch. Turning my back to him, I held the cross toward Dion. A glance back over my shoulder told me Roberto was still unsure of me.

"You better come with me," I said. I backed toward Daddy's station wagon, keeping the cross aimed toward Dion. It struck me odd that a man dressed like a priest would be so repelled by the cross. He was entirely willing to keep his distance.

I opened the driver's side door of Daddy's wagon and got in, rolled down the window, and held the cross out while I started the station wagon. I looked to the passenger side. Roberto hadn't gotten in yet.

"Come on, get in!"

"I want to, but I can't," he said. "You've got to get rid of that thing."

That alone gave me reason enough to keep holding the cross. However, I trusted Roberto, and I felt it was the right thing to remove him from the threat. Hoping I wasn't fooling myself, I said, "Get in now!" I tossed the cross to the back deck. I rolled up my driver's window as Roberto was getting into the passenger seat. I put the Oldsmobile in gear and floored it. First, I had the tires squealing, plumes of blue smoke billowing out the back, but a few seconds later, we lurched into motion. Veering away from Dion, I aimed for the exit.

"Go faster!" Roberto said. "He's closing on us. He's very fast." I looked in my rearview mirror and saw that Dion was gaining on us. I put the gas pedal to the floor. Smoke again billowed behind us as the tires squealed and the back end of the wagon fishtailed. I eased off the gas, letting the tires regain their purchase on the pavement. I pushed us forward again, accelerating away from the undead man in ersatz priest's outfit chasing us. In seconds, we were out of the parking lot, going down the access road at over fifty miles per hour.

"Faster!" Roberto said. Another glimpse in the rearview revealed that Dion was almost on us. I floored it again.

Whap! Something had hit us. Looking in the rearview, I saw Dion just behind the car, but we were pulling away from him. After touching us, he was giving up, it appeared. He slowed to a jog. I felt better staying with my exit strategy and kept my right foot down. A quick check of the speedometer seconds later revealed we were going 120 mph. Looking back up, I saw that the traffic light that was distant a moment ago was changing right in front of me. It went from yellow to red as I entered the intersection. I hope. I was unable to stop in time and was relieved that no one had entered the crossing in front of me. I back off the gas, slowing the Oldsmobile until we were down to seventy.

"I'm impressed," Roberto said. "You were going damn fast and he still caught up long enough to touch the car. Glad we've lost him," Roberto said. "It would be wise to keep going for a while." He had been watching out the back window.

"Phenomenal car," he said. "I would not have guessed you'd drive a monster like this. You are full of surprises. But I should ask, are you okay?"

"I've got to admit I'm somewhat nervous," I said. "I've had more than my fair share of freaky over the past five days. I've experienced a recovery that is miraculous and grotesque all at the same time. About ninety seconds ago, I was the quarry of Mr. Black—a sort of vampire hunter and his trusty vampire pal Reverend Dion. Now I've just driven almost twice as fast as I've ever gone, run my first red light, and I've got an admitted vampire riding in my passenger seat. Those would be my highlights."

It felt inappropriate that my heartbeat was calm. I pictured Wendy kicked back on a couch somewhere, watching television and snacking on junk food. Maybe the heart was responding to my demands as well. It had made me restless and energetic, but it had never let me down. I wondered—did Wendy sense me around her heart? And I wondered if she felt something for Roberto—I was feeling that I did.

I also considered that I might have made a few mistakes in the past two minutes. My being at Modern Memorials was innocent enough. Running into Mr. Black a second time was unexpected and unlikely. I didn't understand why he was so provoked by me.

"If you don't mind," Roberto said, "would you tell me what you were doing there? Look—Kelly—don't get me wrong. It's really nice to see you again, but I think you should know you scare me some."

"What?" I thought I heard in his voice that he wasn't the only one feeling disadvantaged. I might need to use that.

I took the onramp for the Interstate. It was empty this time of night, an invitation to have some fun with Daddy's behemoth. We were going 100 by the time I merged into the right lane.

"Woohoo!" He yelled, making my ears ring. He was enjoying the G-forces too.

"So," I said, "let's agree to not hurt each other, okay? How does that sound to you?" We were going 120 again.

"Suits me fine," he said. At 130 mph, my outside rearview mirror started shaking. A bit of common sense seized me and I dropped my speed by half. Daddy's project car had even more power in reserve, but my confidence in the precision of its steering didn't justify it. I checked on Roberto again. He looked like he was having fun. Cute smile.

"Roberto," I said. "I have a few questions for you, but I think the first thing we need to do is decide where we're going. I need to understand what we are getting away from. Those people that came after you: did you know either of them?"

"It clearly looked that—until they saw me—they had eyes on you. I've never seen them before, but I think I know who they are. They've got to be from Continental Grid."

"Yes," I said. "They were. I saw their truck earlier."

"And you've talked to them before, I think. What made them decide to come after you?"

"What's Continental Grid?" I asked.

"They are the evil empire. I understand they hunt down my kind. I didn't know they went after other kinds, though. So, I'd love to know, Kelly. What kind are you?"

I felt frustrated because I didn't have an answer. Before I had been devastated by my heart ailment, I could show my temper. A few times I was impressively angry. I remember well how that felt. What I was feeling was not like that. I was having angry thoughts, but the couch potato who was controlling my heartbeat was chilling to music videos.

"I don't know, Roberto. Maybe Mr. Black thought I was a vampire. The first time I saw him he flashed that cross at me and looked freaked out when I didn't react. He backed away from me and looked like he was ready to cut and run. I think he was afraid of me."

"He looked like a sharp guy," Roberto said. "If he's familiar with how strong the undead are, keeping a respectful distance makes sense."

"So how strong are you?" I asked. I thought I should know this.

"I'm as least as strong as a mountain gorilla. Or maybe a polar bear. I can roll this car over. Or I can stand it on end. With a running start I can jump and land standing on a basketball backboard. How strong are you?"

Good question. I realized I had never felt stronger. I had been saved by Wendy's heart.

"Strong enough," I said, though I really had nothing to base the opinion on. This was the first time in my life that someone assumed I was powerful. I liked that he was listening to me and talking with me. There was so much good about him.

Then I had to face the grim issue I'd been avoiding thinking about since Roberto found his way into my life a third time: his girlfriend's heart was in my chest. He might not respond well to that news.

That was not the most important thing at that moment, I recalled. Getting a plan was.

"What's the safest thing we can do right now?" I asked him. "That other vampire? Does he have some type of ESP way of tracking you?"

"I hope not," Roberto said. "But I can't say for sure. Most of what I know about being a vampire I've figured out on my own. The guy who transitioned me wasn't there when I woke up. He was going to train me, but he never came back. So far, the only one I can sense from any distance is you. I wonder—how do they track you? How did you meet them?"

"I was working on Wendy's obituary and thought the details of her funeral arrangements would fill out the piece. I went to that Morty Coil's place and came across Mr. Black talking to some people down in the basement. At first, he thought I was just a nuisance, but then he came at me with a cross. When I didn't flinch, he backed off and looked very worried. I think he was there about Wendy. He was interrogating the staff about how they'd handled her body. So, it might be that Black went out to Modern Memorials next because that's where Wendy's body had been sent."

"Why send her there?" he asked.

"To be cremated. I think that's how they get rid of vampires."

"Oh. Not good." He was quiet for a moment. "Wait, that can't be right. I know she's okay. She woke up. She's been talking to her friend Rose."

"I would have thought you guys would have planned to meet once she woke up."

"That didn't work out. Something went wrong, and at this point you know as much about it as I do," he said.

I realized that I might know a lot more. He didn't know about the organs then, but he did know about Dwight—sort of. I then realized that I must have had Dwight wrong. Roberto was the vampire that changed Wendy. Dwight might not be a vampire. It frustrated me that the vampire sitting next to me knew as little—or likely even less—than I did.

"What can you tell me about Continental Grid?" I asked Roberto.

"Jack—the guy who did this to me—said they were this secretive private organization whose role was to control the vampire population. Jack was part of an underground group that was resisting their totalitarian rule of the undead. He wasn't clear about whether they exterminate vampires, but it sounds like sometimes that might be tolerated. They follow the CG party line. Vampires like Jack and me are considered OTG, which means 'Off The Grid.'"

"That sort of explains Dion, doesn't it?" I said. "Maybe it takes one to hunt one."

"Unfortunately, it does look that way," Roberto said.

"The last time I was being pursued you recommended calling the proper authorities. Correct me if I'm wrong, but I think there is no one to call in our current circumstance."

"That's why I should have stayed in hiding," he said. "Justice is for the living. Mine is a lonely and desperate existence," he said with a theatrical rise to his voice. I saw what I thought was a rueful smile. He was quiet for a moment. "Nothing new there, though. Okay. So, the question is, what do we do? Dion and his chauffeur were looking for you and seemed to know who you are. They probably don't know my name, but they know that I exist. They said 'new target' when they spotted me. We can't count on them forgetting about either of us."

"That would be too much to hope for," I said.

"Can you go out in the daylight?" Roberto asked.

"Yep. I have no problem with that. You can't?"

"For me tanning has severe and lasting health consequences. In any case, you might be better off going to the police. I might be better off going into hiding."

"Assuming I can get a police officer to listen to my story about being pursued by vampire hunters—one of which is himself vampire—I doubt their protection would continue long enough to discourage Dion and Mr. Black."

I didn't mention that the police might be looking for me anyway, at the request of Central Hospital. At minimum, my absence had to be a black eye for the organization. Dr. Garrison speculated I had an infection. By now they might have declared me the new Typhoid Mary.

Then there was the matter of Dwight, who was soon going to work out how to recover a certain critical organ from my chest. Either of my two stories about pursuers was sufficient to get me admitted to a locked psych ward. Perhaps I might have been safer there, come to think of it.

I felt a pang in my stomach. I needed more steak.

"Roberto? Do you have any particular dietary requirements I should know about?"

"Aside from the occasional pint of human blood, my needs are simple," he said.

"I hope you're not contemplating trying some of mine, are you?"

"I have been what's called 'blood drunk' for the last three or four days. My appetite is just now coming back. But no, I don't think I dare try yours. Jack told me that vampires can't drink vampire blood. You might not be a vampire, but you're not exactly human either. I'm not likely to chance it."

"What's 'blood drunk'?" I asked.

"I found out that if I try to drink too much blood, I become irrational, angry, and erratic. It takes a long time—several nights—for a single vampire to drain one victim's blood. It took me three nights to transition Wendy."

Looking down the highway ahead of us, I saw the lights for the I-Way truck stop. They had the steak I wanted, but I didn't dare stop there as my calls on the cell phone the previous night had originated there. However, I remembered that there was another truck stop further down the highway near the intersection for state highway 68.

"Roberto, I need to eat. We might be safer with other people around us. There's a truck stop ahead where we can stop and talk this through while I get some desperately needed nourishment. Does that present any problems for you?"

"As long as we don't sit near any mirrors or crosses, I don't have to cross any running water, and you don't order anything with garlic in it, I should be okay."

I pivoted the rearview mirror to aim at the passenger seat and caught Roberto with a broad smile on his face.

"I'm guessing," I said, "that some of that wasn't true. That cross seems to be a big problem for you, but you don't show any particular effect with photons reflecting from your face to a mirror."

"I never much liked garlic, even when I was alive, but it has no unusual effect. I get my best results combing my hair when I stand in front of a mirror. Running water is not a problem, and great for washing clothes. I can enter a room without being invited—except that would be poor manners and my mother didn't raise me that way. Anyway, we can stop if you need to. Maybe in a public place we'd be less likely to be targeted again. We have a lot to sort out."

Roberto continued to make a good impression on me, far better than any living guys I'd dated. It was too bad he had the monstrous condition of vampirism. Of course, he suspected I was something equally unsavory. Maybe that gave us something in common.

As we passed the exit for the I-Way truck stop, I asked Roberto "What made you decide to become a vampire? Things must have been depressing for you to adjust to such an existence."

A loud "Ha!" burst from him. "Decide? There was no decision involved. Jack gave me no choice. Basically, he lured me away one night after work, handcuffed me to a pipe in the basement of an abandoned building, and killed me over a series of nights."

"Oh," I said. I regretted my question. It was like asking someone why he'd let himself be raped. I couldn't avoid thinking about what it must have been like, to have been trapped there, alone and wounded in the dark, waiting for his assailant to come back and feast on him yet again. "It must have been horrible."

"Horrible does not begin to describe it. The biting wasn't that painful, but the long hours of anticipation and the loneliness and the unanswered calls for help shattered me. I screamed myself hoarse. And then there was the thirst and hunger. I begged him for a bottle of water and something—anything—to eat. For Jack it was all business. He said, 'No. It will take long enough to drink the blood already in you. Diluting it will just make this take longer. Sorry.'"

This felt like a good time to be quiet. I saw in Roberto's reflection that the memory pained him. In other awkward conversations, I'd try to come up with something to change the topic, like "how about those Red Sox?" or "unusual weather we've been having, isn't it?" It didn't think it would help to express how difficult our situation was.

Ahead in the distance I saw the glowing orange globe on a pole, indicating the brand of fuel at the next truck stop.

"So—if I do have something to eat, will you have to sit there and watch me, or will you be able to eat something?"

"I'm quite tough," he said, "so I don't think I'd do myself much harm. However, I'm broke, and it doesn't make much sense to have you buy me something of no use."

Slowing the car for the exit ramp, I realized that I was not all that well off myself. I had a small amount of cash left, no purse, credit cards or ID, and a cell phone with no charger that would lead the police to me. I didn't feel panicked, despite our recent close call with CG, and wondered if my low anxiety level might be yet another gift of the undead heart in my chest. Reason told me we were not in immediate danger. Experience told me that reflection and planning nearly always outperforms a panic response.

Also, I needed that bloody steak.

I pulled into the truck stop's main lot. A central cluster of copper lights illuminated the main building complex. I parked between two SUVs in the automobile parking area. I thought it better to park closer to the cars than the big trucks. A vintage car owner would never chance leaving it amid the big rigs. Leaving it parked there also kept it aimed straight for the access road and, from there, back onto the Interstate.

We decided on a booth that kept us out of the way of foot traffic and gave us a view of the door. I asked Roberto to go in, sit down and get me a glass of water. I stayed outside for a moment. He protested, but I assured him I'd only be a few seconds. I think he might have worried I'd be bringing in the cross. I'd considered it.

Once he was inside, I went to the passenger side of Daddy's station wagon, put my back against the side of the car and began bending my knees, sliding down till I grasped the bottom edge of the rear bumper. I pulled up on it, but little happened. I kept the pressure on, grunting and straining, but only managed to make the car sway slightly. After ten or fifteen seconds of struggling, I had to admit no one should be able to roll it over. If Roberto was that strong, he was many times stronger than I. Despite my exertion, my heart rate was about right for a couch potato. Perhaps Wendy's listlessness was pacifying my heart, keeping me from generating enough power.

I took a red baseball cap from the back of the wagon, twisted my hair up on top of my head and secured it under the cap before going in. I admit I bypassed reason when I decided to enter, unarmed, instead of jumping into the wagon and driving off and leaving this all behind. Roberto had trusted me. As dangerous as he was, I wanted to believe I was safe continuing to trust him. I saw relief on his face when I entered the restaurant. Had he feared abandonment? I know I didn't want to be alone either.

In our booth, we sat side-by-side so we'd both see who entered. A waitress brought menus. I ordered the eight-ounce steak and a refill on the glass of water.

"How do you want that steak done?" she asked.

"Very rare," I said.

"You get two sides with that."

"Could I get more steak instead? I'm eating for two. It's a craving thing, you know." I saw amusement in Roberto's eyes. He must have thought I was joking.

"I'll see what I can do." She scribbled a note and brought it to the kitchen window.

"So," I asked Roberto, "have you spent your whole un-life in Springfield?"

"Yes." He smiled. "It's hard to travel with a condition like mine. I'm originally from the area." I loved that my directness surprised him.

"And you have to hide away during daylight hours?"

"Yes, I must. Every day we must submit to the dreamless sleep of the dead. We must be someplace totally dark or we burn up like a brush fire. It only takes a hole burnt through your arm by a dot of sunlight to help make up your mind about staying hidden."

"Where do you hide?"

"I prefer the basements of old industrial buildings, converted churches, foreclosed McMansions, burned out houses sometimes, that sort of place. I have a half dozen favorites if you can call them that. I've developed a tolerance for claustrophobia."

"Why is that?"

"I think it pays off to be tucked away in a tight dark place. If someone were to find me lying out in the open in a basement and dragged me out into the sun, that would be the end, I think. Completely final. I may be dead, but I'm not suicidal." I think he'd been waiting a long time to say that line.

"Do you have many friends?"

"Well, that depends. If I may count you as one, then the answer is—one."

"Then what is Wendy Allard to you?" Though we were sitting side by side, I sensed that his eyes were now looking down.

"That's complicated," he said. "I've been very lonely. She's the only person I'd ever met who wanted to be my victim, even before I had bitten her."

"Am I hearing you right? Someone you've bitten would want it again? What happens?" Though there was no one sitting near us, Roberto's answer was almost too quiet for me to hear.

"Do you know how mosquitoes inject something like an anticoagulant when they bite? I think we must do something similar except that it makes victims passive. I've seen people respond like they are drunk. I don't know. I get too blissed out while drinking to pay much attention." He continued gazing at the tabletop.

"Roberto? Will you show me your teeth?" I asked.

He turned toward me and smiled slightly. Though he seemed to be feeling down, his smile looked genuine enough. His teeth looked perfectly normal. With a smile like that, he could have been a model.

"I thought vampires had fangs," I said.

"Yeah, got those." Roberto looked around the room, assessing whether anyone was watching him. "Look," he said. He opened his mouth wide. For a moment, it was a perfectly normal mouth, but he tilted his head farther back and I saw something hinge down from the roof of his mouth. Two slender gleaming fangs arced forward, falling into position behind his upper canine teeth. They looked like a rattlesnake's fangs. A few seconds later, they curled back in as he closed his mouth.

"I'm guessing you weren't born with those," I said.

"You guessed right. They were there when I finished my transition. It's funny when I think about it. I felt them up there with my tongue, but I didn't know they would come out on their own until I took my first victim. Poor Walt. When they moved it surprised me, even though I'd seen Jack do it. It took time to develop conscious control. At first they acted as if they had a mind of their own."

While he was telling me, I was exploring the roof of my mouth with my tongue. I wish I had paid more attention to its shape. All my life I'd taken it for granted. I thought that it was possible something smooth and curved lurked up there, just below the surface. What would happen when my steak arrived?

"How did you meet her?" I asked.

"She was having a smoke in the alley behind a club on University Avenue. I talked to her. I was trying to keep her calm. Even alive it's not easy to get near people. She understood what I was right away. She said, 'where have you been?'"

"You were going to bite her anyway, right?"

"That, my dear Kelly, is my un-life—good name for it—in a nutshell. She smelled down and out, like some crazy people do. We talked. She interrupted me and said, 'You're really a vampire?' It took a goth chick like her to hit the nail on the head. Everyone else I'd approach thought I was an undercover police officer, social worker, prostitute, or missionary. So, I said 'Yes, I am.' She said, 'Do you want to bite me?' and cleared the hair away from her shoulders and tilted her head back."

"So, you bit her neck right there in the alley?"

"Actually no. Necks are wide and messy—hard on my jaw and more dangerous to the victim. It was more comfortable to bite her on the arm. There's a good place at the elbow where medical people draw blood. That works well for me."

"But she died at home, right?" I said. He looked shocked.

"Are you a mind reader? Psychic? How do you know these things?"

"I have a few skills, but I came across that bit researching her obituary." He looked relieved for a moment, but then looked away. Something wasn't making sense. He turned back to look at me, his face serious.

"What I'm having trouble with is this: the first time I saw you—three days ago, right? You're in a hospital bed hooked up to monitors and oxygen. You were weak. Then yesterday I find you behind the desk in the medical records office, and you're worrying about a stalker and protesting being returned to your hospital bed. Today you're a reporter covering Wendy's obituary, and now we're on the run from what's supposed to be a vampire's worst enemies. That's three different women—at least—but they're all you. If I made up a story like that, no one would believe me—but that's what I've seen. I can't make sense of it."

"I suppose not," I said, letting myself smile a little.

"So, why were you in the hospital?"

"I received a transplanted heart on Sunday. I was just days away from dead. My own heart fell apart from myocarditis—the doctors think that it was caused by chicken pox." That should have matched up to what he'd observed so far.

"Next scene: I discover you in the medical records office three days later?" he asked. "My father had a heart transplant. Granting that he was a bit older than you, he was in the hospital for weeks, not days."

"I don't understand it either, but that was what happened. Here—look," I said. I pivoted so I was facing toward him. I unzipped the NASCAR jacket and then pulled down the zipper on my yellow tracksuit so he'd see the proof.

My actions were noticed elsewhere. A chorus of hoots erupted from some of the truck drivers sitting on the diner stools. "Hey, Honey—let us have a look too." I zipped and zipped some more, amazed that I could forget such essential modesty. Too much time in the hospital makes modesty unfamiliar.

"That was not what I was expecting," Roberto said. "In so many ways. They didn't do a good job, did they?" He had seen the tangled network of scar tissue over misaligned bone.

From where we sat, we watched vehicles entering and leaving the parking lot. A white passenger van with Central County General Hospital on its door drove by and pulled into a space in the auto lot. The same security officers that came to my room three nights earlier—the young man and woman—left the van and entered the restaurant. They looked toward the seating area, glancing towards us for a second. They didn't recognize me, soon turning away and entering the convenience store area.

"We need to leave," I whispered to Roberto. I got up and headed for the door, leaving a ten-dollar bill on the table and hoping Roberto would follow me. I was ready to run if I had to. As I went out through the door, he was next to me. His speed was astounding.

"Your food?" Roberto asked.

"Not worth the risk. Let's go." I saw the question on his face, but there was no time.

The hospital security team was studying the contents of a beverage cooler as we exited. I was nearly certain they hadn't seen us. Walking as fast as we dared, we returned to Daddy's station wagon. The seats and steering wheel shuddered as the huge engine block shook itself awake. Out of habit I checked my rearview mirror, even though I knew I was going to drive straight out. A pair of headlights—too high up for a car—pulled up behind us, blinding me with my rearview mirrors. Though it was dark, the gold-on-brown design on the vehicle's hood told me it was a Continental Grid van.

CHAPTER 6
DWIGHT

Friday morning

At 3 a.m. in the morning, I made my fourth trip to the hospital.

"I'm here to visit my dear old uncle Frank," I said at the front desk. "Frank Pierpoint. I know it's late, but I've been on the road for days, and I just have to see him. I have to see that he's okay. My mother won't be satisfied with anything less—you know how it is. She can't travel."

"Visiting hours begin at eight," the receptionist replied. My insistence had rendered me invisible. She hadn't been on duty the previous night and was unlikely to recognize me as the kidney thief. "It's pretty late to get a hotel room, so you might stretch out on one of the couches in the family room." She pointed me down the hallway. "There, you'll hear a PA announcement at the beginning of visiting hours."

This worked out about as well as it needed to. I didn't need to go any farther the way I was dressed. I had an idea about how I might blend in.

Besides looking in on my newly adopted uncle Frank, I had to believe that Johnson Cooper had to still be there too, recovering from the nightly punishment inflicted by his new liver. Also, Kelly Williams had to be there too. With a heart transplant, she'd have the longest recovery—or no recovery, if that organ were as dangerous as the others.

The empty family room featured an end table stacked with dog-eared copies of Redbook and Ladies Home Journal, two green vinyl recliners, a matching vinyl sofa, and a TV set in a wooden hutch delivering an infomercial about a cleaning product. I pulled the door closed behind me, took off my jeans and sweatshirt, put on the hospital scrubs, and pulled the cloth footies over my shoes. I'd brought the small cooler and a backpack, in which I'd stowed a pillowcase. Opening the window, I dropped the pillowcase—now holding my street clothes and the backpack—into the shrubs below. I put on a surgical mask and walked out the door, cooler in hand, striding purposefully to an elevator which took me to the ground floor. No one was around to see me traverse that level. I took the stairs back up to the third floor, where Pierpoint was recovering.

My heart was beating hard by the time I got to the third floor, and it wasn't because of poor conditioning. Soon, I'd be walking into a hospital room, rolling Pierpoint—still in his bed—out of his room to the surgical suite where I'd somehow retrieve Wendy's stolen pancreas. Some parts of my plan were tighter than others, and that last detail wasn't quite settled. Might be messy.

Down the hallway, yellow lights flashed next to a patient room, and two men—probably doctors, considering their bearing—were having a heated conversation in the hallway outside. The one with his back to the room had his arms crossed on his chest, leaning a bit back from his colleague whose whispers weren't all that quiet.

"Ten pounds in under twenty-four hours, Steve. He's lost about a sixth of his body weight since the procedure, and he's not dehydrated. He's digesting himself somehow. Urates, blood glucose, and ketones are off the charts. He came in overweight, and three days later, he's got the muscular definition of a pro bodybuilder. His pancreas is in overdrive. He'd be better off rejecting it before it finishes him off."

"Are you hearing yourself?" Doctor Steve asked. "The organ was benign prior to transplant. Young donor, negative on all pathology and pharmacology screens. The answer is somewhere else. We need to revisit this patient's history. There's likely something we didn't catch, or something he didn't tell us."

"I'm lead on this," said Doctor Not-Steve. "He's in a state of panic, delirious from the feast going on inside him, and there's nothing that begins to explain this. And there's this day–night problem also. He stabilizes during the day, and then goes into distress after sunset. How does he even know what time it is? Anyway, we have another pancreas, and it's going in. If the one we're removing still proves viable, we're no worse off. And more important, he'll live. In another four hours, we won't have either the patient or the pancreas. So, let's get him back to the O.R. You there!" He'd seen me.

"Yes?"

"Transport patient Pierpoint to Suite 318, now." Doctor Not-Steve checked his clipboard and then handed me a form from it. "Verify the DOB. Let's get a move on. Go."

"Suite 318, verifying DOB," I said and walked into the room. It seems I'd been given a new job. I heard Dr. Not-Steve saying, "I swear this hospital is cursed. First, that walk-away with the coronary transplant. Then two kidney transplants have matching negative outcomes—and apparently we had a theft."

As I entered room 318, I heard Dr. Steve say, "Word is there's a liver that's gone into overdrive too. Same donor, I gather. Last night, the patient developed instant hepatitis—joint pain, nausea, stomach pain, high fever, black urine…"

I loved my good luck. Anything this strange going on could only mean I was near another part of Wendy. Soon, I would make her whole, and then make her mine. I got busy.

I figured out the Pierpoint part of the doctors' instructions, and his bed was numbered, but I thought I'd have to fake the DOB thing since I didn't know what it meant. My patient smelled like a cross between a locker room and the alley behind a diner. Wendy's pancreas was digesting him from inside and the resulting imbalances made him stink.

It looked like Uncle Frank was already packaged for transport. IVs were connected to hangers on the bed's superstructure, and a stand with the vitals monitors was connected to the bed frame, sort of like a sidecar.

I glanced at his chart. Pierpoint, Frank. My dear, dear uncle. DOB. Date of Birth, that was it! DOB. November 30th, 1948. It matched the one on my piece of paper.

"It's O.R. time, Uncle Frank," I said, as I steered the bulky rig into the hallway. He wasn't entirely out of it. His eyes rolled toward me for a second, and I saw his mistrust. I didn't take it as anything personal, though. Uncle Frank knew something bad had been happening to him, and I simply hadn't made things better for him. Good to be right about something, I guess.

I had no problem finding the operating room, as the two doctors were standing in the hallway waiting for me to roll Uncle Frank in. Two doors swung inward, making the delivery a simple matter.

"Put him in three," Dr. Steve said. Holding area number three was obvious by virtue of the illuminated number above it. If there was anything wrong with how I delivered Frank, no one said anything.

"You're in good hands now," I said as I walked out of the cubicle, realizing that what I said might in fact be true.

"You—nurse," Dr. Not-Steve said. It turns out he was looking at me. "Get into fresh surgical and scrub up. We may need extra hands."

"But I..."

"You have somewhere more important to be?"

I managed to fake washing up and getting into surgical scrubs well enough to avoid notice. Doctor Not-Steve chided me for being slow, but I needed to stay out of the thick of things and watch. So, I made myself stay slow. By the time I eased myself into the operating room, fortunately, two real nurses and an anesthesiologist were handling everything the doctors were asking for. The situation was urgent enough that the doctors didn't notice me. I stood near the door and watched them as they puzzled over Uncle Frank.

"Anomalous scarification at the incision site," Dr. Steve reported. "No trace of a scab. It looks like it was closed a year ago, not three days ago. Except that it's sunken in. Adipose tissue that characterized the wound site has simply melted away. The tissue is desiccated. Anesthesia ready? Proceed."

The gas-passer responded that the patient was under. He was closer to me than the doctors, and I had a chance to watch how he operated his gas equipment. I might not know why I was doing it, but I'd be able to mimic the settings.

They took a scalpel to Uncle Frank. They didn't get much blood for their efforts. In about three minutes, they had the pancreas exposed.

"Where are the sutures?" Dr. Not-Steve asked. "The pancreatic duct looks fully intermingled with the duodenal tissue. Unprecedented."

"Yes, I see it. Yes, it's interesting, but we've admired it enough," Dr. Steve said. "Let's get it out and have pathology assess it—hopefully without destroying it. I think we go aggressive: get all the tissue that's contiguous with the transplant. We leave nothing foreign behind."

Watching two masters applying their skills fascinated me. Despite their sense of urgency, they were precise and deliberate in their procedure. I thought I'd like to try it sometime. In a way I already had, installing a pump and kidneys in Wendy.

Soon they had the elongated organ lifted away and separated. They set it aside in the stainless pan. I left my station near the door and walked up to the tray where my prize rested. As I came around the edge of the room, I realized how jazzed up I was. I couldn't believe I was pulling it off. I was about to break out in sweat.

"The pathologist said he's ready to look at it," I said as I picked it up and headed back for the door.

"He?" Doctor Not-Steve looked up at me. I was glad I was masked. "I thought Grace was driving in from Northwoods?"

"Um, my bad," I said, worried for a second. Their attention stayed with the patient though, even though I thought they might overhear my pounding heart. "I assumed. I'm just passing along a message. Sorry for stereotyping. Anyway, traffic must be light this early in the morning."

"Be careful with that," he said, returning his attention to the next step of Uncle Frank's surgery.

"I'll protect it like it's my girlfriend's," I said. In the prep room, I transferred the pancreas to my cooler, stripped off the latex gloves, and walked as fast as I dared for the back stairwell. My heart pounded with the thrill of my successful theft, but I had something holding me back from my getaway. I still needed to get a liver. Either that organ or the pancreas might fix the caustic stink of Wendy's breath. Also, we needed the heart, but that wasn't as likely to cure the current problem.

I climbed up the stairwell to the fourth floor—all patient rooms—and walked back the length of the building. I needed to visit Johnson Cooper's room, which I guessed was somewhere near Uncle Frank's room. An elevator ride back to the third floor left me off right across from the ICU rooms. A strip of surgical tape next to the door recorded the name of each patient inside, and I found Johnson Cooper's name next to one in sight of the nurse's station. I ducked in and quickly decided which patient he was. His roommate, a middle-aged woman, was clearly the Sandra Bates listed on the door. I pulled the curtain around his bed and tried to capture the spirit of making rounds I had seen on TV hospital dramas. Mr. Cooper was awake.

"And how are we feeling this morning, Mr. Cooper?" The skin on his face looked slack, like a deflated balloon.

"How do I feel? Look at the freaking chart, you incompetent quack. Are you going to tell me what you guys are going to do about this?" He was pointing to a bag of liquid hanging off the side of his bed. Drops of black fluid were filling the bag, emerging from a tube that snaked out from under his bed covers. He coughed. Its acrid smell drove me a step back. It was very much like the exhaust fumes Wendy was exhaling.

"Are you in any discomfort?"

"Idiot! Are you a real doctor? It's all on my chart. Look at the automated morphine drip they've got me on. It's not there for a party favor. Do you see any cake or confetti?" I decided against mentioning that the skin on his face was rolling outward from his mouth as he spoke, like waves rippling from the splash of a rock tossed into a pond. I saw the sharp outlines of bone and muscle under the slack skin. His body fat was gone.

"I'll take that as 'no' then, shall I? How often is it set for?"

"I can push the button every eight minutes. My mind wanders and sometimes it takes me ten or fifteen minutes for the pain to force me awake. Could you make it five minutes? I just pushed it three minutes ago." The countdown timer on the gadget said we had five minutes and a few seconds to wait.

I had an idea, driven by my need to stay out of sight, at the same time arranging to retrieve a certain organ from Mr. Cooper.

"Look, how about I just stay here for a few cycles and make sure you get it promptly? Will that work for you?"

"Really? Are you messing with me? After the way you guys have treated me, it's about time. Sure, go ahead." While we waited, he filled me in on his situation, clearly happy to have someone listen to him kvetch. Bottom line, everything was fine by day, but he started burning up with fever and passing black urine at night. It was the same the day before. The liver's juices were marinating him.

The doctors had told him there'd been a problem with several other transplants over the past few days, and it was keeping the specialists busy, but they'd be back to see him soon. Johnson had been getting that message all day.

When the five minutes were up, I pressed the dosage button for him.

He nodded off after the next cycle, eight minutes later. After pressing the dosage button a third time, I noticed his blood pressure and oxygen numbers were going down. I wanted to get him to surgery while he couldn't yell or say mean things to me. Time to retrieve Wendy's liver.

I ventured out into the hallway, making my way back to the operating room where Uncle Frank had just gotten a new pancreas in exchange for Wendy's supercharged version. Uncle Frank was gone. The operating room was empty. I returned to Mr. Cooper's room, hid my cooler with the pancreas under the covers between his legs, and moved what connections and tubes I could to his bed. I rolled him to the operating room. As the doors closed behind us. I heard a warning beep repeating from the nursing station. No time to waste.

I found a facemask and a throat tube in the anesthesiologist's cupboard and connected them to Johnson's head. I didn't have a drug to squirt into his IV, but I could always hit him with more morphine in a few minutes. Meanwhile, I turned on the gas gauges and started pumping oxygen and nitrous into him. I didn't have the heart rate and blood pressure monitors any more, but I felt the carotid pulse in his neck. He still had one. He stayed asleep.

I found a tray full of cut-em-open tools in a cabinet on the other side of the room. Time to get to work. I'll spare you the details, but I'll summarize by saying I was better at installing organs than removing them. Still, Johnson Cooper was quite alive when I left the operating room with the organ that would hopefully cure my stinky-mouthed princess. I stripped off my outer layer of scrubs and gave Cooper one more push of the morphine button as I was leaving.

I started for the back stairwell, but then had a thought. My patient might have been better off without Wendy's liver, but that would only be for a short while as he'd need another one soon—much sooner now that I was leaving the building with his current one. So, I attempted to do the right thing. I made sure my nose and mouth were covered by my surgical mask, pulled my surgical cap down to my eyebrows, and walked up to the nursing station. I guess I was carrying myself right, as I got immediate attention.

"Hi. Someone left a patient on the table without a liver in that operating room over there. Yes, that one. His transplant didn't go so well, so the latest one had to come out. Could you organize another liver for him? That'd be great." I turned and walked away, going about ten steps toward the stairwell when someone finally left the nurse's station and hurried to the operating room. I figured that might keep them busy.

I returned to the back stairwell once again and descended. I went out the side exit, around behind the building, and retrieved my pillowcase of clothing and backpack from the shrubbery. I still had a few hours left to work on Wendy before sunrise, so I hustled back to my car. My latest haul of organs would really impress her, I thought. She might even forgive me for not having the heart yet.

I took an indirect route home to be certain I wasn't being followed. As I turned onto my street, I noticed the lights on in a few of the houses along the street, almost certainly the homes of older neighborhood residents. Old people don't sleep that well. I turned off my headlights to prevent advertising my late return.

"I'm hungry," Wendy said as I walked into my kitchen through the carport door. I saw the hunger in her eyes and knew I needed to dial her back to human.

"That's all going to have to wait." I bowed grandly. "Your pancreas awaits you, Madame, followed by a full course of liver."

I planned on recruiting Tanner to act as my surgical assistant while restoring the retrieved pancreas and liver, but she explained he'd gotten very tired and was napping on the sofa. I decided to let him rest, even though I was burned out from the stress of my new calling as a transplant surgeon. Two more procedures and I could call it a night.

"Give me some so I can relax while you work," Wendy said.

"Hey, let's look at history. We're most likely to lose blood during these installs. We'll top you off once I've finished closing, okay?"

"Okay," she said. "Don't forget." I set to work knowing she wouldn't forget.

ROBERTO

Friday, an hour before dawn

"Not good," Kelly said. The Continental Grid van had pulled right up to our rear bumper. Backing up hadn't been her plan, so our way out was to drive forward. Kelly had us moving before I buckled my seat belt. Though we weren't moving that fast yet, our pursuers were forced to move slower still—the space we'd parked in was scarcely wider than their van. We eased between the two towering SUVs and were accelerating toward the highway access road when the van's headlights started closing in on us again. I thought they were going to ram us. Kelly thought so too because she floored the gas pedal, and we fishtailed out onto the access road. The speedometer needle was leaning toward my side of the car.

"How did they find me this time?" Kelly asked. I didn't think I was expected to answer. The big car lurched and swayed as she aimed it up the on-ramp for the highway. I worried we might become airborne as we merged into the right lane. I couldn't see where the tip of the speedometer needle was pointing because it was so far to the right. My only other experience with speed so great was on an airliner lifting off for a transcontinental flight.

"Maybe you can back off a bit now," I said. Neither of us had spoken for a minute, but I'd glanced back several times and saw no one following us. "I doubt that van can go anywhere near this fast." For a moment, I thought she hadn't heard me for the roar of the wind blowing past us, but then she let up on the gas, and soon, we were down to eighty miles per hour.

"Is your clock right?" I asked, pointing to the dashboard.

"Yes," she said. I thought I heard a note of irritation in her voice. "This car is Daddy's pride and joy. If something isn't original equipment, it's because he found something that looked and worked better. Is there someplace you need to be?" Now it felt like she was teasing me.

"I have less than an hour before sunrise," I said. "To avoid becoming a pile of ashes, I need to be someplace light free before then." Looking over her right shoulder at me, she was taking my measure. She returned her attention to the road.

"In that milk crate on the back deck—along with jumper cables, oil, tranny fluid, fan belts, and headlight bulbs—Daddy keeps a Handi-vac. I don't think it's big enough to clean up after you, though. Hiding you in our basement isn't that good an idea either considering the attention I've been getting. I'm not looking forward to spending the day without your counsel about Continental Grid, but I guess neither of us have much choice in the matter. So, where should we hide you?"

"This highway loops around the southwest corner of the city. You know that place with the silos where they grind corn meal? There's a warehouse building there I've hidden out in a few times. You could drop me off there."

"How about we put up at the Extra-Z motel up ahead? Oh wait—no credit cards and not enough cash. That won't work."

"There are a couple of other problems with that. With our luck, today would be the one day where the chambermaids choose to come in and open the blinds. And Continental Grid apparently has a talent for spotting your car. You'd need to either hide it or keep doing 120, and I don't know how long you can keep that up."

"We're barely going 100, but I see your point. Okay, let's go on to the grain elevator." I heard a catch in her voice. "I wish I knew where I could go to be safe."

In the two years since Jack made me into a monster, I had seen and heard fear in my victims. The capacity for sympathy erodes while giving in to the compulsion to drink blood. Something about Kelly's sudden display of vulnerability made me feel human again. Maybe it was because, this time, the monster pursuing a victim wasn't me. I understood the power our pursuers could bring to bear, and it seemed Kelly did too.

While I was alive, I'd wanted a woman in my life who was strong and capable but who still needed what I could provide. My wife had been very dependent on me. I had no certainty I'd be able to protect Kelly from the threat Continental Grid offered, and it pained me that I'd have to leave her to fend for herself. She might be more than mortal, but neither of us knew if that was going to be enough.

Kelly asked, "What do vampires dream about?"

"Dreaming." I'd noticed that a week or two after I transitioned. "It isn't the same. When the sun rises, I just pass out. It's like fainting, but slower."

"I used to be afraid of my dreams," she said. "I kept dreaming that I was dying—because my heart was falling apart—and I'd wake up still alive. I wasn't sure which part was worse: dreaming of dying or waking up ill."

"What are your dreams like now?"

"It's hard to say. I haven't slept much since I left the hospital." Her eyes were fixed on the road ahead. "Work," she added. Hearing her say it out loud, I realized that it didn't add up.

"It's not like you owe me anything, Kelly—you may have saved my life back there—but I'm not buying that. Both you and I know you're not completely normal, but I don't see your editor sending you out on assignment straight out of the hospital after a heart transplant. I've been completely straight with you. I don't think you're a liar, but I don't think I'm hearing enough truth."

She glanced at me in her mirror and returned her eyes to the road ahead. The grain silo was a shadow on the horizon ahead, vaguely illuminated by the approach of dawn.

"Back at the restaurant," I continued, "you decided it was time to leave when the hospital's courtesy shuttle pulled in. What was that all about? Unfinished paperwork?"

"Something like that." She wasn't going to tell me, even though it felt like she wanted to. She flicked the turn signal on for the exit ramp that would take us to the granary. We slowed to a reasonable exit speed and merged onto county route 22, going east.

Had it been the fall harvest, there would be a line of trucks waiting to transfer their payloads of corn to the silos at Pollard Processing, but that season was a couple months past. There was a single pickup truck parked next to the farmhouse that was the facility's office. I pointed to a long one-story wooden building paralleling the road.

"Drop me off there."

Kelly switched off the headlights and eased the big car off the pavement onto the gravel lot surrounding the facility, pulling up next to the long building on the street side. Apparently, another row of trucks could line up on the other side of the building.

I knew of a hatch with a short ladder leading down to a dirt-floor basement where they stored wooden pallets and rusted-out contraptions with motors and belts. It was comfortingly dark down there.

"This is your stop," Kelly said as she braked the car. She turned and looked at me.

"Where are you going to go?" I asked, hoping she'd come up with something that she hadn't yet mentioned. I would have fought to my last to protect her, so long as it was nighttime.

"I don't know. I'll probably call my father from a pay phone and see if he can help me sort it out."

"So, I guess this is goodbye, then," I said.

I watched as her face worked its way through the things her mouth refused to say. A tear, then two, both clear like water, streaked down her face.

"The words make sense, Roberto, but…that's not right. I don't think this is goodbye."

Her eyes and mine were saying what we didn't dare use words for. I didn't want her to leave, but the risk of staying near her was much too great. Somehow, Continental Grid kept finding her. Maybe it was because of me. Maybe it was because of her. If we split up, perhaps they'd only find one of us, and it was better if it was me.

"I don't want you to go, but I'm the new primary target, if I heard Mr. Black right. You're better off far away from me."

"What's that? Oh my, Roberto, there's a…" Droplets of liquid pooled in the corners of my eyes, an echo of our shared anguish.

"There's red in your tears," she said.

"I'm not happy about our choices, and I'm really hating the idea I might not see you again. You're someone amazing Kelly. If I was alive…"

"Do I dare ask you for a hug?" she said. "I don't want you to leave, either."

"It's that or the Handi-vac." I released my seat belt and inched at human speed across the seat. She met me halfway. Her left hand came to rest on my right as I curled my left arm around her shoulders. The moment she touched me, a radiance spread through me, reminding me of the warmth I used to soak up sitting out in the sun.

"I thought you'd be colder," her eyes still on mine. My victims had never mentioned anything but cold. This was yet another of her mysterious powers.

"I think it's your gift to do this to me. I scarcely remember warm. Please, I must know—what are you?"

"Right now, I'm just a very scared woman who wants to stay alive. And who wants you that way too."

The sun brightened the horizon. Soon, my consciousness would fade.

"I must go, Kelly. I'm sorry. Good luck." That sounded so horribly lame.

"I'll come back for you, Roberto. Hide well, and I'll come back and get you tonight." I knew she'd silently added, "…if I can. If you're here."

She put her hand behind my head and pulled my face to hers. I couldn't resist. My strength was nowhere to be found.

KELLY

If I'd been thinking right, I'd never have opened my mouth to one hiding fangs that might make a rattlesnake jealous. My heart—or was it Wendy's?—wouldn't let him go without some sign of what had been boiling up from deep inside me. I didn't just like and respect Roberto, I needed him.

I've never written about a kiss, because it always ends up sounding like the sloppy, juicy interplay of the upper ends of two people's digestive tracts. So, this must not have been a kiss, because it meant something so indescribable yet real.

Roberto's cool lips warmed as mine met his. My hand touched his cheek, also cool at first touch and just as suddenly warm. Our lips, still dry, brushed and rolled against each other's, finding only perfection in the touch. Roberto put his hand between us, pushing me back with his palm against my chest.

"What are you doing to me? It feels so good. Too good." I saw confusion in his eyes and heard longing in his words. "My kind doesn't kiss. We bite."

"You don't sound so sure. That was a wonderful start." His lips looked a little redder, less perfect. More human. I pulled him back to me. He came to meet me.

His lips were full of life, warm like mine, pressing and caressing like there could be no other purpose for them. I held him tight and kissed him harder. If there were to be only one kiss for us, everything I could be as the woman who loved that man was going into it. He wrapped his arms around me, returning the kiss with a feverishness that matched mine. I was certain he was restraining his phenomenal strength as he enclosed me, sharing his aura of power to comfort me. His strength was there to protect me. He could never hurt me. I parted my lips to invite him in.

His tongue was warm and moist, its quest for mine urgent, and its motion a reassurance that I'd been right to trust him. If there was hunger in our kiss, it was for union, not just animal need. Our mouths spoke of acceptance, of trust, and of the timeless need that binds two together with hope for a future.

Then we both erred, asking by exploring each other's palate. We probed for each other's fangs. I found his, but he found I had none.

We broke away from each other. The lingering taste of him was slightly bitter and salty, like endive and celery salt. I'd feared tasting corruption and decay and ended up awed by the arcane process that merged man and monster.

"I never thought I'd kiss again," Roberto said. He smiled. "A kiss to die for, and I've done that already."

"You've got to go," I said. "I'll be back at sunset." He looked back at me.

"Be careful. Do what you must to protect yourself. If you can get back, fine, but only if you're certain there's no risk. I've survived this long. So, go." He let me go and climbed out the passenger door. I watched him as he walked around behind the car, heading for the utility building's door. He stopped as he came around behind the car.

Daddy's wagon swayed as Roberto seized something on the back. I thought for a moment he was in range of the cross and was feeling weak. I heard a brief metallic shriek followed by a pop. He came up next to me at the driver's side window, holding a saucer-sized disc in his hand. I rolled down the window.

"It's a transmitter," he said, holding up the disc for my inspection. One side had the Continental Grid logo, and on the other, a tiny flashing red light.

"That's how they found us at the truck stop?" I asked. He nodded agreement.

180

"Dion planted it on the back of the car when he ran us down. They're probably headed this way right now. You better get out of here while you can. They're probably just minutes away."

"Give it to me!" I said. "I'll lead them away from you." He stepped back, avoiding my grasp.

"Best you live to fight another day, Kelly Williams. It's been great. Go. Now." He turned away from me and ran to the utility building, the disc still in his hand. He dragged a cargo bay door open. I saw through to the opposite side of the building where there was another door like it. They could load grain out either side.

Once inside, he began pulling it closed. The last I saw him, he was thrusting a finger in the direction I was headed, mouthing the word "Go." The door closed.

The sky brightened again. The sun would be up any minute. I stepped on the gas and rolled back onto the county road, with an empty feeling in my gut.

The only other time in my life I recalled feeling so inconsolable about departing was when I left mom in the hospital and Aunt Meg drove us home. I was young, but not so young that I could ignore the truth that no one shared with me. Mom died that night. They all knew it was coming, and they all tried to hide it from me, but they didn't do it well. Aunt Meg—Daddy's older sister—was staying at our house. She drove me home from the hospital and put me to bed. She came the closest to being honest with me. I asked if Mom would be okay, even though no one spoke of her recovering anymore. She said it didn't look well. She told me to say my prayers and go to sleep, and then we'd go back in the morning. I didn't know how to pray, and maybe that's what I did wrong. Morning came, but by then there was no reason to go.

Morning was coming, that time when you wake again to loss. Was Roberto gone forever? How could I feel this way about a man I'd met only a few days earlier? It had to be my heart's fault. Love must live in the heart, I thought, and I had stolen Wendy's love for Roberto when her heart was put in my chest. The sun wasn't up yet, so she must still be awake and sensing a void in her feelings where an immortal love should have been. How awful it must have been to find emptiness where a love like this used to be. I was in possession of stolen property. This love was such a precious and magnificent feeling.

The sky was growing brighter. About a half a mile down County 22, the road curved left through an underpass beneath the Interstate. Just on the other side, I saw a road that let me cut back toward the granary, so I had a view back to the other side of the highway. The county road passed through undeveloped land. Patches of brush and trees allowed me to park the car where it couldn't be seen from Pollards. I switched off the motor and headlights and walked to the back of the car. The metal on the tailgate was pulled outward and torn. Roberto had not exaggerated his strength. Worried about Daddy's reaction, I tried to press it back down. I made a little progress, but I didn't have the strength to flatten it.

I walked another thirty yards down the road and found a good view of the building Roberto had entered. It was cold out and the NASCAR jacket wasn't enough to make up for the warmth I missed from the car.

I had been watching for less than a minute when the Continental Grid van pulled up next to the building. Even though I was on the other side of the highway there was no mistaking that it was Mr. Black who came out of the driver's door. Dion met him at the back of the van. He extended his arm toward the building, holding up a cell phone or a device that size. He was scanning the building. His arm went past and then came back to the door through which Roberto had gone. He turned his head and spoke to Mr. Black, who put one hand on Dion's shoulder and pointed at the sky with the other. Dion shook his head no. Mr. Black was speaking continuously. My guess was that Dion wanted to enter the building and Mr. Black was advising against it.

Mr. Black opened the back of the van and with Dion's help removed two rectangular black boxes somewhat larger than a refrigerator. Both appeared to have small wheels on one end, with pushcart handles over larger wheels at the other. They reminded me of food vendor pushcarts. Dion opened the door to the utility building and helped Mr. Black roll one of the boxes into the building. It looked like a lot of work. Dion rolled the second one in on his own. He laid his palm flat on the top and it lifted open like the trunk on a luxury car. He climbed in, pivoted, sat down, and pulled the lid closed over himself. Just then the rising sun glinted red off the metallic cap of the tallest grain silo.

Mr. Black slid the building's door shut and returned to the van, secured the rear doors, and drove off, returning the way he'd come. He was returning to the Interstate. The rising sun was lighting up the cap of another of the silos. I went back to the car and got in and put the key in the ignition. I held off starting the engine.

I supposed the black boxes were something like coffins. Maybe Dion was going to wait out the day, capture Roberto at sunset, and secure him in the other box. So maybe they really weren't going to hurt him. Maybe there was a better safer place for him to go where a kindly society of vampires would look after their prodigal child. It could be Roberto had nothing to worry about, and his maker, Jack, had been misguided about the dangers of Continental Grid. Dion hadn't tried to hurt Roberto. The intent appeared to be to get

Roberto to come of his own accord. The hows and whys of Continental Grid were hidden to me, as they were to Roberto.

Then why was it that I felt sure Roberto was in terrible danger? Maybe I was being misled by the connection that Wendy's heart had to him. Wouldn't she be panicked, knowing that her partner through eternity was being taken away to a community for the undead? That had to be the explanation. It was true that I had never had a committed relationship with an adult man, so it was possible I was being misled by the passion Wendy felt for him.

All of this was probably none of my business.

I reached for the ignition key. I was about to turn it, but the man responsible for the car came into my thoughts. Daddy would have said, "Always do the right thing," and "Pay your debts." It was Wendy's heart that was keeping me alive even as it was misleading me about my feelings for Roberto. I couldn't imagine how she could survive without the organ beating in my chest, but I knew that, somehow, she did. I owed it to her to save the man that I—or she—loved.

I drove back to the utility building at Pollards, stopping my car at the door where Mr. Black had left the two black crates. My car was still the only one around. The sun was now shining on the top edge of the door in front of the two boxes. I felt my pulse speed up as I walked to the door and put my hands up on the edge to slide it open. I braced myself and yanked it to the side. It offered almost no resistance.

The crate that held Dion was closest to the door. The matte-finished plastic crate displayed the Continental Grid logo on each side, and each such logo had the universal biohazard icon next to it. A label beneath the two graphic items warned "Biological hazard. Do not handle unprotected. Contact Continental Grid for proper disposal. Call 888-555-01234 (US) for further information or to arrange pickup. No user serviceable parts."

On the top of the crate, and on either side of where I knew Dion's head to be lying, there were hockey-puck-sized portholes. Could he be watching me? He might still be awake. I considered stepping back and waiting for the sun to fully illuminate the crate before attempting to open it. If I understood Roberto correctly, the sun would turn Dion into a pile of ash.

On the other hand, if he was watching me already, he might burst out and imprison me in the other crate. I felt like I was in a flee-or-fight situation. I couldn't bear waiting the five minutes it might take for the sun to provide me its protection. I went around to the handle end of the crate and attempted to roll it out of the building. It must have been fear of Dion's speed and strength that was causing my heart to beat so fast. An adrenaline rush helped me move the crate outside with almost no effort. Unfortunately, the sun was still not high enough to illuminate the crate. I hoped Dion would not chance emerging.

I looked over the seam across the top of the crate and was disappointed that the means of opening it were not obvious. The only feature I saw looked like a credit card swipe on a gas pump. I went to the back of Daddy's station wagon, dropped the tailgate to check and see if there was a wrecking bar in his plastic crate of useful tools and automotive supplies. Nothing likely presented itself, but I found a heavy-duty chain with an S-hook on each end. I knew it had something to do with the trailer hitch on the back of the wagon. I took the chain back to Dion's crate and found that there was a loop near the bottom edge of the handle side. Just above the loop, the word "Thanatote" was embedded in the plastic, with the raised trademark symbol to its right.

My heart was pounding harder than ever. My strength was beginning to fade. I oriented Dion's crate to the back of the station wagon, closed the tailgate, connected the chain, and hooked Dion's crate to the trailer hitch. I decided that I could at least move him far enough away from Roberto to buy time when sunset finally came. I got back in the driver's seat and drove back to the Interstate, following the route that Mr. Black had taken. The plastic on the front edge of the box made a horrible scraping sound as I dragged it over the gravel and back onto the roadway. I found that very satisfying.

Though I was still nervous about what I was doing, my heart wasn't pounding as hard. Roberto would have been amused at the timid speed I was driving as I entered the right lane of the highway. The sun was now in my eyes, and the punctuated screech of the plastic crate scraping behind me as it bounced off the pavement was making me hesitate. I was going under fifty miles per hour. A semi tractor-trailer swerved around me and sounded its horn. I must have been going below the minimum speed, but the tugging and dancing of the poorly tethered crate behind me was distracting. In the rearview mirror, I saw another big truck closing in. I was going to have to either speed up or pull over.

Then it dawned on me that the sun was up completely. I sped up.

The crate began bouncing up and down, providing momentary relief from the screech of plastic dragging on the pavement while it was airborne. I felt the hard tug of each bounce through the steering wheel, and I hoped that the chrome steel of the Oldsmobile would outlast the plastic of the Thanatote. A few seconds later, at eighty miles per hour, my impulse was rewarded.

The crate caught on a repair patch in the roadway, bouncing so high I saw pavement underneath it. It hung in the air, tilted to one side. For a moment, I thought it was becoming a kite. It wobbled twice and then rocketed straight down. The black tote landed on the pavement, jolting the station wagon. Its rapid descent broke the tote into three pieces, one fragment still dragging behind me. The lid went flying off towards the edge of the road. Something man-shaped fell onto the roadway.

Steam, smoke, and then flames rose from the mass behind me in the roadway. A flaming figure gathered itself and stood, shooting sparks and swirling tendrils of black ash. I started braking and pulled over to the shoulder, still towing a screeching sheet of shattered black plastic.

The flaming man-shape standing in the roadway was facing the big truck speeding toward him. He stretched out his arms. Flames flickered above his head. Fingers from both hands broke off, trailing sparks as they cascaded to the pavement. His arms broke off at the elbows. His head tilted back and snapped off, falling behind him, shattering and scattering smoldering blobs the size of apples. The blobs burst in a series of flash-bulb bright flashes.

The truck driver honked long and loud as he drove through the conflagration, smashing the standing figure into a cloud of ash and cinders. I heard brakes screeching.

I expected to hear a thump when the truck made contact. It was more like a loud poof.

I was parked on the shoulder, a piece of the tote still trailing the Oldsmobile. The truck pulled over and stopped just beyond me.

I got out and inspected the chain attached to the remains of the black crate. Daddy's car was fine. The crate looked damaged beyond salvage. The final score: Oldsmobile, one; Thanatote, zero.

The trucker climbed down from his cab, inspected the tractor's grill, looking back at me a few times as if deciding if it was wise to approach me. I turned my hands outward at my sides, hoping to express openness. He walked up to me.

"Dammit, lady," he said. Sweat was beaded on his forehead. "What the hell are you carrying? Mannequins? No way you should be out on the road with flammable materials like that. You could have killed me. That was no DOT trailer, either." I think he was deeply unnerved by my actions.

I tilted my head down apologetically. "I'm so sorry. I didn't think any-one would be out so early, so I took a chance. I should have known better. Is your truck okay?"

He turned and went back to the grill of his cab-over. I followed. There was a coating of grayish dust that extended up the grill and lower edge of its windshield. I dabbed at the ash with my finger. The chrome work underneath was undamaged.

"So, what was that?" he asked. "Thermite?"

"Just some oily rags," I said. "I've never seen spontaneous combustion before." Looking back down the highway to where Dion had landed, I watched the last wisps of ash drifting across the road.

DWIGHT
Friday Morning

I was driving Tanner to the hospital when I realized we'd missed a bet with Wendy. We'd been inefficient and wasteful. We should have figured it out while installing her modifications and restoring her kidneys. If we'd just waited until she was asleep for the day, she'd lose almost no blood while we worked on her. She'd miss all the discomfort, which in turn would spare her meatball surgeons her terrifying critiques of their effectiveness. Despite the pressure, Tanner had no problem focusing on Wendy's needs. He'd come up with a potential solution for holding her upright with some surplus theatre tech stashed in his car trunk. His supply of gadgets, mechanical or technical, seemed endless.

I think I was having these thoughts because I didn't want to face the possibility that she might have killed Tanner, and I could be too late getting him to the hospital. I was the first to feed her that night, dozing off as she finished, assuming she'd go easy on Tanner.

She woke me just before dawn, tapping me on the leg with her hockey stick crutch.

"I want a bedtime story," she said. She had the cutest fake pout. "It's getting light out. Time to get away from windows." I helped her downstairs. After laying her out on top of the washer and dryer, I let her have ten more sips from my arm. It hardly hurt at all. I puzzled about how it was her cold lips sucking at my arm made me feel so warm.

She sighed and went flat. Therefore, it was daytime.

I found it disturbing seeing her that way. Cold, inert, unresponsive—there was no way to tell the difference from her condition and death. She was just as cold.

I found Tanner stretched out on the sofa where Wendy had been sucking at his arm. I had planned to take him out for a big breakfast. I figured we needed a lot of nourishment to make up for stress, exertion, and the blood we'd surrendered to Wendy.

The problem was, Tanner wouldn't wake up.

My first impulse was to call 911. However, a quick survey of my kitchen would reveal to emergency personnel or police that something awful had happened there. I rejected the idea of attempting a cleanup while waiting for the ambulance—not enough time. Also, there was the non-zero chance that someone might wander into my basement and discover the female corpse laid out down there on top of the washing machine and dryer. I already had enough difficult things to explain with Tanner's condition. I dragged him out to my car and heaved him into the back seat. He still felt warm, which was reassuring.

For a few minutes, I was angry with Tanner. He'd developed an unnatural attachment to Wendy's thirst for his blood. It was his fault—he'd let her drink too much. He should've paid attention. Still, I remembered also feeling pleasure as she sucked on my arm, but I attributed that to feeling philanthropic toward her. She was beautiful, even as she drew bits of my life out of my arm. I started thinking she'd been injecting me with a sort of drug while she fed.

What I told the emergency room personnel was nothing like that. I pumped my car's horn as I pulled up to the sliding door for the ambulances. The door opened and two attendants in pistachio green scrubs and white caps hurried out to inspect. I was opening the rear passenger door when the first one, a middle-aged man asked, "What's happening there?"

"I found him unconscious. He's got some holes in his arm. I think he's lost some blood." The younger attendant, also a man, went back into the emergency room to get a gurney.

Middle-Aged Man pressed his stethoscope against Tanner's chest while probing his neck with fingertips.

"Pulse is weak," he said, "but it's a pulse. How'd this happen?"

"I can't say. He was like this when I found him. Maybe a suicide attempt?"

"Not a lot of blood on him." He surveyed Tanner's clothing. "What did you see where you found him?"

At that moment, the second attendant returned with a gurney and two more people in scrubs. I let Middle-Aged Man's last question go by unanswered.

They conferred about how he "presented" and asked me questions about how he was situated when I found him. They transferred him to the gurney after establishing a low likelihood of spinal injuries and hidden lesions.

"You shouldn't have moved him," Middle-Aged Man said.

"My...His address is hard to find," I said, knowing I needed to keep them from taking interest in my townhouse or the solar-sensitive corpse in my basement.

A young woman with a clipboard led me to a small cubicle that allowed her to speak to me through a porthole in the plexiglass. Her stated intention was to obtain payment and the patient's details, and about in that order of priority. I foresaw there would be difficulty as I explained Tanner was a friend, not a family member. She offered me a piece of paper to sign where I would take responsibility for his hospitalization. I declined, suggesting that they might find a medical insurance card in his wallet. She brought out an array of forms, demonstrating her deep personal commitment to get me to sign something, and began explaining the dire plight of hospitals and the need for the community to take responsibility for the demands they meet, et cetera. I was starting to fume. She reminded me of Vivian at the hospital records office. I was happy to be away from Wendy. I was starting to worry about the unholy appetite that been inserted into my life. She'd nearly killed my best friend.

I delayed signing her forms, but I did agree to let them charge $100 to my credit card to cover Tanner's likely minimum co-pay. When Ms. Bureaucrat stepped away from the desk to gather yet more forms, I left by the main door, circled the building to return to my car, and drove away from the hospital. I hoped this was the last time. After all my previous trips there, how could I not show up on multiple hospital security videos?

I had one mission left in my quest to make Wendy whole and make her mine, and that was to get her heart back. My next step was to track down the chest it was hiding in.

Back at my townhouse, I visited the basement to look at Wendy. Though she appeared dead, it was easy to imagine her active and animated. It had only been a few hours since sunrise. Seeing her in the unguarded moments between bullying us and feasting on my best friend, I remembered the unique and vibrant woman who more than once stopped me in my tracks.

She was looking so much better. She'd healed a lot each sunset. Only the exposed bone at the ends of her toes and on her left hand's fingers highlighted the crematorium injuries. Her scalp and hair had grown back completely, and the charred flesh on her face, arms, and legs had been replaced by smooth undamaged skin. With the return of the originals or my approximations of the missing organs, she was functioning amazingly well. All she needed was blood and old school funk to keep her happy. She was laid out flat across the top of the washing machine and dryer. I bent over her and kissed her cold dead lips. They were wonderfully tender. I wished I could feel them respond.

Looking at her lying there, I remembered her request for clothing. Tanner had written down her sizes and favorite stores. Maybe if I got her something nice to wear, that would help.

Help what? I asked myself. She was in love with this Roberto, the master vampire who was to be her partner for all time. Maybe, a few centuries later, she might remember me and think of me kindly. That might be all I'd get, but I still wasn't ready to quit. I wanted more. I went upstairs to the kitchen.

I opened the folder I'd borrowed from Vivian and paged through the various transfer forms and related communications notes. Wendy's heart had been transplanted into the chest of Kelly Williams. I hoped Kelly hadn't grown too attached to it.

A call to the hospital switchboard got me forwarded to Kelly Williams, but the voice that answered sounded official.

"North Austin 5. How may I help you?" a woman's voice said.

"Can I speak to Kelly, please?" I asked. "Kelly Williams."

"She's not available right now. Are you family? Is this Mr. Williams?"

"No," I answered. I instantly regretted not saying "yes" and working the role of Mr. Williams. "Just a friend of the family. How's she doing? I'm guessing the transplant is working good so far?"

"I can't give out that information. You'll have to contact someone in her family."

"Who do you recommend?" I asked, but the call was cut off. I got the sense that the woman who answered was happy she didn't have to say anything more. The few words she said made me think more than patient information was being protected. Why had she asked if I was Mr. Williams? Was he Kelly's husband? Her father? A son, or a cousin? What news did they have that was just for him? I was tempted to call back right away, saying I was Mr. Williams, but the chances were high the same person would answer. I'd have to wait and try again after some time had gone by.

I was not pleased with the situation, and it wasn't just that I'd have to go back to the hospital. Regardless of whether Kelly was getting any benefit from Wendy's heart, it was unlikely I could just drop by and collect it as they pulled it out of Kelly's chest. After having lost a pair of kidneys, a liver, and a pancreas, I suspect they'd have tightened up their security.

I was exhausted. I knew I needed rest, but I had much to get done before sunset. I made a shopping list and a to-do list, went to my bedroom, set the alarm for noon, put my head on the pillow, and closed my eyes.

Right away, I felt guilty about wanting three hours sleep, but I would soon be useless if I didn't rest. If only I knew how to find Kelly, then I'd be able to relax. I could plan. I looked for Kelly's phone number in the folder but didn't find it. The next of kin however, Harlan Williams, had his phone number in the appropriate space on the form. Time to make a call. I dialed.

"Hello?" A man's voice answered.

"Mr. Williams? Is Kelly there?"

"I'm sorry, she's not available." I couldn't read anything from his tone.

"I'm calling about a problem with Kelly's new heart," I said, trying to match the delivery manner of Dr. Not-Steve from the night before.

"Who are you?" Again, nothing was revealed. If I'd upset him, I couldn't tell.

"I'm Doctor Tanner…from the hospital."

"That's not the hospital's number you're calling from," he said. He was an active observer of his caller ID display. "Aquariums?" He sounded slightly puzzled, but not hostile.

"That's correct," I answered. "You deserve an explanation about what is going on." He was a while responding.

"And you can provide that?"

"Yes, though it's not simple. I thought I might come over to see you and work through the details." The details of what? I had no guess as to what he was aware of. Maybe Kelly was still in the hospital. Maybe she was there with Mr. Williams. Maybe she'd died, consumed by a vampiric heart, somewhat like my dear old uncle being consumed by Wendy's transplanted pancreas.

"I'm a simple man, Dr. Tanner," he said. "Say what you've got to say now. I think I can help you sort through it."

"It'd be better if I came over."

"Goodbye," he said and disconnected the call. I redialed three times, but each time only got the answering machine. I got the idea he had something to hide, though, when I didn't hear his phone's announcement: it only played the leave-a-message tone. He'd been getting a lot of unwanted calls. What was the story there?

If he was there, at home, then there was some chance that Kelly might not be as bad off as I'd feared. Also, he picked up the phone to talk to someone calling from a non-hospital phone number. He'd chosen to answer a call from an unfamiliar location. What was he waiting to hear?

I closed my eyes and focused on the possibilities. It occurred to me that Mr. Williams was speaking as if he thought his phone was being tapped. Still, he answered his phone so he must be waiting for contact from someone. The phone book confirmed I was calling him on a landline. Mr. Williams was Kelly's next of kin and was at home, waiting for a call, and apparently open to hearing some explanations. At last: a road trip that wasn't going to take me to the hospital. Even better, I wrangled my route to Mr. Williams to allow a visit to an adult video store I knew of. It had several alluringly dressed mannequins in its window.

I took advantage of the keys to Tanner's car to acquire some useful props for my trip across town. He always had props and tools in his trunk from the various theatre productions he'd volunteer on. I guessed among the props he might even have a handgun. I was wrong: it turns out he had many, and none of them were props. I chose a blue-steel revolver with 22 on the barrel. It had bullets in the cylinder.

KELLY
Day 6: Friday Morning

One benefit of living in a house that borders on a schoolyard is that all possible trails are blazed. Like the action of water and wind eroding a landscape, the travels of children redraw property lines and establish new rights of way. I remembered a short cut from grade school that got me from the convenience store parking lot to my back door. I'd wondered if I'd been spotted walking along the edge of the schoolyard while classes were in progress. The now-grungy yellow tracksuit with the blue NASCAR jacket should have made it easy to describe and recognize me. So far, no one had noticed. I made it to our backyard and looked around the front corners to check the street. Seeing nothing suspicious, I recovered the emergency key and let myself in through the back door.

"Daddy?" I called out, but no one answer. All the lights were off except for the lamp above the kitchen table where Daddy and I had breakfasted together so many times in recent years. I was becoming alarmed. Normally, the only interior light he would leave on was the one in the hallway where the garage door opened out.

There was a handwritten note on the middle of the kitchen table, anchored at the top by a dirty coffee mug. I didn't have to read the note to know that Daddy was in trouble. Whenever he left me notes on the table, he anchored them on the corners with the salt and pepper shakers. Those two items were mysteriously absent from the table, moved to the top of the dishwasher. He would not have left the house without putting the dirty coffee mug in, or at least on top of, the dishwasher.

One more item out of the ordinary was the absence of a pen resting on top of the note. Daddy always left a pen nearby so I could write a reply if leaving before his return. He and Mom had come up with that habit together. Ours was once a busy household. Sometimes, their traded replies could flow over to the backside of the sheet. No pen left meant he didn't expect to read a reply.

There was also the fact that the note was written in pencil. Daddy had dozens of souvenir pens from NASCAR events or auto parts stores, and one of those was always the instrument of choice for notes.

Daddy had left under duress.

"Dear Kelly,

I have to step out to help a friend, but I'll call in a little while. If you need to use my car, the keys are in the usual place.

Love you,

Pop."

Daddy had left with a gun to his head.

He'd always refuse to acknowledge the speaker when called "Pop". Eventually, everyone gave up. I guessed he'd written it there to invoke a favorite reference, to the cheap handguns criminals once carried called "Saturday Night Specials." He called them "punk criminals with flimsy pop guns." One of these wannabes had escorted Daddy out of the house.

I opened the pantry where we kept the canned goods, took down the solitary can of root beer soda, and twisted off its top. It was empty. Its secret interior should have held the keys he'd mentioned. Where else could he have meant?

Starting at our front door, I looked about for the obvious places that Daddy might have advised against. In the entry coat closet, there was a board with hooks where Daddy would have guests leave car keys. It simplified rearranging vehicles when six or eight cars clogged our driveway. I found his keys there, hanging on a hook. All the others were empty. "Leaving them there is almost as good as giving the car away," he'd say. Nevertheless, he'd left his there.

I felt ill. I steadied myself on the door jam and managed to stand up a bit straighter for half a minute, trying to focus only on my breathing. This was very bad. I was exhausted. How long had I been up? More than a day except for the nap at the library.

I wondered why someone would find it necessary to take Daddy. Why were the stakes so high that it was necessary to use threat of harm? Imagination failed to reveal why he would allow Daddy to leave such a chatty note. Why not leave instructions, or a demand?

I realized I'd been thinking "he." My subconscious was trying to answer the question I had yet to form. I had three choices for enemies—four, if I wanted to err on the side of including Roberto—and the one I wanted least was Dwight.

If it was someone from the hospital, why had they let Daddy go in the first place? That didn't make sense. If it was Mr. Black or someone else from Continental Grid, why not just wait for me to arrive? So far, their tactics were direct.

Of all the people I wanted to avoid, Dwight made the top of the list. He was clearly unbalanced. His was a quest driven by some dark passion, nothing like the hospital's effort to protect their reputation, or Continental Grid's campaign to secure OTG vampires. Dwight was the one that would show the most extreme behavior.

I reached for the phone to call the police. Exhaustion and hunger were clouding my judgment. I thought I remembered deciding that I shouldn't call the police, but just then I couldn't recall why. Fear and fatigue and the desperate need for a friend pushed me to dial 911.

"What is your emergency?" a woman's voice answered. I said that my father was missing. I was explaining the situation to a police detective a few seconds later.

At first, my observations generated cheerful sounding platitudes about Daddy's likely return from a walk or a visit to a neighbor, maybe a friend. He had not been gone so long that it deserved police intervention. "Ninety-eight percent show up in twenty-four hours," he said. I felt the welling up of a gusher of hysteria, but my focus on Daddy sustained my resolve.

"I know it sounds far-fetched, but my father is a man of precise and considered habits, and he uses deviations as a means of sending messages to me. That's clearly what has happened here. I just got out of the hospital yesterday, and he would not leave the house until he was certain I was well taken care of and settled. He's not that old, and this just isn't like him. You've got to get over here."

"Why were you in the hospital?" the detective asked.

"I was there for a transplant procedure," I said.

"Please stay right there," he said. "I'm detective Waller. I'm sending someone right now."

I went right to the refrigerator. I was already starving when I was diverted from my meal at the diner five hours earlier. Daddy must have been on my wavelength because he'd gone shopping that morning. On the second shelf, secured in plastic wrap was a juicy looking thick cut T-bone steak. The only preparation I made was to cut half of it away from the bone with a steak knife, put it on a plate, and start carving off bites with knife and fork. Steak had never tasted so good before, and that was an uncomfortable reminder that, up until my transplant, I'd preferred my steaks medium well.

As I'd expected, eating made me feel much better. What surprised me was the energy boost that came with it. I always thought it was carbohydrates that did that, but the raw red meat kicked me into a more alert state.

Expecting the arrival of the detective, I tried to make efficient use of the moment. I put Dad's cell phone on its charger. I took my own cell from its charger where it had been while I was hospitalized. It was very warm. I collected my wallet from the dresser in my bedroom and collected a wad of fifties from our cash stash in the basement.

I was desperate to shower. It had been three days since my last hospital sponge bath and I smelled strongly enough to cause distress to anyone within two yards of me. Still seeing no one in front of our house, I brought some fresh clothes into the bathroom with me and attempted some quick touch-up with a washcloth. Mainly I needed to change into something—anything—else.

For the first time since I left the hospital, I had a moment to study the bizarre configuration of my chest. I thought—maybe even hoped—I'd have to clean the wound site, perhaps claiming a little credit for the unnaturally quick healing. The healing looked quite complete. The alien organ residing in my chest had taken care of its immediate neighborhood: the mad landscape of twisted and misaligned bone down the center of my chest had receded. It still looked like something serious had happened, but long ago, and nothing so serious as having your ribcage cracked open. It was more like I'd been lashed with a braided cable. Where there'd been angry red scar tissue a day earlier, I now saw pinkish white. It felt normal—maybe slightly numb—when I ran the washcloth over it.

I emerged ten minutes later smelling far less toxic, luxuriating in fresh underwear, black stirrup tights under a mid-length black skirt, bloused over by my favorite silk top, a crinkled-up aubergine number that could legally be called a camisole. I covered my mostly bare shoulders with my black silk blazer. A pair of black walking shoes replaced the running shoes I'd been living in for the previous two days.

I waited for the police to arrive, stretching out on Daddy's recliner in front of the TV set.

The doorbell rang, and I realized I had dozed. The TV remote revealed that it was almost four in the afternoon. I opened the front door and found a uniformed officer. His patrol car was idling in front of the house. He looked startled when I invited him in. Apparently, he planned to receive the necessary information standing there on the front step. I insisted he come in.

Officer Peterson appeared entirely out of his element. He had a ticket book clipped to his belt, which suggested to me that he was more accustomed to speeders and parking scofflaws than kidnappers. He tried to ask the right questions, but I found it necessary to guide him to the pertinent facts about Daddy's disappearance. What wasn't working out particularly well was that everything I called out as a clue was either too subtle for him or could be explained by Daddy's having gone for a walk. Peterson suggested that Daddy might be showing signs of old age. He told me to stay there while he returned to the patrol car and called in the details.

"You're welcome to use my phone," I said, "Or you could use that cell phone clipped to your belt."

"Official business, Miss," he said and let himself out. Not only did the officer lack the command presence of a real beat cop, he was also a poor liar.

Through the curtains I saw him behind the wheel of his cruiser, talking to a handset. He was sympathetic, but not convinced, so I expected him to return with a message for me to be patient. I took a moment to go to Daddy's den and check email.

As was often the case, Daddy left his email program logged in. The subject line on the top message read "For Kelly Williams – URGENT." It was from Dwight.

The message read:

"Hello Kelly. If you have questions about your dad's travels, stop by Schlock House Funk on NE 55th tonight at about 9 p.m. Wear a white flower in your hair. If there are police around, that could be a distraction, so do your part to keep the peace and be patient. Ear protection is recommended."

I returned to the living room eager to share the new evidence with officer Peterson, but he'd driven away while I'd been at the computer. I called the police again, saying I had important new information for detective Waller, and was put on hold for a minute.

"Yes, Miss Williams," he said, "the officer will be there shortly. Please try to stay calm."

"But he's already been here," I said, "and he drove off without hearing everything. I've just gotten an email about where he might be and where to go to get more information. I'm certain they've kidnapped him."

"Are they asking for a ransom?" Waller asked.

No, it just says to go to a club on NE 55th tonight at nine o'clock.

"Forgive me, Kelly—may I call you Kelly? I have to ask you this. Is there any chance that you're being set up for a prank or some kind of surprise party? You have to admit the possibility."

"Daddy just wouldn't get involved in that. He would never make me worry or stress me. I mean, I was nearly dead a week ago. After losing mom and then watching me nearly die too—well, he simply wouldn't do something like that."

"Look, Miss Kelly, you haven't given us much to go on and it isn't clear that any crime has been committed. The story we got from you before was that you were out all night and that when you got home three hours ago, he was out. You hadn't called him in over a day, you came home, he was out. No signs of struggle, right? Except for Amber Alerts, we give missing persons cases twenty-four hours. You'd be amazed how many of these calls clear up on their own within that time. Well over 95 percent. When officer Peterson checks in, we'll review the report and get back to you if we come up with any-thing. Try not to worry—it's probably just something you haven't guessed yet."

"No! Please! I'm not mistaken. He really is in trouble," I started to say, but Waller was talking over me.

"We'll be in touch," Waller said. The call dropped. I dialed him back.

"Do you have anything new, Miss Kelly?" He was exasperated.

"It's Miss Williams, and you need to listen to me. My father is in imme-diate danger from someone who is trying to get at me..."

Waller's voice overpowered mine. "I understand that you're stressed and you're worried, but please remember that it's our job to protect and serve, and we've got experience in these matters that you don't. Happens every few days. From everything you've shared with us, the most likely explanation is someone is setting up a surprise party for you tonight at that club."

I was out of arguments. "Can you at least send a detective out to be there at nine?"

"Just a minute." He put me on hold, allowing me to hear a pre-recorded message about the consequences of false reports and inaccurate information. When he returned, he sounded relieved.

"I've got good news for you. There'll be a uniform on traffic detail at that club tonight. He'll be just outside the front entrance. If anything comes up, just call 911, and we'll direct him to you. Okay? Gotta go, another call waiting."

I was on my own until the trouble began, and I was certain it would. The police would only respond to problems that complied with familiar definitions.

Could I deal with this on my own? I had to face the possibility I might have to. What would I be up against? It was certain I would be dealing with Dwight, and that looked like a big challenge. If he'd become so quickly angry with "Vivian," how nasty would he be when he learned who I really was? And if his probably-undead girlfriend Wendy was involved, I'd be severely outmatched physically and at a psychological disadvantage by being outnumbered. With the police insisting on following protocol, I could think of only one person who might be an advantage at my side, and he was asleep under a warehouse in the southeast corner of the city.

Roberto had been respectful and trustworthy. With the strength of a mountain gorilla—strong enough to tear sheet metal like it was cardboard—he could protect me.

I thought I might be fooling myself. The heart—my heart—had been installed with a passion for Roberto already built in. That had to explain why I was so ready to put my trust in him. My mind was in the same place, as he'd been kind, caring, and protective toward me. It was Roberto I wanted at my side that night, even knowing that he might act completely differently once he was reunited with Wendy. If I was going to reclaim Daddy—and do whatever it took to make good with Wendy and Dwight—Roberto would be the most powerful and moral person available to me.

I would have to get back at the grain silo just before sunset, when Roberto would emerge. I had just over an hour to get there. I decided I could spare twenty minutes to shower away the stink of fear I knew was clinging to me.

Normally, a long hot shower is a time of relaxation and reflection for me, but this time, I was preoccupied with Daddy's situation, the ill-defined danger I would be walking into, and the vulnerability I felt being naked. What if Dwight or Wendy was lurking outside, waiting for the moment when my guard was down? I washed quickly. It wasn't until I saw my hair frizzed out while attempting to blow-dry it that I realized I'd missed using conditioner. Mousse was sorry means of management, but I chanced it, in my haste converting a ball of ash blond frizz for a darker hair helmet. I put on my previous outfit over the yet fresher underwear and slipped out the back door, retracing my route to Daddy's station wagon. I had two charged-up phones, cash, a cross, and as much of a plan as I could carry. For the first time, I wished I owned a gun and had the training to use it.

DWIGHT
Friday Afternoon

So. Everything pretty much sucked by the time we were heading out for Worship except that I didn't end up giving Wendy anymore blood—at least, no more of mine. But I'm getting ahead of myself.

I'd already guaranteed myself a minimum ten years in jail by kidnapping Kelly's father, compounded by assault. I'd pistol-whipped him to take the fight out of him. I guess that would add gun charges to a judge's sentence. Old Dude hadn't hurt me, but I was certain he could deck me given another chance. His hands were big and calloused, and his forearms belonged on Popeye. I hit him from behind while I was making him write a note to Kelly at his kitchen table. I'm not proud of this.

Keeping the gun on him, I forced him into the trunk of my car and then herded him into the basement of my townhouse. With his hands tied behind his back and being gagged, he behaved quite well until I got him into my basement. He saw Wendy lying across the washer and dryer. His eyes went wide. I held the revolver to his head to restore his focus.

"You're not going to end up like that if that's what you're worried about. If Kelly does the right thing, this'll be nothing more than a brief time-out for you. So, sit. There, against the wall. Try to relax." That was easier said than done with his hands tied behind him. With the liberal use of rope, I anchored him to the water pipes next to the washer.

"You'll excuse me," I said. "I have a few upgrades to complete before sundown." I turned my attention to the gadgets and gear—and particularly to the clothing I'd bought during the day. The new outfit may not have been the perfect solution to all of Wendy's wishes, but she'd always acknowledged any improvement in function I could provide. Giving her the ability to stand up straight should qualify for praise as well.

And then there was her new outfit. She'd commissioned me to buy her new clothes. She was going to have to settle for one new outfit of my choosing. I knew the kinds of things she could wear that would look hot. I'd seen similar garments at the Hipshot Adult Video store, just a few doors down from my favorite aquarium supply. The vinyl bustier-and-corset mini-skirt combo was going to be worth every cent, and not simply because the corset helped restore structural integrity to her torso. Vinyl forearm gloves complemented the top, also hiding the exposed bones of her left-hand fingertips. There was a matching set of stiletto boots. My one regret was that the zipper holding her closed was visible between the waistband of the skirt and the bottom of her bustier. I went to work on the next phase of the installation.

Old Dude on the floor was none too happy about the demonstration I was putting on. Though muffled by the gag I had stuffed into his mouth, he said something that rhymed with "you sick bastard."

I thought he'd at least behave himself, but he caught me off guard while I was engaged securing a battery pack in Wendy's abdomen. He managed to get his legs out straight, snagging my ankles and yanking back, throwing me off my feet onto my side. I came down hard but didn't hit my head. My left shoulder hurt like hell, though.

Yes, I was mad. However, I couldn't blame him. I had to place priority on controlling him and getting ready for the evening's finale, for better or worse. With the instructional presence of Mr. Handgun, Old Dude submitted to my lassoing one leg and then the other. I secured the rope to the bottom of the stairs so he couldn't kick at me again.

With the careful application of an electric drill, four lag bolts, and a socket driver, I installed the structure that would support her upper body. My last step was to wire up the electronics that would set Wendy's position. I zipped her abdomen closed and turned my attention to getting a dead woman dressed up in an outfit that looked two sizes too small. Not my fault, by the way. I bought the sizes she told me.

It wasn't as much fun as you'd think getting her into the new outfit. Dead chicks don't cooperate by sucking in their stomachs or wriggling into tight-fitting clothes. I've had more fun getting toothpaste back into the tube than I did handling a cold-as-concrete corpse. I was gaining appreciation for what Annie and Basil faced on a daily basis. Still, Wendy ended up looking great, even considering the two chrome-plated actuators I'd bolted onto her from ribcage to hip. This last trick was Tanner's innovation.

Theater tech geeks are an incredible resource. They can fix anything with next to nothing. Tanner had a steamer trunk full of tech gear from the last production of Phantom he'd teched for. The show had a lot of special effects, and the parts for a some of them had wandered into his kit bag during set strike, so he said. "They would've just trashed them, most likely." The actuators were simple foot-long metal rods with half-inch metal loops at each end. A walnut-sized motor at one end turns a screw inside a chrome sleeve, extending or contracting a narrower chrome rod. By bolting the motor end to her hip and the rod end to her rib cage, I could control the distance between pairs of anchor points. With one actuator installed on each hip, connecting to the nearest rib above it, the motor control wires were run in and out of her abdomen at the bottom of her stomach zipper, connecting it to the batteries and radio-control systems Tanner borrowed from my remote-control toy car collection. I also wired in an extra connector for recharging her from an automobile auxiliary power outlet.

I sealed up the new wiring conduit with silicon caulk to prevent leakage. I rolled her onto her side to cinch up the corset from behind. The motor wires were tucked under the waistband of the black miniskirt. Even with the space taken by the batteries and remote controls, her waist was no bigger around than a CD. I laid her out straight, arms at her side, and stood back to admire my handiwork.

"Okay, Old Dude," I said. "Let's take her for a test drive." Using one of the remotes, I rocked the controller's thumbwheel toward me. The actuator motors started whining and she began to sit up. I reversed the controller, though, because her head was hanging backward—it hadn't gotten the message to stay with the torso. I pushed the thumbwheel away from me: the metal rods extended, lifting her tiny waist off the table, while her hips and ribs were pushed away from each other. I tried moving her side to side and around in a circle, but the commotion was causing her to wriggle off the top of the washer and dryer. She wouldn't notice if it happened, but I didn't want to drop her on Old Dude.

"Impressive, isn't it? I suppose you have some questions about what's going to happen here. Here's your bottom line," I said and paused for dramatic effect. I had his attention.

"No one knows where you are. There's something I want—I can get it in exchange for you—but not at the risk of being convicted of kidnapping. If you try to get away, I'll have to stop you. Do you understand me?"

His eyes told me I was lucky he was tied up. I went upstairs and considered the tech I'd need to do a little bit of one-to-one video streaming with Kelly. The starring cast of my little production awaited in the basement. The sun was dropping below the horizon. I had one more thing to do before going face-to-face with Kelly at Schlock House Funk. I worried that Kelly might be tempted to organize help from the police. It was time for a clear message steering her away from any such strategy. This needed Wendy awake, so I had a few minutes to spare.

I sat back on the sofa, picked up my landline phone, and called Central Hospital. "Lehane Tanner's room, please," I asked. The phone picked up on the second ring.

"Tanner?"

A woman's voice responded. "Dwight? Is that you, Dwight? What the hell is going on?" It was Tanner's mother. She seemed upset.

"How is he?" I asked.

"Was that you who dropped him off? What happened? What were you two doing? Was he at your place?"

Old Dude moaned. I could hear him even though I was around the corner from the stairs. No, he was yelling with something in his mouth.

"What in G... what the Hell!" Wendy's alarmed voice told me she was awake. Time to go look in on my two troglodytes. I heard the sound of thumping on metal. Maybe Wendy was kicking the dryer.

"Sorry, Mrs. T. Gotta go."

KELLY
Friday Afternoon

I peeled off way too many fifties paying for the many gallons of pre-
mium gas Daddy's muscle car required. Back on the highway, I contemplated
the savings in fuel if I could just drive slower. I abandoned that attitude in
short order, as my need was to get back to Roberto. I sped up from doing the
speed limit up to "going with the flow." I tried to stay in the wake of larger,
faster moving vehicles on the perimeter highway, hoping there'd be no rush
hour back-ups. Springfield was sleepy enough to make jams a rarity, but an
accident would always back things up. I didn't want to cause one, so I com-
promised. I was still certain I'd get back to Pollards before sunset. I wanted
to be there when he woke up.

Traffic was sparse nearing the exit. No other vehicles followed me off
the Interstate onto the state highway. I stayed well below the speed limit to
give me time to survey the area. Mr. Black could be parked in a different
vehicle. He was probably pissed off.

As Pollards came into view, its similarity to a ghost town occurred to
me. There was no one around—no pickups, no cars, no motorcycles. Four
big rigs were lined up in a fenced yard—the lights in the office building and
entrances to the utility buildings were off. The sun was still touching the
domes of the tallest silos, so the coppery yard lights hadn't turned on yet.

I eased the Oldsmobile around behind the long building where I hoped
Roberto was resting, turned off the engine, and sat there in the driver's seat.
The building opened through to the street side. Mr. Black had parked his van
there on the previous visit, so I entered, planning to go peek out and look for
him. First, I stopped next to the empty Thanatote.

The container had no obvious latches, handles, triggers, or switches.
The card slot was the only clue. I placed my hand on it as Dion had, but got
no response. I decided against tapping my chip card.

A look out the building's side door reassured me I could start my search for Roberto without interference.

I would have cried if I let myself. I was panicky. Daddy being in danger was—no, I told myself. You can't dwell on what hasn't happened yet, or on what you can't know. It's almost never what you think.

Then there was the matter of Roberto: why was I so excited that I might be seeing him in a few minutes? It was more than the hope of recruiting him to help save Daddy. Roberto had proven to be an ally, but it was Wendy's heart that loved him, wasn't it? And her passion for Roberto might be spilling over into me. Was I letting my hopes and fears blind me to greater danger? This strong-as-a-gorilla vampire was going to wake up hungry, and I couldn't rule out that his needs might overwhelm my preference to keep my blood. How could I protect myself if his thirst sent him after me? The sun sets, the vampires rise, and they own the night.

What kills a vampire? I had one answer. If I were to use sunlight against Roberto, it was too late. What else? A wooden stake in the heart? I could not imagine getting that done. Not to Roberto. Not to anyone. But there was something else. The cross lying in the back of the station wagon had intimidated both Roberto and Dion. I dropped the rear window, got out and went around to the back. Daddy was not going to be pleased when he saw how the two vampires had abused his restoration project. I tried to press down the bulge where the metal had been stretched out. It felt softer than the first time I tried it, but I couldn't improve it enough. The result was bumpy and uneven. Daddy would notice that, and the hole made by Dion's tracker.

I gathered myself and leaned in over the tailgate to reach for the cross. I hesitated. What if I had become susceptible to the power radiated by the cross? Would I hurt myself—or worse?

It's better to know now, I decided, because I was out of time. I closed my hand around it and lifted it out of the car. It was about the size of a carpenter's hammer, made of a heavy wood. The white paint on it was glossy, making it feel durable and utilitarian. Still, it was effective. And it hadn't hurt me yet.

I was holding it nearly at arm's length, like it was a snake or a stick of dynamite. My heart was beating faster. I rationalized that it was my anticipation that was responsible and that I was not actually affected by the icon. Relaxing my arm somewhat, I brought it closer. Nothing changed.

It was odd holding the cross and realizing that I'd had no history with it. Mom and Daddy had been married in a Christian church, but that's where my family's religious devotions had ended. Christmas was a time of Santa Claus, reindeer, and shelf elves: I knew about the Christ child from some of the seasonal songs, but the story was never discussed at home, and I was spared—so I thought until then—the endless hours in church, at Sunday school, and in confirmation classes. I understood that many doubted that Christ was "God made man." Some denied he'd even lived, saying he was a composite character, invented to play the proclaimer of nice-sounding platitudes intoned from a mountainside.

However, I was relieved of all doubt. The cross I was holding, the product of human design and manufacture, could channel divine power. It warded off the undead. They were unable to resist it. Both Dion and Roberto had shied away from it. If the cross had such power, it came from beyond the mortal artifice that carved it. There must have been a Christ if the mundane object in my hand could become an instrument of faith.

There was so much I needed to learn about the world that religious symbol revealed. However, the setting sun called my attention back. Roberto would be rising any moment. And Daddy had been kidnapped.

The area between the sliding doors on the street side and the backside was planked with thick, rough boards, stained by heavy equipment oil and sprinkled with the chaff, dust, and the pollen of the various grains transported through the building. It was getting darker outside, and I realized that, wherever Roberto was hiding, it was going to be darker than where I was then. He had to be hiding below where I was standing. I cast about for a stairway or ramp, finally spying a hatch on the floor at the west end of the building. A recessed wooden handhold allowed me to lift it open. Despite the thick boards, I decided it must be cantilevered somehow, because I was able to open it with little effort. A wooden ladder provided access to the low space underneath. I called down into the dark.

"Roberto? Hello?" There was no answer. It was too early for him to be up.

Slipping the cross into my belt, I climbed down the ladder and found myself on a dirt floor. The overhead clearance was fine for me, but Roberto would not have been able to stand up straight. There were a few light bulbs hanging from the ceiling, but no switch was apparent. All I saw in the dim space were burlap sacks and white plastic tarps, like the ones covering the bales of hay out behind the building.

I climbed back up and out to look for a light switch. As I returned to the space between the doors where the Thanatote sat, the street side door slid open. Mr. Black walked in.

Through the door I saw Black's Continental Grid van. He stopped on the wooden deck when he spotted me.

"Miss Williams. We meet again." He had another cross holstered on his right thigh, the twin of the one I'd taken from him the night before. He blinked his eyes several times, making me think the low light was bothering him.

"You should leave," I said. "Now."

"You killed Dion, didn't you?" he said. "He was a good boy, working hard to spread the good word. He never hurt anyone, but you snuffed him out." Was Mr. Black Dion's father? The catch in his voice as he spoke hinted a relationship beyond coworker.

"Mister Black, I have to deal with an urgent problem. Sorry, but I have no time to talk to you. Please leave now!"

Mr. Black stepped back, again showing that I'd somehow intimidated him. He stopped. His eyes were glazed for a moment. Then he charged me, the cross held high in both hands.

I braced myself and thrust my right hand out to counter his momentum, slapping him square in the middle of his chest. It sounded like the crack of a whip. His cross went flying behind me. Black stumbled backward and off the deck, landing on his butt outside the door, gasping and wheezing. Blood ran from the corner of his mouth. He clutched his chest where my palm had hit him.

It was dusk. The sun no longer lit any of the scattered clouds in the sky. As Mr. Black rolled onto his side groaning, I sensed that Roberto was nearby.

ROBERTO
Friday Sunset

Kelly was nearby. When had she come back? I was grateful she was there because it meant she was still alive. I couldn't wait to see her. First, though, I had to unwrap myself.

Breathing is the prime necessity for the living, but not as much for the undead. The habit stayed with me even though the need was minor. I'd rolled myself up in a white plastic tarp up against the sidewall of the building, waiting to finish pulling the plastic over my head until I was certain I was about to become a corpse again. Never certain exactly when I would switch off, I must always fight off panic as I breathe over and over the air trapped in the tarp with me. Anyone would become claustrophobic instantly, but they'd be trying to fight their way out. I had suffocated myself until I blanked out. A coffin would have been a great luxury.

When I woke, the air was no better than when I'd blacked out. The tarp shredded as I tore it from my face. Once I emerged from my plastic chrysalis, I was covered with its tatters. I brushed them off as I ducked under the low wooden beams and made my way to the ladder. There was a dim glow of light at the hatch. I'd closed it when I'd selected the cellar for my sleep. Someone else had opened it and left it that way. I heard voices above, a man and a woman exchanging heated words. I imagined someone could be waiting for me to climb up the ladder. Someone like Dion.

So, I didn't climb the ladder. Standing under the aperture, I crouched and launched myself straight up through the hatch. Landing with my feet straddling the opening, I'd planned to roll off to one side, but what I saw froze me in place. There was Kelly. She was putting her hand out to ward off Mr. Black who was running at her with a brilliantly shining cross held high. It happened fast. I heard a sound like a firecracker. He bounced off her palm and, arms pinwheeling, stumbled backward out of the building and off the deck, landing sitting on the ground. He groaned as he rolled over onto his side. Couldn't have happened to a nicer guy.

As I was uncertain the conflict had ended, I stayed quiet for fear of distracting Kelly if Mr. Black retaliated. I didn't move. She turned her head to look at me anyway, as if I'd spoken her name out loud.

"Roberto," she said. "I need your help." I hurried to her side. She was looking out the door again. Mr. Black was on his knees, attempting to stand up. He held his arms crossed over his chest. He was protecting it. Kelly had damaged him.

He stood, turned, and staggered to the passenger side of his van.

"I better stop him," I said. The red trickle at the edge of his mouth reminded me he might have a lot of blood in him too.

Kelly put her hand on my forearm to stop me. She was warm.

"No," she said. "We're not hurting him again. And it would be wrong to hold him." Placing his hand on a black square on the side of his van, the door rolled open and Mr. Black climbed in. The door slid shut behind him.

"He has blood," I said, pointing out what should have been obvious to her. The van's engine started.

"I hit him pretty hard, didn't I?" she asked. She looked surprised. Gravel sprayed in the driveway and rattled off the undercarriage of the van as it lurched into motion. Mr. Black was gone. Kelly was right there.

"You didn't tell me you know kung fu," I said. "Another thing you've been keeping from me. Are you okay?" I might have been babbling. Kelly was beautiful, intelligent, and radiant. I was entranced. Also, I was deeply thirsty.

"Roberto, I'm so glad to see you." A smile blossomed on her face for a second, but then her lower lip trembled. She looked down for a moment. "My dad has been kidnapped. I think he's being held by this madman Dwight who wants something from me. I must meet them in about two hours. Would you come with me?"

My answer was stuck in my throat. I had to go to Worship and meet up with poor Wendy who'd been on her own since she'd reanimated. She was waiting for my guidance and mentoring. We had a relationship to grow.

There I stood, wanting desperately to help Kelly, yet unable to. I was entranced and delighted with her. I was in love with Kelly.

"The problem is I have somewhere I need to be tonight. And I need to feed. Couldn't the police be helping you with this?"

"They're no help. At least, not for our sort of thing. Now I'm guessing you won't be either," she said. Though her words sounded discouraged, the way she carried herself told me she was ready to move on. She straightened up, turned toward me, and held out her hand.

"Good luck to you, Roberto. I've got to go."

I reached out to shake her hand, but the turn of her body revealed a cross hooked through her belt over her right hip. I staggered back.

"What do you need that for? I would never hurt you," I said.

"You just said something about being thirsty. I'm presently your most likely source of nourishment."

"That would be nice," I admitted. "But it would have to be okay with you. Look, could you take that thing off, or at least turn it away? That's really uncomfortable."

"Just the same…" she said, reaching for it. Her hand never got there. She clamped the palm of her right hand on the middle of her chest and covered it with her left. Her head was cocked a little to the side, as if she was listening. She held her hands as if she was waiting to feel a baby's kick.

"Just the same…" she repeated. Her eyes focused, and she looked hard at me. I couldn't read her face. Was she angry?

"Kelly, are you okay?" I'd have held her, caught her if she fainted, or given her a shoulder to lean against if that's what she needed, only the cross glowing on her hip pressed me back.

"Oh, Roberto." She took a breath. "I love you," she said. I was thunderstruck. Those were the words I thought I'd never hear again, spoken by the best friend I'd made since Jack transitioned me. What made her say that? Her eyes showed surprise.

"If I let you feed on me," she said, "will you promise not to hurt me?"

"Sure," I said perhaps too quickly. "At the worst, it might make you a little dizzy. It takes days to kill someone that way. It's nothing I want to see again."

"You have to agree to come with me," she said. "I know you've probably got to meet your friend—that's it, isn't it? Can't it wait until a little later? I don't have any choice about when I have to be there." For a moment she was gone in thought.

"Oh darn," she said. "I've got to get a white flower—to wear in my hair."

"Why a flower?" I asked.

"I guess because he doesn't know what I actually look like. He needs it to find me in the crowd."

"I get it," I said. Thirst drove the next words I spoke. "So, yes, I'll go with you, if you'll let me feed and maybe give me a ride after you settle things. I'm not going up against someone like you, I hope." Could there be others like her? I only knew one other like me, and he'd disappeared.

"I don't know," Kelly said, "but it seems unlikely. The ride afterward may not happen right away, depending on Daddy. If they've hurt him…"

"Sure, okay," I said. "I need blood now. You'll need to get rid of that icon first." Kelly looked as uncertain as I'd ever seen her. I imagined she was deciding whether she could trust me doing to her that which killed Wendy. She turned and walked toward the cross dropped by Mr. Black and extracted the one in her belt and knelt. She left hers on the floor side by side with the one Black fumbled. That one had gone dark.

Kelly rose and walked back to me. Light faded from the cross she'd left behind. Curling two fingers inside the collar of her black jacket, Kelly pulled it to the side, exposing her neck down to her collarbone. I made myself walk calmly toward her.

"I feel silly saying this," she said as we met. "Please be gentle with me. And try not to get blood on this blouse, okay? It's one of my favorites." She looked lovely in purple and black. My desire to hold her in my arms surged. For a moment, I forgot about her offer of blood.

"Is this okay?" she asked. She looked uncertain, perhaps puzzled by my hesitation.

"No," I said, "Let me use your arm. It'll be more comfortable for you."

"Which way is the fastest?"

I reached for her gently and brought her to me. I put one arm around behind her right shoulder so I could support her head in my hand. The heat of her body was like a furnace. The smell of life on her was narcotic. With my other hand on the small of her back, I brought my mouth towards her neck and she rolled her head back, exposing her throat. I dropped my jaw low to let my fangs pivot out.

They refused.

"What is it?" Kelly asked.

I helped her straighten up, keeping a hand on her warm relaxed shoulder. She wasn't frightened. I didn't think I'd ever be able to take her blood. It wasn't like there was a forcefield around her, or that I had suddenly detoured to a new diet regimen: I was simply incapable of harming her. I was unable to keep an intention.

"I'm sorry, this has never happened before. My fangs won't descend." Until then, I'd thought I'd developed voluntary control of them, like any other joint in my body.

"That's okay," she said, "I'm sure it happens to everybody one time or another." She was grinning impishly.

I laughed. She giggled. It was like music.

"But you're serious," she said, "You can't bite me? What are you going to do? Should I cut myself? Look, I need to get going, and you promised to come along. You've got to come."

"I know what I'll have to do, but first let's get going. We'll see to your dad." I felt awful knowing I was deferring Wendy, but the irresistible woman standing in front of me was having a very real crisis and I needed to help her.

"Okay," Kelly said. She went back and collected both crosses, keeping them on the far side of her. We returned to the center of the building, passing a large black cart that hadn't been there that morning. It had the CG logo on it.

"What is that?" I asked.

"Coffin, I think," she said.

It looked like a small fortress. The black material looked rugged.

I touched the raised panel on the top to sense the texture. The box hissed at the contact. I retreated out the front door and Kelly hustled out the back. I looked back inside to see if something was coming out. It had opened at the front edge, the top lifting back like the door of an exotic sports car. I saw hints of what looked like navy-blue satin lining.

Nothing more happened. I ventured back in, and Kelly returned from the far door. We looked inside the crate. It looked like it held an astronaut's couch, but with fabric and trim more likely found in the lobby of a fine hotel. The inside of the door had a dead bolt—it could be locked from inside. There was a video display on a swing arm rotated into a recess on one side. You could lie back and watch decent-sized visuals. Cushy.

"Roberto! Are you okay? Stay away from this thing. CG stuff."

I pulled the top back down, and it slammed shut with the same authority as the door on Kelly's station wagon. It finished pulling itself closed from inside. Kelly was walking out to her car.

Unable to resist, I touched it again and it opened again. I slapped it shut and ran out to Kelly who was standing at the open door of the big Oldsmobile.

"Yep, coffin," I said. Nice improvement over being wrapped in a tarp.

"Get in. We've got to get moving." I went around the far side and got in. We slammed doors simultaneously, and she drove us out from behind the building and back onto the road. We went back the way we'd come that morning.

"How'd you get it open?" Kelly asked.

"The coffin? I just touched its panel. It popped right open."

"Hmmm. It didn't open for me. At least the other one didn't. I had to use more extreme measures. I'll tell you about that later." The car was tearing along. I glanced at the speedometer. We were doing seventy miles per hour already, and we'd just started up the access ramp to the Interstate.

"Okay," I said when she'd finished getting us onto the highway. "So, tell me everything. Where are we going? What happened to your dad?"

"My dad was supposed to be home, but when I got there, he was gone and had left me a message with some important clues. Someone had held

223

a gun on him. I found an email from someone anonymous saying that if I wanted to know where Daddy is, I had to go to a club called Schlock House Funk tonight. And wear a white flower in my hair. I need to find a florist. Aw heck, they could all be closed by now."

"No worries, miss," I said. "There's a strip mall on a frontage road at the next exit. It has a huge grocery store."

"They'll have flowers," she concluded. "That's where you go to buy them, right?"

"It's the thought that counts, isn't it? Anyway, on our budget, how much could you afford?"

"Okay, we're going. Anyway, I think this guy who took Daddy wants something from me, and…"

She stopped talking and put her right hand over her heart. The car started slowing. She was pulling off onto the shoulder of the road. We came to a stop. She slouched back in her seat.

"Kelly?" I asked. "What is it? What's the matter?"

"I think she's feeding."

DWIGHT
Friday Night

Tanner must still be alive, I reasoned. I hurried back down to the basement, switching on Wendy's heart as I descended, and found her lying flat on her back, her head up and looking at me. She pointed with each hand at the nearest actuator rod. Old Dude on the floor was wide-eyed. I guessed he hadn't seen anyone rise from the dead before.

"What the hell is this?" she asked. She had her hands on the bars over her stomach.

"That's what will help you stand up straight. Just a second. Let me help you up." I pivoted her so her knees were off the edge of the dryer and worked the remote so her abdomen contracted. With my free arm guiding her, she sat up.

"This is just so wrong," she said as she examined the actuator rods and the lag bolts threaded into her hips. I rocked the controller thumbpad and she tilted from side to side. A brief push returned her to the full and upright position.

"That is…" she started. "How are you doing that?"

I showed her the controller I was using to control movement, demonstrating the basics.

"Give me that," she ordered. I hadn't planned on letting her operate it. I guess I'd imagined working it for her, united in choreographing the turns and gyrations of her iconic figure. I would dance by radio wave with the deadly robot dolly.

Instead, I surrendered it. The way she ordered me—it got right in my head and I was putting my hand out. Her will had plowed past my vaporous fantasies and put an impulse in me. It wasn't that she'd commandeered my motor control—it was that I yielded to the impulse to do the wrong thing.

After a few false starts, she grasped the principle of the thumbpad, finally settling on holding it in her right hand, where she had some intact fingertips and presumably a sense of touch. Her control was superior to mine. Though her movements were angular, the play of her upper body above her mechanized waist made me witness to the birth of a new form of dance. She made it beautiful. The robot torso mated with the floating undulation of her arms and shoulders and head. She'd unlocked the secrets of movement in the span of forty-five seconds.

I pointed out a mirror I'd propped up on the other side of the basement. She gyrated her way over to get a better look, continuing her posing exhibition.

"Dwight," she said. "I'm grossed out that you fiddled with me while I was sleeping. That's just rude." She was right. I couldn't wait to ask her permission though. The work was far neater this way. Very little blood loss. That applied to both of us.

She flipped up the front edge of her skirt. The mirror reflected black panties. "Thank goodness," she said, relinquishing the hem and turning toward me.

"I love it. Thank you, Dwight."

"I hope you like what I did with the makeup. I didn't know what to do with your hair."

She posed with her hands on her hips and lifted her chest up high. She looked imperial.

"Totally amazing," she said. "Wow, you got rid of the power cord. How'd you do that?"

"You've got a rechargeable battery pack now. I'll show you the connector later."

I was transported, elated and giddy. She loved how she looked and worked.

"Now, let me reward you," she said. She started toward me, lowering her jaw so her fangs could swing into position.

"No," I said. I'd already decided that giving her more blood would be as bad for me as it had been for Tanner, so I explained my little theater piece starring her and Old Dude. I had decided to record the performance on my cell. I could send it to Kelly William's phone using the number off a conveniently annotated phone bill I saw in Old Dude's house.

"So, Old Dude, I guess this has been an unusual day for you. You got to watch me wire up a corpse, and she turns out to be a lot less dead than you thought. Miss Allard here is in fact a vampire. Vampirism is a condition requiring the regular taking of someone else's blood. I can tell you that it's not that bad, even the first time. But, please, tell me what you think—later." I started recording.

Wendy knelt next to Old Dude. He tried to lean away from her. Still on her knees, she laid a shin across his lap and pressed his head back against the wall. He pushed back against her—I saw the muscles in his neck go taut—but she was like a truck spring pushing back at him. Irresistible. She was on his neck, feeding vigorously. I silently counted swallows as I moved in closer so there would be no mistake about what was happening.

I stopped recording and shouted "Twenty! Stop!" Wendy stopped feeding and looked at me, puzzled.

"We need him in good health, okay?" I said. "He's how we're going to get your heart back."

"This is not so much fun so far, you know. He tastes so good. I'm not used to being on such a narrow diet. I hate having to stop. I need more. C'mon, Dwight."

Were we having an argument?

"I don't know how to help you with that, but I do know you can hurt people. You nearly sucked Tanner dry. I had to take him to the hospital. They think he'll live. Either that or you'll be competing with him for any spare blood here in the Springfield blood bank. Good luck with that." I was trying to imply she'd be on her own, ignoring the fact that, in about three hours, she would be under the wing of the master vampire Roberto. I wondered if he'd thank me or tear me apart.

"Okay, you're right. I knew I picked the best geek, Dwight."

I was the best.

"Roberto will be able to straighten this all out."

I felt like the worst. She was using me.

I sent off the video message to Kelly's cell. Wendy made her way up the stairs, moving a bit too much like Robocop. "I'm going to put on some music, okay?" she said.

"Sure. Whatever."

ROBERTO
Early Evening

"Who?" A phone on Kelly's hip vibrated three times. She looked at its display.

"Don't know this one," she said. I guessed she meant the phone number. "It's a message. With a video."

I slid across the bench seat to get a better look. She pressed a green triangle and the video started. It showed a dark-haired woman kneeling, sucking at a man's throat. Her victim was sitting on the floor, legs straight out, roped to the pipes next to a washing machine and dryer. The display was small and grainy, but I'd seen the woman's face and mannerisms plenty of times.

"It's Daddy," Kelly said. "Oh damn, damn, damn; he's feeding Daddy to a vampire."

"It's Wendy," I said. "That vampire is Wendy."

The video was replaced by a text message. "Give us what we need and he goes free. 9pm Schlock House Funk. White flower in your hair. No police."

She looked at me. "That's your Wendy—who you made into a vampire—preying on my father, isn't it? And because she's showing up in a video sent to my phone, I'm almost certain Dwight is behind this."

"Dwight?" I said. Who was he and what did he have to do with Wendy? I asked her those questions, but Kelly had only one thought.

"How bad is she hurting him?" Her voice quavered.

"She just woke up and is probably feeding on him for the first time. He won't be any worse off than if he'd donated. It took seven feedings before Wendy lost consciousness. It doesn't hurt all that much. After fifteen or twenty seconds, they calm down and stop struggling. So, who is Dwight?"

"Yet another person I met at the hospital. Right before you found me, this Dwight guy had been in that office talking at me, trying to find out where Wendy's organs had gone."

"What are you saying?" I asked.

I realized she didn't want to discuss this. I gently rested my hand on her knee and waited.

"Wendy's stepsister found her body. You probably knew her parents were away." I did, but how did Kelly know?

"Tisha had legal power of attorney for her," Kelly said, "and used it to change things like the funeral and other services at Morty Coil's. She pocketed the refund."

"That doesn't surprise me. Wendy detested her. Tisha shares her father's obsession with growing money." Kelly was still sitting with her head looking down. I hadn't heard the worst yet.

"What else?" I asked.

"Her stepsister also authorized the harvesting of Wendy's organs, like the heart, liver, kidneys, and pancreas. That was done before she was cremated."

"Not part of the plan," I said. How can she function? "Amazing. Could she have regenerated them? I always wondered if we could heal from that much damage. Hey, it's getting dark. Maybe you should put on your parking lights."

She pulled out the light knob and the dashboard lit up. She sat there unmoving, still locked in tight to some secret.

"I'm not so sure, Roberto. You see—that's why I was in the hospital. I was in for a heart transplant. They gave me hers."

Kelly caught me off guard. I felt betrayed. I wanted it to be a lie. But how else could she have been out of the hospital so soon after a heart transplant? My ability to regenerate at sunset had been granted to Kelly when she received Wendy's heart.

"It's so strange," she said. "During the day, this heart beats just like you'd want it to. When the sun sets, the feeling in my chest changes. Its beating has nothing to do with my actions or thoughts. I can be sitting absolutely still, and it will beat like a trip hammer. I can be running flat out, and the heart will laze along like someone drifting off to sleep. After sunset, it beats for Wendy. What we just saw proved it. I figured something else out." She relaxed a little and then sat up a little higher in her seat.

"What is it?" I asked.

"I thought that, as it beats the way it would in Wendy's chest, the love she felt for you came along with it. I wasn't sure it was my own emotion."

"Oh." I got it. "That's why you said that back there. Has something changed your mind?" I started understanding why she'd been so reserved.

"I was so surprised to find out that the feeling was mine. I knew that while Wendy sleeps, the heart becomes my heart, keeping me alive like my old one did. I saw you and then I understood. What I felt for you didn't change from the daytime. I love you without any help from the heart."

"I...we need to get going."

"Yes," she said. "Yes, you're right. Let's find that grocery store." She was all business again. She dropped the car back into gear and forced a roar out of the car's engine. The acceleration pushed me deep into my seat.

I was twisted up inside with Kelly's confessions. This amazing woman had told me she loved me. It was as much a revelation to her as it was to me. It put definition to how I felt about her.

But she had confessed to having Wendy's heart in her chest. The video of Wendy feasting on Kelly's dad was the first proof I'd had that Wendy had survived. What was she doing with this Dwight guy? And I had begun to believe it was Wendy's heart calling out to me from Kelly's chest. That explained my being summoned to her hospital room. Wendy's heart was woken up by the heart transplant procedure. Jack had said he'd be able to find me once I'd awoken, using the sire-and-victim link. I'd expected to have that connection with Wendy. I was unsettled by how things had gone awry.

Kelly trusted her feelings toward me, but I wasn't sure I could trust how I felt toward her. I'd never experienced the connection before. I didn't know how it might leave me vulnerable. When it came to Wendy, I had to admit I'd been far more lonely than passionate. Those feelings, now directed toward Kelly, were magnified. Did it work differently for me toward her? Might it be supernatural?

Things felt chilly in the car. No one was talking, so our descending onto the frontage road and going into the supermarket provided a welcome break from the silence.

We found a florist's display just inside the supermarket entrance, offering many colorful bouquets. One choice was a cluster of white flowers from which she extracted a single chrysanthemum. Scissors chained nearby let her trim the stalk. She placed it above her right ear.

A look of realization came over her face, and she strode off toward the meat department, the flower in her hair and its stalk in her hand. She moved too fast. I caught up with her as quickly as I dared, unable to rely on my nobody-here-right-now skill in such a well-lit space. She stopped in front of steaks and roasts.

"This one looks juicy." She seized a package of steak tips, then turning her attention to the kitchen goods aisle where a cheap steak knife was added to the collection. We took them to the self-checkout where she produced a bill from what looked like an infinite roll of fifties. She paid the full bouquet price for the single flower in her hair.

We were back in the station wagon in two minutes.

She took the steak tips package, poked holes in the opposite corners of the plastic wrap, and offered it to me.

"Will this help?" she asked.

I took it and sucked out the bloody juice. It tasted awful. My stomach grumbled, but then some deeper need took over and I felt a sense of clarity return to my thinking. It helped, but not much.

"It does help," I said, "but the meat part does me no good."

"That part will be for me," she said, reaching out toward the package of steak tips. I surrendered it and she widened a tear in the plastic. She sliced half of it into strips and speared a strand of meat with the steak knife and took a bite.

"Heaven," she said. Something about that word really bothers me. "Let's go," she said. The Oldsmobile thundered back to life and we were hurtling back onto the highway. She appeared quite comfortable driving the massive vehicle at something-beyond-posted speeds, spearing the occasional bite of raw steak.

"So, we're going to a rock club, right?" I asked. We needed to be talking and that was a practical question. "Do you know where it is?"

"NE 55th, on the ten thousandth block." That matched where I needed to go.

"Is that where they have Worship?" I asked. "Rose tells me it's a goth event that shows up at different clubs."

"I don't know," Kelly answered. "I think there's only one club out that way. There are a couple roadhouse bars, but only one dance club."

"That's where I need to go too," I said.

"And I really appreciate it," she said. I heard relief in her voice.

"No," I said. "What I'm saying is that I'm supposed to meet Wendy at this event called Worship. I suppose the good news for you is, if she shows up there, it's good news for your dad. She won't be feeding on him if she's with people."

"I see your point," Kelly said. "And the good news for you is you'll make your date on time." Her voice started out frosty, ending up sounding like buddy-talk at the end. There was a war of emotions underway, and Kelly was the battleground. I knew how she felt. As much as I wanted Kelly, my focus had to be on Wendy. I could lead her away from the diabolical Dwight and spare Kelly's father in the process.

We rounded the northwest corner of the city. The weakening glow of sunset was behind us as we hurtled through the dark toward NE 55th.

"Is that the right time?" I asked her, indicating the analog clock on the dashboard. "Not quite eight thirty."

"Of course, it's right," she answered.

"We've got more than enough time to get there at this speed, with a greater possibility of being pulled over for speeding. We'd get there late. Or not at all."

She tensed, then sighed and eased off the accelerator. The speedometer needle dropped down to within an inch of the speed limit. She needed distracting, at least for a few minutes.

"You said there was two of those coffins?" I asked.

"Oh. Right. After you hid, Black and Dion showed up in the van and took two of them out and pushed them inside the building. Dion got into one and pulled it shut on himself. I figured he was going to wait you out and try to capture you after sunset."

"Then you didn't go away. But they didn't catch you?"

She explained to me what she'd seen from across the highway, and how she'd taken Dion out for some coffin surfing. It was both her matter-of-fact delivery plus the memory of seeing her toss Black ten yards backward that had me believing her story. I asked what had happened with Mr. Black before I'd woken for the evening.

"I'd come back to get you," she said. "I wanted your help. Also, I'd guessed Black might show up again, and he did. I thought he'd come back for Dion and you."

"That explains the second coffin." I had to be open-minded, I realized. "Maybe they really are there to help us." Maybe Jack Murphy was simply paranoid.

"Who?" Kelly asked.

"Continental Grid. Maybe Dion was just trying to get me to see that there's someone out there who looks after and cares for us."

"I believe there is, but I don't think it's CG."

"Who then?" I asked.

"Roberto, do you believe in God?"

CHAPTER 7
DWIGHT

Friday Night

I'd left Old Dude alone in the basement, closing the door at the top of the steps. From my kitchenette, I looked around the corner and saw Wendy dancing. She had Prince on so loud my speakers were starting to rattle. I compounded a bowl of grain flakes, raisins, and almond milk, and took it to the doorway to watch her invent new moves for motor-actuated fetish corset vampire chicks. It's something you don't often see.

I was nervous and stayed that way until we arrived at Schlock House Funk. I'd seen enough crime shows and thrillers to be aware that I'd undoubtedly made some mistakes in trying to get Wendy and her heart back together in the same room. As far as planning failures went, my biggest shortcoming was not knowing how I'd restore the heart to her chest. I couldn't make myself think what an actual method might be. It might be bad for Kelly, I guessed. Maybe this Roberto guy could explain how to handle this.

At 8:30, I interrupted Wendy, announcing it was time to go. She surprised me with a look of disappointment.

"Roberto is meeting you there, right?" I asked.

"Yeah, that's what Rose said."

"But?"

"I was just thinking he would have found me by now. That's what his maker said would happen—that you'd get a radar for your creation."

"Did it work for him?" I asked.

"Well, no. That guy Murphy never came back for Roberto. So, no experience with it from that side." She sounded resigned.

"Nothing to go on, then. Look, it's time to leave. I could use your help getting Old Dude back into the trunk."

"Sure. Mind if I have another taste? He's got high test in his veins."

"No time, and I plan to keep my word to this Kelly Williams chick. Your guy should have a solution for your dietary requirements anyway."

I led the way downstairs and grabbed the ropes staking out Old Dude's legs. Any interest that might have caused disappeared when he saw Wendy approaching.

"I'm going to untie his legs. Can you stand him up?"

"Sure," she answered. She stood between him and the dryer, put her right hand around the back of his neck, and lifted him straight up, the ropes around his chest sliding up along the pipes. It looked wrong. No one was that strong. Old Dude's face was quite red.

"Thanks. You can let him down now. We don't want to damage the merchandise." Wendy lowered him down and set him on his feet. I gave Old Dude a serious stare.

"You're going back in the trunk for now. All goes well, you'll be free in an hour. Understand?" He was not pleased, but he didn't look poised to fight.

"You follow him up, okay?" I asked her.

"Sure," she said. I detached him from the pipes and led the way upstairs, relieved that I had her strength and speed on my side. She trailed him all the way up and even helped lift him into the trunk. Before we left, she asked if she could borrow my karate jacket.

"I want to keep my new look under wraps until we're inside." We agreed that the dark blood stains on the jacket made it unappealing, so my alternative offer of a black trench coat was happily accepted.

As we hit the road, I estimated we'd be at Worship on time.

KELLY

Friday Night

"I do," Roberto said. He'd flinched as I asked the question. "How could I not believe? My condition wouldn't be possible if the divine didn't exist."

I realized I'd been slow on the uptake. My agnostic upbringing—baptized but never educated—blinded me to the meaning of his fear of crosses. Both Roberto and Dion had retreated from one.

"It's just now occurring to me that I didn't see all the implications of our condition. There is a God, and he was somehow here on earth and put power into the symbol of the cross. That was Jesus, wasn't it? He was 'God made man,' I think the saying goes." Roberto had retreated from me, pressing himself against the passenger door.

"Please stop that, Kelly. Please. You don't know how painful that is. You've got to stop."

"You mean stop talking about religion? It hurts you somehow?" I felt my pulse rate going up and wondered if my heart was reacting to the powerful words I'd been using, or if it was a response to the tense situation we were heading into. No, it was nighttime. Wendy was making it beat faster.

"It's heartbreaking I'm unable to be near anything that represents divinity or hear the words that describe it. It isn't pain, exactly—it's more like magnets with like poles. A positive pole pushes another positive charge away. I suppose I could walk into a church, but there's a pressure in my mind and my heart that screams 'stay away, you'll come to harm here.' I never had a feeling like that before Jack transitioned me. I believe that what he did to me has drawn me towards something evil."

"Were you a Christian before you died?" I asked.

"Please be careful of your choice of words. I'm along to help you, but I won't be much good if you keep doing that. Okay, yes, I'd gone to a church when I grew up and stayed with it most of my life."

"Is what happened to you why you can't say certain names or use certain words?"

"Yes," Roberto said. "You're getting it."

"But you've tried?"

"No, I guess not. I just know it would be bad for me."

The sign for the exit to NE 55th lit up in my headlights. I located a gap between the big rigs in the right lane and signaled my intention to move over. It was less than a mile. We had only a few minutes left before we got to Schlock House Funk. With our arrival imminent, panic grew in my gut. We had nothing resembling a plan, and the stakes were high. Daddy was in danger, and my life might be ending. My time with a borrowed heart might soon be over.

"Oh G..." I started. "Heck! What are we going to do?"

"You mean at the club?" Roberto asked.

"Yes, of course. This Dwight creep will be there. He might make me go somewhere with him saying that's how I'll get Daddy back. Daddy could be vampire food, for all I know, and giving the heart back to Wendy won't change the fact that she's a vampire. Daddy and I could both end up dead." I turned onto the exit ramp.

"We'll figure it out as we go," Roberto said. He was trying to sound reassuring. I let it pass.

The ramp ended at a traffic light intersecting NE 55th. It was green when we got there, so I turned left and headed north for the club. It was easy to spot—there was an animated neon sign, a meat cleaver that dropped down, changing from white to blue to red. When it hit bottom, a purple neon sign proclaiming "Funk" lit up. We were there.

A heavily tattooed guy with an orange-tipped flashlight waved us around the side of the building, past the entrance, to parking in the back. Though late in the evening for me, it was early for the club crowd, so I found a spot quickly. I oriented the big station wagon aimed straight for the exit. The one thing I could anticipate was the need to get away quickly. We got out of the car.

"Wait," I said, and went around to the back. I took one of the white crosses and slipped it into my belt. It looked a little obvious, so I put on the black silk blazer I'd brought along. Though it still bulged out, the black fabric over the cross went a long way toward hiding it.

"What's that for?" Roberto asked.

"Vampires," I answered.

I headed for the entrance with Roberto next to me. An elderly uniformed officer was at the door, a few feet away from a very big baldheaded man, the doorman, who was collecting the cover charges. The elder officer had to be the one Detective Waller had said would be there. I walked up to him.

"Officer, I'm Kelly Williams. I spoke to Detective Waller at headquarters this afternoon, and he said he'd let the duty officer here know about my father's kidnapping." The graying fringe showing under his cap and the drooping skin on his neck told me this man wouldn't be in his sixties much longer, and unlikely to do anything courageous on his own. I hoped I was wrong about that.

"Just a minute," he said. "Stay here." He started walking away from us speaking to his walkie-talkie. "Janice, I'm out here at the dope exchange, and there's this woman..." his voice trailed off as he left our hearing range. About thirty seconds later, he came back and spoke to us. "We don't have anything more about that, but we don't think you need to worry. Let me know if anything unusual comes up, okay?" He was done with us.

The doorman collected a fifty from me, which let Roberto and me inside. We were bathed in the roaring force of overdriven electric guitars, a battered drum kit, and thunderous bass lines. A male bodybuilder type and a female linebacker patted us down. "Any booze, drugs, weapons?" she asked as she frisked me. Before I could answer, her hand came to rest on my cross. She pulled it out of my belt and hefted it, smacking it on her palm. "This is a mistake, honey" she said, "or are you planning to leave right now?"

"That's my cross. It's a religious icon," I protested.

"So, you're leaving then?" she snapped. Decide now, is what she meant.

"I'll pick it up on my way out." She gave me a claim check for it. As we walked into the heart of the din, I heard the bodybuilder say to her, "Her boyfriend just came out of the meat locker," He'd just patted Roberto down and was rubbing his hands together, attempting to restore warmth.

"He would have been tasty," Roberto said, reminding me of another liability in my plan. My ally was a thirsty vampire.

"Flower!" he shouted at me.

"What?" I answered. "I have it on." I touched my hair and felt it where I'd put it over my right ear.

"No! No, what I'm saying is hide it. It might buy us some time. He doesn't know who you are, right? Might give us some time to listen and learn something."

I dropped the carnation into my cleavage. Fortunately, it caught on something.

"But Wendy will sense you're here, right? She'll have that vampire radar thing going."

"Yes, you're at least part right," he said. "I'll have to watch from the shadows."

"What shadows?" The club was dark, but all the space was devoted to tables, chairs, bar counters, band stand, and dance space. Roving spotlights and mirror balls cast light randomly around the room.

"Watch me," he said. He stepped a few feet back. A couple passed where he'd been standing. I'd lost track of him for a moment. I turned my head to the left when I felt a tap on my left shoulder. Roberto was smiling back at me.

"You're hard to fool, but I think I had you for a second," he said.

"At least my radar is working," I answered. "How do you do that?"

"It's an attitude, I think," he said, "but, however I do it, it's an excellent trick, don't you think?"

"I admit I'm impressed. Okay, let's see if we can spot them. I might recognize Wendy from the cell phone video." I looked the room over. The space was probably designed to be a warehouse, laid out in a rectangle about half the size of a football field. There was an elevated walkway going around the edge, filled with couples and small clusters of people watching the action on the dance floor. The suspended pathway passed through two patio spaces, one in each of the far corners. Stairs near the front of the room and at each patio gave access to the walkway.

"Let's look from up there," I said. Roberto had been looking at the same place I had. He led the way. My heart was beating solidly, but not in time to the music. Wendy must not have arrived yet.

"They might be up here also," Roberto shouted as we started down the catwalk. Unfortunately, some of the loudspeakers deluging the room with sound were installed shoulder high along the catwalk, and we had to walk right in front of them. We had to yell to be heard.

"I don't think they're here yet," I said, after a quick scan of the room. I still hadn't felt Wendy's music passion being communicated to my heart. Its rhythm wasn't mine at night, but I was sure it gave me information about Wendy. My link to her that way gave me a brief burst of hope. I knew what it felt like when she fed, and I hadn't felt it since just before I received the video message. Daddy might still be okay.

"I'm not seeing either of them," Roberto confirmed.

"Maybe we should be holding drinks," I said. "It might help us blend in."

"Good thought, but there's nothing at the bar I'd want to drink, and we might need the fraction-of-a-second advantage of response time if something happened. Anyway, eventually we'll have to get face to face with them at some point."

We made our way to a corner patio. My thought was to take a table that let us watch the entrance from the other side of the room. The table nearest the edge had a couple sitting at it. Roberto spoke to them while I hung back, and they immediately got up and moved to a table near the wall.

"What did you say to them?" I asked as we claimed their vacated seats.

"I suggested that the other table might be better. It's like a Jedi mind trick, I guess. No idea why it works."

That reminded me of when Dion had first spoken to Roberto. Apparently, there were some undead mind skills, but Roberto had only anecdotal and intuitive information about his abilities, having been neglected after becoming a newly-minted vampire.

Over the din of the distorted guitars, overdriven keyboards, and a relentlessly pumping rhythm section, I heard a chorus of girl-screams. Looking back to the main doorway, I saw someone making an entrance. A dozen young women in black leather, black vinyl, and black satin dresses were circled around the couple. I recognized Dwight. A moment later, I felt my heart begin pulsing to the music. Wendy was feeling the beat.

The ring of people—with Dwight and Wendy in the center—floated through the crowd, making its way nearer the center of the dance floor. Somehow, the rest of the crowd sensed the prodigy among them and parted ways for the entourage.

The music had infected Wendy. She was striding and swiveling with the beat. I wanted to stand up and dance, and I would have except that I saw that Dwight was looking around the room. He was looking for us. I was glad I'd concealed the flower. Too much was happening too quickly.

"That's Wendy?" I asked Roberto.

"Yes. That's Dwight, right?"

I nodded agreement. "You're not getting the connection sensation?"

Roberto looked at me. His expression told me he had just figured something out. "If there's anything there, you're drowning her out." He looked back to the scene on the dance floor. "It looks like we're not the only priority tonight. Those are Wendy's buds down there around her."

"Do they believe?" I asked. "You know—that she's a vampire?"

"Look at the distance they're keeping, I'm guessing they believe. Rose, the girl with the bright red hair? She always hugs everyone when they meet, except me. She didn't hug Wendy tonight."

The urge to dance was becoming a distraction. I looked down at the circle of people containing Dwight and Wendy. She was swaying, but not yet fully dancing. She started unbuttoning her trench coat.

"Let's get down there and see what we're up against," Roberto said.

That sounded very different to me. "Up against", he'd said. Maybe his reunion with Wendy would take a different course than I'd expected. Regardless, my priority was Daddy. I would do whatever it took to get him away from them.

"Okay," I said, and got up from my seat. I led the way down the steps to the dance floor and walked up to the edge of the circle of people surrounding Wendy and Dwight. He was accepting her trench coat, draping it over his arm as he backed to the edge of the crowd. I heard gasps and mutterings from her entourage.

Wendy walked around the edge of the circle, her pale skin a contrast to her black hair and black vinyl outfit. All eyes were on her, and more jaws than not were hanging slack in disbelief. When she came around to where I saw her straight on, it was apparent what had electrified the crowd.

Her waist was impossibly narrow. It was cinched in by a black vinyl corset, no bigger around than a tea saucer. She had two metal rods connecting the lowest rib on each side of her chest to the hipbone below it. Big metal screws connected two metal rods to her. The screws were threaded into her ribs through the vinyl of her corset and through bare skin on her hipbones. Her miniskirt started just below the two screws. A wide flat black line ran under the corset, right over her navel. It disappeared under the waistband of the skirt. I thought it might be a zipper.

She spiraled into the center of the space, hit a wide-legged stance, and started moving with the music. I was repulsed by the vulgar modifications made to the once-dead girl posturing in front of me. Worse, I felt abused by my urge to move along with her, needing to dance the same steps she was dancing. My legs were still mine to control, but my mind struggled and failed to placate the intoxicated heart. It was echoing the sensuous call of the pounding rhythms.

I gave in to the urge to dance, and in the most shameful of ways. I started doing the step-to-the-left then step-to-the-right girl dork shuffle that got me by in my teen years. No one noticed me, though: Wendy was the show.

The bizarre metalwork connecting her ribs to her hips was ratcheting her up and down like a robot, tilting left and right with machine-like precision. Her vinyl-encased torso, suspended between the rods, moved with its own agenda. Her waist twisted and coiled, its serpentine movement echoed in the sinuous gyrations of her arms extended out to her sides. Pivot and gyrate. Undulate and extend. She was mating the movements of machine and woman to create a bizarre and fascinating blend.

"Oh my god, he's here!" exclaimed the red-haired woman I'd seen at the crematorium vigil. She was wearing a black lace dress. She was looking at Roberto.

"That's Rose," Roberto said. "I guess this is it," he concluded and started toward the crowd. Rose stepped back, tapping a neighbor on the shoulder. A gap opened in the circle of people around Wendy.

She saw Roberto. I knew because my heart skipped a beat.

The music continued to pound, but everything else came to a stop. Roberto and Wendy were facing each other, a yard or two apart, the circle of people around them watching and waiting to see their reunion. I recognized then that eternal perfection in their faces that overcame any flaws of shape or texture. Having seen Roberto, then Dion, and now Wendy, I came to see there was some pattern to the changes visited on them by their affliction. Their skin looked like porcelain, incredibly smooth, free of any marks or irregularities. Pores, wrinkles, dimples—none of these things had a place on them. The function of skin on the living—sweating and absorbing—was irrelevant to these beings. I found them beautiful.

She spoke to Roberto, but I couldn't hear for the pressure of the music. I think he replied, "I am here." My heart beat still faster as they came together and embraced, her head against his shoulder as he put his arms around her.

My pulse rate increased again as she leaned back from him. The flawless features disappeared into a knot of anger. This time I could hear her. The whole club heard her.

"Where were you? Why didn't you find me? Do you know what they did to me?" Her voice penetrated like a jackhammer or ambulance siren. Her circle of friends took quick steps backwards.

Roberto reached out, trying to coax her head back to his shoulder as he softly spoke, attempting to calm her. The trip-hammer pounding of my heart told me he wasn't succeeding.

The tension between them widened the circle of people around them. This left Dwight inside. He was looking around the dance floor as he took a tentative step toward Roberto and Wendy, probably trying to locate the woman with a white flower in her hair. I made sure to keep watching the reunited couple and avoid eye contact with him. It was just that he knew where Daddy was.

Dwight saw me anyway. I could feel him looking at me as I kept my eyes locked on Roberto and Wendy. They were the center of my focus: I couldn't bear to see Roberto holding Wendy in his arms as my heart—no, THE heart, or was it HER heart?—pounded.

Dwight looked at something else finally. He wasn't reacting, so I made myself look away from the awful reunion and chanced a direct glimpse at him. It seemed he was having a revelation. His brow wrinkled for a moment, and then he looked right at me and started toward me. I wanted to run.

Wendy's circle of friends parted so Dwight could make his way to me. I stood my ground, waiting for the worst. For Daddy's sake.

"Vivian?" he said. "You're Vivian, right? From the hospital."

"I remember you," I said, managing what I hoped was a frosty tone.

"Maybe you can help me," he said. "That heart that got transplanted out of my, my… my girlfriend? It was put in Kelly Williams, and she's supposed to meet us here tonight. Except that I don't know what she looks like. Would you mind taking a look around the room and see if she's here?"

"Look, I don't think I can be much help to you," I said. He furrowed his brows, looking like he'd once again expected more than he deserved.

I was grateful that he'd gotten my identity wrong. I thought maybe I could get some information about Daddy from him, so I decided I'd try to lighten up a little bit and engage him.

"I never saw her there and I haven't seen the news photos of her, so—sorry."

"Okay. Say, have you seen a girl with a white flower in her hair?" he asked.

"Sorry. No again. Wish I could help. So, you're with robot girl?"

He tilted his head as he looked right at me. Something new had occurred to him.

Dwight locked gazes with me, as if he'd been desperate to share something with someone, with anyone…

"I made her."

"Wow," I said after much too long a pause. "That's…quite an accomplishment. You built that roll cage?"

"Roll cage, eh?" he said. "You know something about cars?"

More than I'd first realized. If Daddy was nearby, he might be in Dwight's car or van. If I could just get there first, I thought.

"My dad has a muscle car," I offered. "He talks about them a lot. I know his biggest motor is a 455. Or it started that small."

He looked away. "That's great." He didn't like hearing from a woman whose motor was bigger than his.

"Do you have something like that?" I asked.

"I've got an okay Pontiac Le Mans with the 400 CDI."

"Horsepower?"

"Three hundred thirty," he answered. "1968." It sounded like he felt vindicated of something. I saw my opportunity with him.

"Hey cool. That's totally a GTO."

He lit up. "That's what I'm saying! Only the body is different. Engine, chassis, frame, suspension, tranny...exact same parts."

He'd just told me Daddy was in a 1968 Pontiac Le Mans, out there in the parking lot. I felt a tap on my shoulder.

"You're that reporter lady, right? Kelly?" Rose had seen me. "That is you, isn't it?" She took a few steps to get next to me. "Thanks so much for saving Roberto from those crazy delivery guys."

Dwight noticed.

"You're Kelly?" he asked.

My anonymity was gone. The angry heart—a distraction while I'd played for Dwight's confidence—now said, "hit the bastard."

It turns out I must have hit him, because what I saw next was Dwight staggering backwards and falling flat on his back next to Wendy and Roberto. He looked unconscious. Wendy looked at me and then back at Dwight, who was coming to. He was massaging his jaw, trying to puzzle out how to return it to its normal position. I felt a stinging sensation on my right palm, confirming that I was the origin of his discomfort.

Wendy was looking at me again. She had to suspect who I was. I guessed this because my heartbeat slowed a little, thumping like it was gathering its energy to do something. I saw anger on her face.

I slid my hand into my cleavage and retrieved the white flower. Placing it over my right ear, I gave her what I hoped was a look of defiance. My heart raced as she charged me. She took a few quick steps and leaped at me, aiming for my belly, but she missed me entirely. I'd leaped up, catching the scaffolding of the elevated walkway overhead. Wendy landed flat on her face, the metal rods at her waist clicking and scraping on the floor. A small remote control she'd been holding in her hand tumbled a few feet away.

I was still hanging from the scaffolding by my fingers. As a kid I couldn't make it across the monkey bars, but here I was, locked onto the metal structure, surveying the dance floor and marveling at how far above the floor I'd gotten. Wendy was still flopping around on the floor, trying to find the right orientation so she could stand up. My hands hadn't tired, and then I understood. It was nighttime and I was strong at night.

I turned around by reversing my hands so I could watch what was happening. Roberto was at Wendy's side, helping her roll onto her back. He offered her a hand to pull her up. As she rose, I noticed her grace and how Roberto blended his strength with hers. Any questions I had about his character disappeared. His first instinct was to be helpful and proactive. It hurt to see that excellent nature focused on the beast I'd seen feasting on my father.

Roberto picked up the dropped remote and returned it to Wendy. She was arched a little too far back, but once she had the box in her hand, the metal bars on her belly contracted to fix her posture. Roberto escorted Wendy back the way they'd come. They stopped just underneath me, Dwight joining them.

"Kelly?" Roberto called out.

"Bitch!" Wendy screamed. "She's got my heart." She tried to jump and grab me, but got her coordination wrong, arching backward but catching herself before falling. I didn't wait to give her another try. Hand over hand I pulled myself up the metal scaffolding and threw my leg over the railing. A couple of young men helped me over. They weren't necessary. I was strong.

"Wow," one said, "robot chick is mad at you!"

"Or she's in love with you," the other said.

"She doesn't mean what you think she means," I said, scrambling toward the stairway near the front of the club. I thought maybe at last I might get police help.

At the bottom of the stairs, I looked back, expecting the three of them to be following me. They'd gained the attention of a bouncer. I hustled to the exit. "No reentry," female linebacker said as I passed through her security check area.

"No problem. What I need isn't in there. I do need my cross back." I gave her my claim check. She was back in a few seconds, smacking the wooden icon against the palm of her hand.

"How do you use this, Hon?" she asked me. My assumption was that she meant "as a weapon."

"I'm not sure. I'm going to need to learn fast."

Once outside I went over to where I'd last seen the police officer, and then around the 55th Street side, lit by the club's animated neon. No sign of him. I continued around the building.

ROBERTO

An immense man walked up to us. His bearing made me believe he was a bouncer.

"What seems to be the problem here, folks?" he said. He'd decided already that we were the problem judging by his tone. The crowd that had circled us in the middle of the dance floor reassembled around us. Wendy's spectacular dive and Kelly's leap upward to almost twice her height had startled several witnesses.

I looked just below the bouncer's right eye, let go of myself and imagined I was his best friend ever. It was my sole reason for existing to get him to understand, for his own good, that he needed to know something.

"Shouldn't you do something about those guys who dragged that woman up there?" I asked him. I pointed at the two guys who had helped Kelly over the railing. "You can't let them do that again."

It worked. He looked where Kelly had climbed over the railing. His problem had moved to the balcony, and he was on his way to deal with it. He headed for the stairs at the back of the club, intent on the two troublemakers I'd invented for him. It was his good fortune he was suggestible: if we'd ended up struggling, I would have bitten him. Lots of blood in him, and servings to spare. Dining in public is a bad idea, though. It draws unwanted attention, if not interference.

"Let's go find Kelly," I said to Wendy and the guy with her. "Who is this anyway?" I asked. I'd seen him before, but he hadn't seen me.

"I'm Dwight," he answered. His voice sounded a little frayed, like he was quite tired. I sensed that his blood had been drained—but not completely. Wendy had been feasting on him was my guess.

"Dwight took care of me when you didn't show up," Wendy said.

Again with the accusations. My beloved—my partner for all eternity—was all over me like I'd cheated on her. I'd expected a warmer greeting, but she was on my case instantly. I had done what I'd promised and been where I said I'd be on time. Sure, something had gone wrong, but I wasn't the cause, and Wendy was trying to shame me for not being the cure.

I started for the club's front door where Kelly had gone. Wendy's gaggle of friends stood aside. Wendy and Dwight followed.

"Don't you want to know what happened to me?" Wendy demanded as we neared the club entrance. I mustered what calm I could. Between being hungry and being harangued I was irritable.

I looked around us and said, "Let's get outside where we can be away from human eyes and ears, okay?" Dwight's face grew even paler, but he followed me and Wendy out the door. The company of two vampires was unnerving him. It was new for me too. I was impressed he chose to stay with us. That took real courage. He trailed Wendy and me out the door as the body-builder guy stood back. "No reentry," he said as I passed. He sounded relieved.

I led them to the edge of the parking lot, at the side of the club. Kelly was still near—I felt that pulse that had drawn me to her hospital room a few nights ago—but I didn't see her. Perhaps she was around the other corner of the club?

"Wendy, look," I said. "I'm sorry I couldn't find you, but we both know this didn't go as planned. I heard some of what happened to you. I didn't know what to expect. It's good to see that you're getting around. How are you?"

Wendy gave me the predator stare. There was a big problem with me, and I was about to hear about it.

"I woke up in a burning box, damn it!" Wendy said, taking off the black glove to show me her left hand. The bones were exposed on her fingertips and thumb, revealing knots of scarred flesh encasing her knuckles. I was repelled, and she noticed. She put the glove back on.

"Wicked stepsister screwed me over. Bitch canceled my funeral, pocketed the refund, and signed some papers to get me cremated. She let them gut me like a fish. They took out my heart, my kidneys, my...what else, Dwight?" She looked at her exhausted companion.

"Right and right. They also got her liver and pancreas. She's got most of it back, though."

He'd put them back. That's what I thought he was going to tell me.

"You rebuilt her?" I asked Dwight. "What's with the metalwork?"

"Do you realize I'm standing right here?" Wendy said. "Don't talk about me like I'm a shop project."

I had to sort through a lot right then. In three minutes, I'd learned more about vampire physiology than I'd ever dreamed. Wendy's friend Dwight knew more than anyone, maybe even Jack. I had so many questions.

But I was also understanding that Wendy was feeling neglected. Where was our connection? I sensed Kelly, who was somewhere out of sight, but not Wendy who was standing next to me.

"Sorry. You're right," I said. "How are you? What do you need?"

"Well, okay," she said. She let her head tilt down a little. "It was really messed up, but Dwight helped me."

"Were you afraid you weren't going to make it?"

"Not that. I was afraid of never being whole again, just winding down and down slower until I'm paralyzed meat with a thirst. What if that's forever? That'd be hell."

"He helped you out?" I asked, indicating Dwight. Despite his valuable knowledge, I was tempted by the nearness of someone with blood flowing in his arteries.

"He made everything work," Wendy said. "He got my parts back—except for the heart—and sewed me up and helped me stand straight again. Did you see how I can move now?" Her sudden brightening took me off guard. She'd become instantly happy.

She took a step back and struck a cocked-hip dancer's pose, the metal rods whirring and whining as they adjusted the tilt of her rib cage. She offset the movement of her ribs by tilting her head and angling her arms all around her. I saw that her right hand was closed around the gadget she'd dropped on the dance floor. As she squeezed and kneaded the object, her metal rods extended and retracted.

"And what is that?" I said, pointing to the black band running down the center of her belly. It was stitched to her skin.

"Zipper," Wendy announced. "I didn't heal up there, so this keeps everything in place. I thought we were supposed to heal from any injury. Why didn't that work?"

"It's because you return to the state you were in when you awoke," Dwight said. "When you woke up in that burning box, that was your baseline state. Count Darkness here must have been in better shape when he woke up." He was referring to me.

"What should I do, Roberto?" Wendy asked. "How do we fix this?"

I didn't agree that something needed fixing. Wendy was at least as much enchanted with her tricked-out body as she was perturbed by the absence of her heart. There she was, three days into her new life, and getting around fairly well. She moved quickly and looked powerful. My mind was full

256

of questions—there were things about being a vampire I didn't understand. This Dwight guy knew more about us than we did.

"Tell me what you did," I asked Dwight.

"I had to improvise. When I found her, she was a bloody mess. First, we duct-taped her, but we kept having to redo it. She was much weaker but still quite, uh, aggressive. We worked all night to get her stabilized."

"Who's 'we'?" I asked.

"My buddy Tanner was helping me. Brilliant guy, but in a sort of out-there kind of way, you know? Anyway, he's still in the hospital. Wendy nearly sucked him dry. So, it works out that you don't have to have vampire parts exactly right. You just need to do something enough like it. I've got a fish tank pump hooked up inside her, moving the blood around."

"That works?" I asked, and Dwight nodded yes. "What keeps it running?"

"Rechargeable NiCad batteries. There's a recharging cable tucked into her—it's under her waistband."

"You look like you've been feeding her too, pal." I turned my attention to Wendy. "So, you've fed on three people in three days. That's a lot. Even worse, you nearly killed one of them."

"What are you saying?" She asked. "That I'm not supposed to eat?" Her defiance melted as she added, "I guess. Actually, there's been four."

I had forgotten about the crematorium worker. He too had just barely survived. Wendy had fed on Dwight, his buddy Tanner, the crematorium worker, and Mr. Williams. She should have been blood drunk.

"Remember when I transitioned you, how spaced out and angry I was when you were about to die? Have you had that feeling, you know, or behaved impulsively since you woke up?"

I was surprised by her amused smile. "No more than usual," she answered. "But the answer you're looking for is that most of the blood I've drunk has leaked out of me. Dwight did more work on me last night. With that plus the zipper I'm finally keeping it in. I don't need to drink as much."

Those last few words set me off. I had to feed, and I wouldn't need to compete with her. Wendy's was the last blood I'd had to drink. I was two days overdue, and my next meal was right in front of me.

DWIGHT

"So good of you to help us out, Dwight," Roberto said to me. He was no longer listening to Wendy. "You've done incredible work, selfless work, and I hope you'll get some satisfaction looking back on what you've accomplished. You do feel good about it, don't you?"

"Yes," I answered. Roberto was so right. I had done hard, selfless work to take care of Wendy. It was so nice he'd noticed and said something. "Yes, I do. I like to help." It felt good to be recognized.

"You've even fed her a few times," he said. "I hope it didn't hurt too bad." Roberto was grateful. "I want you to know I'm grateful."

How odd it felt that he said the word I'd just thought, but grateful was a good word. I might have expected him to feel that way, but I hadn't expected to hear it. "It's not that bad. She makes it kind of pleasant."

"She was in good hands, Dwight. You took her in, cared for her, fed and clothed her, and took her where she needed to go. You've done well by her." He took a step toward me, offering his hand. We were going to shake hands. I would accept his thanks.

Wendy stepped between us, pushing Roberto's hand aside.

"Run, Dwight. Now! He's going to bite you."

In vampire time, it must have taken an eternity for me to work out what was happening. That "run" order was excellent advice. In human time, it felt slow too. Wendy's words and action took Roberto off his plan. She'd held onto his arm, buying me time to get away. I ran for the back of the building where I'd left my car. I was already stressed about my blood loss. Roberto wouldn't be making me feel any better.

"You're not biting my geek," I heard Wendy saying as I recovered from running in my run-down state. I was light-headed. I saw stars. I was breathing hard by the time I came around the back corner of the building. A last

259

glimpse told me Roberto hadn't started after me. I hoped I could get back inside my car before he caught me. I worried he might be fast. Wendy often moved faster than I could follow.

As I rounded the corner, I saw my car had been moved. Then I realized it was still moving. Vivian—no, Kelly—was between my car and the wall, pushing with her back low against the rear bumper. The tires were squealing in protest from being forced across tarmac. I was barely able to roll my car when it was in neutral, let alone push it across the pavement with its brakes on. It became clear to me that I was one of the few there without superhero strength. About eight feet out from the wall Kelly stopped pushing. Smoke rose from all four tires.

"Daddy? Are you okay?" She was shouting at my trunk. She knew Old Dude was in there. I heard his muffled voice. Kelly saw me coming.

"Wow. Hi Dwight," she said. "Nice car. You said this was a 1968 Pontiac LeMans, right?" She was looking at me like a boxer watching her opponent. At least she didn't look like she wanted to bite me, but she might have been ready to tear my head off.

I nodded yes to her question. I'd already told her when we were inside.

"Yes," Kelly said to my trunk. "'68".

The rumble of the music from the club masked the sound of Roberto and Wendy's arrival. As they came around the corner, Wendy was still holding Roberto's arm. I backed up toward Kelly and my car.

"Leave him alone!" Wendy was shouting at Roberto, who had spotted me. His eyes told me he was seeing a vampire happy meal. I really didn't want to become a vampire myself, but a few more donations might get me membership in the club.

The trunk of my car opened with a pop and the screeching of ungreased hinges. I looked in to see Old Dude kneeling in there, his hands behind his back where the latch connected inside. He started climbing out. Kelly came to his side and helped him. She quickly untied the rope around his wrists.

"Daddy," she said. "Oh, thank God."

Kelly didn't notice it, but I saw Wendy and Roberto both freeze for a second when she said the "G word."

"There he is," Wendy said, pointing at Old Dude, still restraining Roberto with her other hand. "He's fresh and nearly full. And he tastes really good. Dwight, step out of the way."

I'll never forget the look on Wendy's face. She was talking right to me, straight from the heart. The only thing that mattered to her then was getting me out of Roberto's way. I had the same goal.

A blur of movement started from where Roberto had been standing. I was no longer between him and his target. He blew past me, snared Old Dude with an arm around the waist, and ran off with him to the far end of the parking lot. It looked like he was going to vault the chain link fence at the back of the parking lot. He stopped at the last possible moment. Kelly started running toward them. As she ran, she pulled a white cross-shaped object from her belt and held it in front of her.

"Smack!" Old Dude had punched Roberto in the head, causing him to sway from the impact. New tally: I was the only one without any physical power. Even Old Dude was dangerous. I was lucky he hadn't taken me out when he tripped me in my basement.

Roberto tangled himself around Old Dude from behind, his right leg somehow coiled around Old Dude's right leg. Roberto had locked Old Dude's left arm out straight and was about to sink his fangs into the exposed elbow joint.

"In the name of God, let him go!" Kelly said. Roberto dropped Old Dude and flattened himself back against the fence. Kelly helped her dad back to his feet, still holding the cross aimed at Roberto. His head was turned to the side, his face twisted with pain and his eyes shut hard.

A cold hand closed around my arm. Wendy pressed against my side as we watched Kelly hug her dad. I was dazed by the horrible thing I'd done, kidnapping that amazing man and causing someone the panic and worry I'd caused Kelly.

"I'm sorry," I heard Roberto saying. "I was about to take some from Dwight, but they made him the easier target. I'm sorry. I'm just so thirsty. Please, you can put that down. I'll be okay."

"Are you okay, Dwight?" Wendy asked. "Somehow I felt his attack coming while he was chatting you up. I won't let you lose any more blood."

"Roberto seems to be under control again," I said. "Did you feel what happened with Kelly and the cross?"

"How could you not see it?" Wendy said. "When she spoke, it lit up like daytime. It's still too bright to look at directly."

"I don't see any light," I told her. "This must be like a citronella candle for vampires." With Wendy at my side, I was feeling courageous. Roberto had proven to be useless, and I was going to show her again how I was the one pulling for her.

"Let's finish this," I said to her. She looked up at me, with a look I think said "It's your show."

"Kelly," I shouted.

The cross still aimed toward Roberto, she turned her head to look at me. Old Dude was walking off a leg cramp. He was also massaging the fist that had stunned Roberto.

"You have something that doesn't belong to you," I shouted. "You've got your dad back, right? Do the right thing."

Kelly spoke to her dad for a moment. He came to her and accepted the cross from her. She began walking back toward me while he held it toward Roberto. He was backing away, coming back toward my car. Kelly was almost there.

KELLY

Daddy had it sorted immediately. I'd given him the cross so he could protect himself from Roberto. Daddy had had most of a day to observe and experience the workings of the bizarre reality I was living in. He was ready.

Though Dwight had lost control of Daddy's hostage situation, I'd come to the club believing that I would have to pay a price. Ever since the heart had shut itself into my chest and proclaimed its intention to stay there, I'd hoped that somehow it would remain—though I knew it wasn't mine. I was looking at the woman it belonged to.

Dwight had called me out. Time was up. As I approached his car, he came forward to meet me.

"I'd supposed this was about the heart," I said.

"You supposed right," he said. "You have no right to it. It was never supposed to have been taken." Wendy was watching me from a few steps away. I noticed that, though it was her heart that was stolen, she was letting Dwight manage the situation.

"I've got to ask, how can she be doing this well with all those organs missing?"

"I fixed her up," Dwight said. "I put in an aquarium pump to cover for her missing heart. Runs on rechargeable batteries. I closed up the leaky abdomen with a plastic zipper. The other organs I got back from the hospital and re-installed myself. And check this out," he said, pointing to the metal bar bolted to her hip and rib-cage. "My buddy Tanner and I came up with this."

"I'm guessing they didn't just hand the organs back to you?" I asked.

"No, everything had been transplanted to other people already. It took a few trips," he said, "but I was able to get almost everything back."

Dwight was as dangerous as I'd thought. He was a kidney thief and freelance night surgeon. How many corpses had he left in his wake in his quest to restore Wendy? And why was he doing this? She and Roberto were supposedly the reunited couple, yet Wendy was clinging to Dwight's arm like they were that couple.

Dwight looked desperately weak, but he continued to be a presence.

Nevertheless, he'd certainly done one thing wrong.

I hit him in the face with the heel of my palm, like I did inside the club. Dwight ricocheted off the passenger side of his car and landed on his hands and knees on the pavement, losing his grip on a silver-and-black gadget like the one Wendy held.

"That's for kidnapping Daddy," I said.

Wendy tackled me. My heart had ramped up as I saw her begin to move. The next thing I knew I was on the ground with her sitting on my stomach, her left hand holding my neck to the ground. I suddenly remembered how much I like air.

"No hitting my geek," she yelled at me, so loud they must have heard it in the club.

"Kt… Kt…" I tried to say. I was desperate for air. My effort to speak somehow triggered something in her. She released my neck and moved her left hand down to rest over my collarbones. I was gasping, still breathless.

She set her gadget on the ground and shook loose the glove on her left hand. Her hand was a network of scars, tipped with bare bones on the middle three fingers and thumb. She hooked her index finger inside the collar of my blouse, and tore straight down, exposing the scarred centerline of my chest. I'd been trying to grab and hold her arms, but I couldn't match her strength. I grabbed the tattered fabric of my blouse and tried to pull it closed again.

"Time to give it back, thief," Wendy said. She held her left hand flat, the three bony fingertips clustered in line like a chisel tip. She cocked her arm back, preparing to stab it into my chest. I felt her excitement growing, my heartbeat speeding up in synchronization with her words and actions.

"Grunch. Grunch." The tips of my ribs twisted around and down and up, ripping the skin on my chest from the inside. My heart contracted into a knot in my chest, yanking and pulling inside me. It was cramping like a bad charley horse. It didn't want to go. Wendy stayed her thrust, fascinated by the horrific tableau on my chest and maybe by my moans and grunts of pain.

"Wow, girl, your cleavage is a hazardous waste site," Wendy said, marveling at the grisly scene below her. I didn't think much of the zipper sewn into her chest either but saying that would not have helped my situation.

"Wendy, wait," Roberto said.

I saw Roberto now standing nearby. Daddy was closer still, holding the cross. Roberto was staying back.

"Wendy," Roberto said. "I don't know what to do about this, but you're sitting on a good person who deserves to live. You look okay—quite okay really. Are you going to be better off with her dead?"

ROBERTO

"You've been with her all this time, haven't you?" Wendy said to me. "You've been just a few inches away from my stolen heart all this time."

"I didn't know until an hour ago," I said. "I know our plan went off course, but couldn't you have found a way to get in touch with me?"

"I don't recall you having a cell phone. You said it was over your budget, and you had no place to receive bills."

"CAN I SAY SOMETHING?" Kelly yelled. She was looking right up at Wendy.

"You're right," Kelly said to her. "It's not my heart. It's not my fault it ended up in me. I guess—maybe it's not mine to keep. Daddy?"

"Yes, Kitten?"

"Your car is in the next row over," she said. "The spare key is where you'd expect to find it. Please leave now and stay far away from these people. Please. I've been on borrowed time, and that's over. Please, just go."

"Sorry, Kitten," her father said. "I'm not into protecting my own hide first. Anyway, this cross seems reliable."

"Wendy," I said. "Do you really need to do this? How do you feel right now?"

"I'm angry, Roberto. You neglected me. And you've betrayed me."

"But you're healthy?" I asked. "You have undead strength and speed now, don't you?" While she was holding my arm to prevent my attack on Dwight, I'd realized she was stronger than me. Her grip was like iron.

"This bitch is way stronger than her old man," Wendy said. Kelly was struggling underneath her. "But you can see she's not going anywhere now. Not with my heart still in her chest."

"But why do you need it?" I asked. "Are you in pain?"

"But it isn't hers, it's mine. It's just not fair. Nothing went like it was supposed to." Her voice quavered. I'd never heard that before. "I was gutted like a fish and burned up in a box. And now it's clear to me. You're all about Kelly now. You don't want me now, do you?"

"And I'm supposed to think you weren't enjoying Dwight's attention? He saved you, hot-rodded you, and you're hanging it all out there like a badge of honor. Look at how you're dressed. What were you thinking? You can't have an existence out in the open like this. I told you about CG. They've probably got teams on the way here already."

"Where is my heart, Roberto?" She aimed her bone chisel at Kelly's chest. "It's right here, isn't it?" Kelly crossed her arms entirely over her chest in an attempt at defense.

With her right hand, Wendy seized Kelly's throat. Kelly grabbed the choking arm with both hands. Wendy used her free hand to drag Kelly's right arm down, pinning it against her side with a knee. Kelly struggled but failed to free it. Switching the hand on Kelly's throat, Wendy trapped the other arm. She pressed Kelly's chin back with her right hand and poised the bony fingers on the left at the middle of Kelly's chest. She was deciding where to go dig.

"Okay, that's enough," Dwight said.

Wendy froze. Her face turned dark red.

DWIGHT

Wendy stiffened. Her face, neck and arms puffed up, turning blackish red. Air whistled out of her mouth as the metal rods at her waist tilted her to her left. She fell off Kelly, rolling onto the pavement. Except for her shivering, Wendy looked frozen.

"What?" Kelly asked as she scrambled away, massaging her throat with one hand, the other pulling the tatters of her blouse closed over her bloodied chest. Old Dude stepped next to her to support her.

"I switched her off," I said. I held up my remote. "I keep a spare. I just had to get it back from under that car. Anyway, I just put her in reverse." I clicked a red button on my remote and the indicator light went from green to amber. Wendy went limp.

"There. That's off—well, standby actually."

Old Dude looked over towards Kelly, who looked equally concerned with him. He was still holding the cross between them and Roberto, who was keeping his distance. Roberto was about eight yards away.

"Wendy, I can't let you do that." I flicked the switches that set her heart and kidney pumps to their normal operating direction. "Look, I hate what happened to you. You always seemed perfect to me, and then this happened."

"You did?" she asked. "You must think I'm gross now."

"No, I think you're something better than perfect. You're unprecedented and amazing. You totally fascinate me. More than ever. And you like funk."

"Oh, Dwight, I can't believe I'm hearing you say that. You never gave me any hint. Oh G…" Her voice choked. "Oh, Mother Gaea. Dwight, I love you."

"Wow. Wendy, that's so…So can you let them go?" I asked. "I'll keep you running—but you've got to promise not to ever bite Tanner again."

269

Wendy looked over to Roberto, looking for his reaction.

"Okay. Yes, I love Kelly," Roberto said to Wendy. He looked across the gap to where Kelly was standing with her arm around Old Dude, still brandishing the cross. "In my life—and in this unlife—there's been only one time where I felt so connected to someone. I thought it would never happen again, so..."

"So, you settled for me," Wendy finished for him. "You're so noble."

"I planned to do the right thing all along, but who could've seen this coming?" Roberto asked.

Roberto turned to Kelly. "You...are the light of my existence. I love you. Yes, I'm torn up with thirst, but I swear to you I'll go a hundred nights more this way rather than inflict myself on someone dear to you. Please forgive me, Mr. Williams—I'm sorry."

"Roberto, I love you," Kelly said. "I don't know what else to say."

"That's rare," Roberto said. He smiled at her.

"I want you to be part of my life," Roberto said. "I just can't imagine how it can work." He turned his attention back to Wendy.

"Look," Roberto said to Wendy. "If you can make it work without killing Kelly, I'm all for it. Short of that, you're facing me, a tough old guy with his wooden mallet set on high beams, and a surprisingly strong woman. Maybe we should each just back off and go our own ways."

Wendy fixed her gaze on Roberto. "Well, I hope you'll be happy—if that's what you want," she said. "Anyway, I'm not what you want, am I?"

"You rescued me from a miserable existence," he said. "You appeared and for the first time in two years I thought of the nights to come with hope. We'd be companions and soulmates. But then my heart led me to Kelly, and she is..."

"Alright, alright," I said. All eyes were on me. I continued.

"No one is ripping out any hearts or carrying people off to feed on them, right? Good." No one arguing with me, but Wendy was still focused on Kelly's chest.

"Wendy, stay with me," I said. "I'll take care of you. I…I love you. I have for years. Please—let this go." I felt like I should kneel and offer her a ring. I thought I saw her face brighten.

"Oh, Dwight, that's so perfect," Wendy said. "I want to be with you, too." She turned to Kelly. "Okay then. Maybe we should have a truce."

"Okay by me," Kelly said. She was massaging her throat. "That's incredibly good of you."

"Thanks. Okay," Wendy said. "So, the heart is yours—at least for now."

Kelly's eyes went wide.

KELLY

I was feeling the measured, composed rhythm of Wendy's heart as we spoke. I felt it beating with the compassion I detected in her voice. Then she said this:

"...the heart is yours..."

And just like that the heart was beating for me. It sped up as I began realizing what had just happened. It was that same shift of rhythm that happened when Wendy went to sleep for the day, but it was still nighttime. I felt whole. I was amazed by Wendy's act. I wondered, did she just feel the loss of what I'd gained?

My eyes welled up. I'd done so well staying focused and disciplined in order to get to my father. I'd kept it together. Now he was here, and he was out of danger, and the heart I'd hoped for was beating in my chest. Daddy wrapped his arms around me as I shook with emotion.

He reluctantly accepted my assurances that the bone dance he'd seen on my chest wasn't entirely unusual in my life, and that I would be okay again at the next sunset, despite what he'd witnessed.

"Come on, Kitten. I've got a jacket in the Oldsmobile that'll cover this catastrophe. That's a shame. You looked great in that blouse." He walked me over to his car. Freshly adorned in another shiny blue NASCAR jacket, Daddy and I rejoined Dwight, Wendy, and Roberto, who were next to Dwight's almost GTO.

Dwight had unlocked his Le Mans and put it in neutral at my request. Why waste gas? With Dwight in the driver's seat, I pushed it back into its parking space—with one hand. The four of us sat in the car while Daddy waited in his Oldsmobile.

I'd assumed Dwight and Wendy would leave together, but she insisted she would rejoin her friends waiting in the club. She'd listened politely to

Roberto and me as we explained what had happened to us with Continental Grid over the past few days, but I soon saw her eyes glaze over. We weren't getting to her.

Roberto repeated the story about how he'd been killed to be revived as an undead resistance fighter. Jack Murphy had proclaimed that CG was a menace to the undead.

"What have they done that's actually bad?" Dwight asked. Despite his geekish demeanor, his intelligence and ingenuity were readily on display.

"I still think Jack may have gotten it wrong," Roberto said, "and I was sure he was unhinged. There's no hiding being blood drunk. Honestly, I've behaved no better than that since I was transitioned. Jack claimed he was organizing resistance against CG and believed one of his co-conspirators must have been snatched by them. That was his hidden motivation when he'd tricked me into going with him to the abandoned building where he killed me. He needed others with undead strength to take on CG and liberate the missing vampires. Of course, my chief concern was getting away from Jack before he killed me, so I wasn't as good a student as I should have been. Of course, I didn't get away."

"Couldn't it be that you've got Continental Grid all wrong?" Dwight said. "I've let Wendy drink four times, and I still haven't become one. You've been a vampire for two years, and you had to focus on it for three days to change Wendy. What I'm saying is there may not be that many vampires because it sounds like a lot of work to make one." Wendy was sitting next to Dwight, who was in the driver's seat of his car. She rested her head on his shoulder.

"CG clearly has something to do with vampires," I said. "I incinerated one who was part of a team that was hunting me and Roberto. When I ran into them this morning, they'd left a vampire called Dion behind in a special crate, probably so they could catch Roberto—or maybe me—and box him up in the second crate."

"How'd you incinerate this Dion guy?" Dwight asked. Wendy was now paying close attention.

"I cracked open his box in full daylight. He went up in a puff of smoke, flame, and ashes in maybe ten seconds."

"Those boxes are decked out like a coffin inside," Roberto said, "but with a whole communications and entertainment center."

"Sounds very practical," Dwight replied. "I understand you spend your day hours wrapped up in tarps under the floorboards of old buildings. A coffin might be more comfortable and a lot safer."

Again, I was cursed with the problem that had dogged me since my undead heart woke up in my chest. Either I didn't have direct proof of something, or someone in authority was more attached to an alternate theory loosely incorporating the same facts. I'd been trumped. I'd gotten that far on deduction and gut instinct, but no one else was picking up the scent.

Roberto and I repeated our admonishments, but it felt like I was a parent talking to rebellious teens. There was enough age difference between us and Dwight and Wendy, the same dynamic might have held sway.

We climbed out of the back seat to go join Daddy in his car. Dwight was going to nap in his car while Wendy went back in to join her friends at Worship.

"Dwight," Wendy said, "I need cover charge money."

Ping. Ping. He tapped one of the metal rods bolted into her hips and ribs. "No, you don't. You'll be fine. They're going to let you right in. You'll probably never pay another cover. Hey," he said after a yawn, "maybe don't feed on anyone inside the club, okay?"

"Sure" she said. I thought she'd do it right away.

"Roberto," I said as we left Dwight's car and got into the back seat of Daddy's Oldsmobile. I saw the cross sitting next to him on the front seat. Roberto probably didn't see it because he gotten into the seat behind Daddy.

"Yes, Kelly?" he said while closing the door.

"If CG is what we think they are, they'll be swarming all over Springfield soon. Even if it isn't Mr. Black, someone else will investigate. That's at least one more van with a vampire priest and handler, with hi-tech tracking devices and undead technology we don't understand."

"There's a lot to call attention to Springfield now," Roberto said. "I'd stayed out of sight, being cautious like Jack said was wise. Now CG has me as one of their OTGs, and they've got questions about you too. Mr. Black thinks you're some sort of vampire. Add to that Wendy showing herself in public, proclaiming herself as robot-assisted queen of the undead. They should be on their way back now. It'll be likely tomorrow night, and a certainty in a week."

"Daddy?" I asked. His eyes looked a little unfocused. "I'm sorry. This must be so confusing."

"No, Kitten." His gaze sharpened. "It's too damn clear. When you were suddenly up and around and begging to go running, anyone else getting a transplant would be begging for more morphine. I knew it wasn't natural then."

"Mr. Williams," Roberto said. "I'm terribly sorry. I apologize if I hurt you when I grabbed you before."

"That was not welcome," Daddy said. "I'm still in knots from hours in the stinky trunk of that Le Mans. I could have figured out the trunk latch by touch, but my hands were tied. Say, this cross works quite well, doesn't it?" he said, nodding his head towards the seat. He was keeping Roberto on notice of his readiness. Roberto leaned away.

"Please, I can't bear it. I promise you, you won't need to use it. I was about to feed on Dwight, but Wendy helped him get away. Then she recommended you..."

"There's never a good excuse for attacking someone, Bert."

"No, Mr. Williams," Roberto said. "You're right. There isn't. By the way, I prefer to be called Roberto."

"I like his name, Daddy," I said, hoping to head off some of his generation's male bonding and hazing rituals. He studied my face.

"You have feelings for him, Kitten?"

Once again, I was left with my gut to trust. I wanted Daddy to understand my love for and connection to Roberto. Still, I'd seen Roberto's attack on Daddy. I reminded myself I had teased Roberto with a foiled opportunity to feed many hours earlier. I'd had him doing the vampire equivalent of chewing tree bark when I gave him the steak tip juice. All I'd ever seen him do is the right thing, or he'd try to do whatever I asked him.

"Yes, Daddy. I love him." I reached for Roberto and drew his face to mine. An instant touch of cold melted away as our lips met. Though more restrained than our earlier kiss, we were unable to separate ourselves for a long time.

"Wow, Kitten," Daddy said. "Look what happened to his face. He's got some color. Did he take blood from you just then?"

"No, just the effect I have on men," I said. "Or at least this man. Anyway, we don't think he can drink from me."

"I will need some soon," Roberto said.

"Then let's try again," I said as I pulled up my left sleeve, gathering the shiny blue fabric on my upper arm to expose my elbow. I held my arm out in front of Roberto. He cradled it like he was holding a baby. He inclined his head towards my offering.

"Aw hell no," Daddy said, snatching the cross off the seat and holding it up. Roberto slammed back against the seat, releasing my arm. He was pressed against the door and trying to slide down onto the floor.

"No, no! Please!" I said. I grabbed the top and the bottom of the cross and ripped it out of Daddy's hands. I hated using my strength against him. I put it back down on the front seat within Daddy's reach. "Roberto, you can get up."

"Thanks. That's just so awful," Roberto said. "I remember I once loved it. Now I can't bear to look at it."

"Daddy, listen. He's got to feed somehow. It's not his fault he's like this. He was given no choice. He'll be a danger to himself and others if he doesn't. You've got to let him try. I trust him." At that moment, I knew that I did. Despite the horrid things vampirism made him do, the person animating the vampire was a good one, always proposing to do what was moral and responsible.

Adjusting my sleeve again, I offered Roberto my arm. He took it gently and brought his mouth to my elbow. He kissed the skin and backed away.

"No use," he said. "My fangs won't descend. I simply cannot do anything that harms you."

"You've got fangs, eh?" Daddy said. Roberto released my arm.

"They're up in here." He opened his mouth wide and pointed inside. The fangs curled down and took their customary position.

"Dear Lord!" Daddy said. "Like a timber rattler." He edged his hand closer to the cross on the seat. Roberto flinched with the word "Lord." Daddy saw his reaction.

"Now they come out?" I asked.

"I really don't like admitting how well protected you are from me," Roberto said. "You'll take advantage of me for sure."

"Get used to it," I said.

"So, what are you going to do?" Daddy asked. "Kitten, you've still got the hospital in an uproar, and if I understand this, Bert here—and probably you—are in the crosshairs of some vampire bounty hunters or the like. After spending some quality time with Fish Boy and Robot Girl, I'm thinking they will attract all the wrong kind of attention. You're probably better off getting away from here, Bert."

"Please, I prefer Roberto. And you're right, I don't see any other choice."

"I think I've got to leave with him, Daddy. If he hadn't created an undead heart, I might be dead by now. And it connects me to him. It's like our hearts have a walkie-talkie. Also, CG was interested in me, even before they knew that Roberto existed. They'll be getting details about all of us from the staff at Morty Coil's. They inspect corpses for possible vampires. We should hit the road, probably tonight."

"You trust him?" Daddy asked.

"Yes. I know it hasn't been long, but I can feel it. We're in this together."

"We better get you two organized then," Daddy said. He started rolling up the shirtsleeve of his right arm. "But first, let's secure this loose cannon."

Daddy laid his right arm over the backrest of the front seat where Roberto had access to it.

"Can I trust you, Bert?"

"Please, I prefer…"

"Yeah, I know. Bert is too informal, but if I'm offering an artery, it should be to someone I'm comfortable with. You good with that, Bert?"

"Yes, sir. Yes, I'm sorry. I'm fighting to control myself, but I'm managing. Thanks for your great kindness. I swear I will not harm you."

"Go ahead, then, son. Let's get you settled."

Roberto hesitated a moment, closing his eyes and mouthing something to serve as a blessing. Red-flecked tears leaked from Roberto's eyes as he gently leaned into Daddy's arm.

EPILOGUE
KELLY

We were hoping to settle down soon.

We drove east from Springfield the next night. We both thought it was inevitable that Wendy would attract CG's attention. Their agents would blanket the Springfield area. And who knew how many more Hygiene Outreach Committee members worked in funeral homes in Springfield?

After leaving the nightclub, Daddy drove us back to our neighborhood, dropping us off a few blocks away so we could take the back route to the house. He drove right down the street and noticed no unusual vehicles waiting.

We were in the house by the time he came in.

"So, Kitten," Daddy said, "you've got speed going for you too."

"It's crazy," I said. "At night I've got amazing power and speed. Then the sun comes up and I'm a mild-mannered reporter again. It's all very weird... and now I'm very tired."

Daddy stood guard while Roberto and I slept through the daylight hours.

"You know I don't feel right about this, Kitten," he said as I pulled the curtains shut in my room. Roberto wedged himself into the utility crawlspace under our kitchen. He asked for a tarp to wrap up in, so Daddy fetched him one of his fabric sports car covers. Once Roberto was settled, I tried to provide a logical argument for our deep connection but came up short. Daddy gently unwound the tension.

"Have you been getting enough rest? They recommend that for heart transplant recipients." Walking through the doorway to my room he said, "What time should I get you up?"

As requested, he woke me at five in the afternoon.

Roberto and I were given the use of a Ford Taurus station wagon that Daddy had arranged for us through a fellow muscle car hobbyist. It wasn't a Klingon Heavy Cruiser like the Oldsmobile wagon, but it was two decades newer and emphatically bland—or so it appeared. Daddy called it a "sleeper." The largest possible V8 that fit under the hood had been shoe-horned in this car as well, and an added "nitrous" canister would provide a sudden burst of acceleration for twenty or thirty seconds. Half of the trunk space had been given over to an additional gas tank. We could drive from sundown to sunup on one tank of gas, providing we drove near legal speeds. We didn't always. Though the Taurus could sustain twice the speed limit all day and night, traveling at 120 mph draws attention. Even to a Taurus. We drove closer to half that fast, dogged by our fear of Continental Grid's reach. Also, our speed, the large engine, and the multiple gas tanks rapidly consumed fifty-dollar bills.

Our favorite tactic was to travel perpendicularly to the routes where we'd see Continental Grid vans. Occasionally, we'd see convoys of the gold and brown trucks, as many as six in a row. When we saw Continental Grid vans driving north or south on I-35, for instance, we'd drive east or west on state Rt. 30.

I'm sure CG trucks were painted that way to evoke United Parcel Service, borrowing on the respect and trust people have for that service. Our illusion expired on our first night on the road. We'd see another one of their trucks about every couple hours. We stopped thinking of the trucks as cargo boxes and started recognizing them as mobile homes. Some elite caste of vampire clerics and their human handlers, quick on the draw with a cross were crisscrossing the country. With their unknown mind skills, our being anywhere near a Continental Grid vampire would be unwise. And they might be harboring a grudge against me. I'd taken one of theirs. I'd destroyed Mr. Black's beloved ward.

We talked about whether I'd done something sinful by destroying Dion. We both wanted to say no, but I felt that I had no right to end someone's existence. Unless I was not actually killing him. What if the undead had no souls? Or might it be true that, once you're dead, your soul returns to your body three days later and you reanimate? What else could cause that?

We felt like Bonnie and Clyde, like they were played in the movie: on the run and unrepentant. I was running to a new life with the man I love. My heart sped up when he said "I love you," and it was a joy to have it working just for me all the time, not only during the day. Still, I worried that my heart was on a trial separation from Wendy, and that they might reconcile later—perhaps over my dead body.

We traveled with a pre-paid disposable cell, so we'd be hard to trace. It was how I kept in touch with Daddy. Daddy started having visitors the next night after we left. He reported more CG vans than police cars were patrolling Springfield. CG began driving past our house every few hours. Daddy suspected the house had been bugged, so I never called our landline. He used a pre-paid cell too. He carried his original cell also, but I decided to leave mine behind as it was likely being traced. I believed this because I'd surrendered to the paranoia that comes along with being on the run. I didn't dare risk failing to believe. Disappearing from town and restricting contact with Daddy was the best way to let the pressure on him dissipate. It wouldn't be long before Continental Grid would be distracted by Wendy's presence in the area.

They'd be looking for her soon, and they would focus on her because of the information from the Hygiene Outreach Committee, and from Black's experiences—and injuries. They'd have Wendy identified by name within a day. Wendy was frighteningly strong, but she'd be no match for a trained team like Dion and Mr. Black. And she'd been unable to resist the power of the cross in the hands of a believer. If CG could find her, they'd take her in. No one knew what might happen next.

Roberto was a joy to travel with. We had different degrees of passion about various things like arts and entertainment, and we learned a lot about each other by challenging each other. It takes a confident man to endure such intimate probing.

We often talked, within his curse's limitations, about philosophy and religion. A matter on which we'd spent considerable time was the unfairness of the curse being visited on a murder victim. Being drained of your blood over a period of days is a frightening and disturbing journey to oblivion. The horror resumes three days later when you are revived and forced to feed on the kind you once were. Worse, your beloved family becomes your probable feeding target due to proximity. There is a core of pure evil in the curse of vampirism. It is instilled in the very substance of the reanimated creature. Therefore, I had to admit the possibility that this evil in some form resides in my undead heart. I was still sorting out how my behavior had changed after my heart transplant. What part of my new life could be attributed to a new heart? Had it changed me? I wondered which of my behaviors are manipulated by the undead entity walled up in my ribcage? These questions gnawed at me while we worked out our destination.

We first drove south, and I saw ten or twelve of their vans during ten hours of driving. Vampires were being chauffeured around in RVs for the undead. If we had already seen that many in just one state in the Midwest, might there be hundreds—maybe thousands—more? How were they all feeding? Why hadn't every man, woman, child, and dog on the continent been turned into a vampire? I had to know the answers. This became central to my growing obsession with Continental Grid. They didn't seem to be the bogeymen Jack Murphy had ranted about. They couldn't be completely benign, though. The same underpinning of evil that animates them, as well as my heart, is repelled by the divinity of a cross, particularly when it's held by a believer like Daddy. Or me. I needed to learn more about Christ and how he influenced the world.

My reading the Bible unnerved Roberto. He said it felt worse than facing a cross. Just the act of reading stirred things up. I read from a Gideon's Bible one afternoon while he lay on the floor between our two motel-room twin beds, wrapped in every possible sheet and blanket. I stood guard all day, reading, watching TV, and hungering for a data connection. I was reading the second book as the sun set. Roberto woke up moaning. He sounded like he was in pain. As I got up to go to him, I closed the Bible and set it aside. Instantly, he was better. We quickly figured out I shouldn't read it while he was awake.

Roberto and I talked about these things as we wound our way eastward, looking for that perfect place to stop and settle down. Somewhere where he could feed without drawing too much notice. Someplace outside Continental Grid's service area.

I needed to be with him, and I needed someplace where I could research Continental Grid and help Roberto—and myself—by learning about vampires. I wondered how much myth and imagination I'd have to sort through to find the truth beneath. Though physically he was far more powerful than me, I felt protective toward him. He was dangerously uninformed of the strengths and limitations of his vampiric condition, and he was now the target of a well-funded organization that fully exploited vampire skills. We needed information as much as Roberto needed blood.

I fended for both of us because I can operate during the day. Being on duty both times of day made me think about being a mother—the one condition of womanhood more exhausting than mine.

I also needed to rest and recover. I was having symptoms of anemia, which I'd had before my birth heart failed. On the road I'd been eating rare bloody steaks nearly every day, a craving that disturbed me. Was it possible my heart was consuming my own blood? Was this the parasite that eventually consumes its host? My impulse was to see a doctor, but who exactly do you go see when your story is that you have a vampire's heart? May I have a transfusion please? And a couple of pints for the road?

Most important was that I needed to understand the cross and what it stood for. Unless they were play-acting, the cross imposed a profound effect on every vampire I met. And in Daddy's hands, with the faith of his youth reinvigorated, it had trumped every vampire capability. This meant that the cross connected to something of demonstrable power. We couldn't discuss this. Even while keeping thoughts to myself, I saw he was becoming uncomfortable. I'd make myself think about V8 engines or impressionist paintings and he would relax.

We had the radio on a lot, staying with news and talk programs. There were no reports of strange attacks, so I concluded, if Roberto was taking victims to satisfy his thirst, he must have strategies that kept them quiet afterward. I was comforted that he wouldn't be killing people.

I think he may have been robbing them, though. He started having cash to pay for the gas. Daddy had given me all the cash from the hoard in the basement letting us avoid using credit cards. Roberto had been penniless when we were at Schlock House Funk. I didn't recall him taking any night jobs since then.

We'd been out on the road for four nights when we rolled onto the tail end of a massive traffic jam. We were crossing the border heading east into Massachusetts. Three lanes of traffic were being squeezed down to one. About a half-mile ahead, we saw flashing blue police lights and rows of flashing white-then-yellow lights along the tops of a line of brown vans. Three lanes of headlights stretched off into the distance leading up to the police encampment and the vans. Only five or six vehicles a minute were emerging from the traffic stop.

"Continental Grid vans," Roberto announced. I was driving at the time. "And police too. We should consider turning around."

"I agree, but we're sandwiched in the middle lane right now. By the time I can break out we'll be near the merge where the blue lights are flashing. That maneuver might attract unwanted attention."

A few minutes later the traffic picked up. Men in blaze-orange reflective vests were moving the lane-marking cones outward, releasing pressure on the merge point. We rolled along at walking pace.

It looked like our queue of vehicles was no longer under scrutiny. As we drew near the clot of police vehicles, we saw they had their hands full. Police, several men in priest's garb, and two handlers—dressed like Mr. Black—were struggling with a small group of skeleton-thin people in convict jumpsuits. Maybe a better description is they were cadavers. They moved fast like vampires, but their eyes were sunken, their skin dry like parchment. In their loose-fitting beige jumpsuits, they looked like they'd been starving.

A few car lengths later we came next to one of the cadaver things, still standing up but his arms braced on each side by two more priests. Three handlers were arrayed around the trio, each holding up a cross. The two vampires had both twisted their heads away, agony on their faces. The cadaver was shaking, convulsing like it was being electrocuted.

"Someone's near," Roberto said. He sounded anxious.

We passed another such creature that was being pinned face down on the pavement. A vampire in a black priest's garb, very much like Dion's, was kneeling on its back. He'd expertly joint-locked its arms behind it. A police officer was attempting to handcuff it, but the creature snapped at her leg each time she tried to step closer. A handler closed in, holding out a white cross—just like the one I kept under the passenger seat—which froze the creature in place while the officer finished secured its arms.

Roberto climbed into the back seat to get a better look through the window behind me. "Who is that?" he asked.

It suddenly twisted its head about, like it was trying to break its own neck. It was looking into our car. It was talking to us. I didn't hear it, but it appeared to be saying "vampires." It mouthed two other words, but I had no guess what they were.

"Just keep going," Roberto said. He sounded stunned.

We eventually passed the bottleneck, the row of police cars and five or six Continental Grid vans. Traffic was picking up speed. With all police focus behind us, I could have wound the car up to 120 mph and been in Neverland before dawn, but Roberto had something he needed to say.

"I need to talk this through with you, Kelly. I'll start by saying we're going the wrong way." I agreed. Turning around at that point would send us back through the traffic jam and the police situation behind us. We couldn't risk repeating the exposure.

"Can't change that just now," I said. "What occurred to you?"

"The things that they were capturing back there, they probably came from where we're heading right now, yes?"

I agreed.

"So, if they're able to set up a perimeter to capture those zombie-looking things and have it work solidly, well, they've got some practice at this. We're driving to where cops and CG vampires manage these cadaver things."

"So, what are the cadaver things and why are they trying to get away?"

"I don't have a good guess. We don't have the facts. Still, my gut says we stay away from there," Roberto said, "and we stop going east. There were six CG vans, and I saw at least five vampires out in the open, wrestling with the cadavers. That one on the ground recognized me as one."

"We're headed for whatever it is they were escaping from."

"Exactly my point," he said. "The direction we're going is where we might learn the most. We need to decide before we get too far in: do we find out what we're about and what Continental Grid has to do with it, and maybe find out what happened to Jack Murphy? Or do we turn our backs on the madness, making do with cow and horse blood, and you keep me warm and cozy in a granite mausoleum with a white picket fence?"

You don't want to keep going?" I asked. "You know zip about vampires, and I know less. With that kind of police action back there, we might be outmatched and outsmarted and just not know it. At least I can get around by day, so I could do some investigating. But I need to sleep sometimes."

"Sleep at night."

"And give up time with you?" I couldn't bear the idea of separation from him. "It's hard to have you—unavailable—during the day. It's not like you're at work or on a business trip. I can't call you or text you. It's like you don't exist between sunrise and sunset. I get lonely."

"I love being with you, Kelly. For me there is only night, so you're always there when I'm conscious. For me, your always there. It's—incredible. Even though we're on the run, it's been wonderful."

That settled it for me. Two weeks earlier it wasn't certain I'd even be alive. Now, thanks to my undead lover, I had my undead heart, and it connected us. We didn't know how much time we'd have together. Heading into a region of conflict would only add to the uncertainty.

"I agree. Let's change course," I said. "I'm not afraid—well, actually I am—of Continental Grid. Let's buy ourselves some time, learn what we can in the safest place we can find."

"We're still not at our best," Roberto admitted. He knew I wasn't feeling well, and it was becoming painfully clear that he'd soon need human blood again. Animal blood only satisfied him for a few hours.

"And we don't know how to be together," I added. He took his eyes off the road to look at me, a question on his face. I'm sure I blushed.

"I mean, we don't even know if we can have sex," I said. His eyes were back on the road.

"I've wondered about that." He was quiet for a quarter mile. "I'd say I'm optimistic. You say I get warm when we kiss or when we curl up together, waiting for sunrise. I like how that feels. That might very well lead to something more intimate." I flipped on the turn signal and worked the Taurus over to the exit lane.

"Route Four?" I asked.

"…will get us to route 95. We'll take that south to the turnpike and head back west. We've still got four hours before we need a motel. We'll be across the state line. We can even stop for a bite."

I was having a hard time with that. When we'd stop, he would wait outside, away from the car, while I ate inside. I'm guessing he'd take his victim just as I was asking the waitress for the check. He'd appear at the side of the car the instant I closed my door. Every second or third day he'd say, "Drive. Now," and we'd make our escape.

"Okay?" he asked. Something tugged at my heartstrings, calling me back to the moment.

"I...yes, take the exit."

We were on 95 south when Roberto said, "We're going to have some problems. Any couple does. We may not be able to get married, but we're bound together just the same. The evil that animates me keeps you alive too."

"Why can't we get married?" I'd considered the idea far-fetched, but not impossible.

"It's what the celebrant invokes during the ceremony. Ideas like 'What G...what the divine has put together let no man pull apart.' We can't be joined that way."

"We don't have to get married in a church—if it came to that."

"Knowing that it can be there, you'd be saying you'd be okay without that blessing on a marriage?"

He took the off-ramp into a rest area and parked us away from the facilities building. He pivoted on his seat and leaned toward me, taking my hand.

"Kelly. I'm about to ask you to do the impossible. Will you marry me?"

"I..." I thought the conversation was headed the other way.

"I know we can't do it now," he said, "but maybe someday, if we can be cured or forgiven for this curse, maybe then we can be united the right way." I saw then he was trying to be brave when deep down he believed it was hopeless.

I lifted my hands to his face and drew his lips to mine. The initial chill was gone in a second. The heat between us grew as our mouths and tongues executed that ancient dance wired deep in instinct. I put my hand on his chest, over his heart, finding its rhythm. Our hearts were beating together. We were two bodies with one pulse.

I took his hand and put it over my heart. He understood immediately.

"Kelly—I don't even have a pet name for you yet—I love you. Until that day comes when we can be married, I'll be okay with this."

"I love you too, Roberto. Let's go find that cozy marble mausoleum with the white picket fence. Want me to drive?"

"You have from the start," he said. He had a cockeyed grin.

"What was that?" My hand was still over his heart. Seized by mischievous impulse, I straightened my arm, pinning him against the driver's side door.

He put his hand around my wrist and squeezed. My hand went numb. As if he were waving off an insect, he pressed me back toward the passenger door.

"Ouch!" I said. He let go. I rubbed my wrist, reminded of his greater strength.

"Sorry," he said. "I guess I overdid that. We've still got a lot to learn about each other. Let's go find a place where we can start. I've got a good feeling about Dallas."

We drove west, trying to put some distance between our decision and the dawn that would inevitably come. As you can tell, because I survived to explain this, that was the right choice.

Cover art by Sarah Adelaide
This could not have happened without WYBW.

Thank you.

BOOK TWO
FAITH OF THE REVIVED

KELLY

    With only minutes left until sunrise, I was ready to wrap Roberto in the blue nylon tarp I was holding and drag him into our house trailer. Our front door was propped open, and I had a fire extinguisher ready just inside, on the hope it could halt the disintegration of a sun-struck vampire. I was prepared for him to come running right to me.

    The sky was so bright, part of me hoped he was hiding elsewhere and would not dare the mad dash across Dallas's maze of freeways to get back to our trailer park. Still, I wanted him back right then. That was the third morning I'd done that vigil. I'd heard nothing from Roberto since he went out to feed three nights earlier. My heart longed for the special connection we had.

    "King Leer", as I'd named him—my trailer park neighbor across the access road—was standing at the bay window of his house trailer, his ever-present can of beer in hand, watching me holding the blue tarp as I studied the skyline. I'd seen him watching me before, from both inside and outside his trailer, starting the first morning I'd gone out to wait. He seemed to be particularly interested in the parts of me below my eyes. I wanted to pull the tarp up to cover my chest.

The peak of the Bank of America skyscraper had become my point of reference. So long as its frame of green lights was the brightest thing on the Dallas skyline, I had hope Roberto would be in my arms in a few seconds.

The story continues in:

Faith of the Revived

Coming Fall 2022

and

The Purpose of Evil

Coming Spring 2023